MURDER AGAIN! HAPPY NEW YEAR!

D.B. ELROGG

A MILO RATHKEY MYSTERY

Murder Again! Happy New Year!
A Milo Rathkey Mystery

ISBN 978-0-999-8200-6-3 (Paperback)
ISBN 978-0-999-8200-5-6 (eBook)
ISBN 979-8-9856252-0-2 (Hardcover)

If you wish to contact the authors, you may email them at:
authors@dbelrogg.com

Cover Art by Jason Orr

Dedicated to Dan who knew the real Alex who wanted to be murdered in one of our books

SPECIAL THANKS TO

STAN JOHNSON
JODY EVANS
ZACH MATTHEWS
DR. ELENA CABB
DOUG OSELL
NICK GOLDBERG
PIPER GOLDBERGER

1

Milo Rathkey woke up on this sunny, cold, December morning to pain. A visit last night to his beloved Excedrin bottle failed to hold off the inevitable. This morning the throbbing in his jaw felt like the pain of broken ribs accompanied by an electrical shock every ten seconds. He downed two more pills and laid back waiting for magic to happen. Fifteen minutes passed—magic did not happen.

After shuffling his way to the bathroom, Milo checked his face in the mirror. Nothing much had changed. The same dark overgrown curly hair, the same brown eyes. He did notice an unshaven lump on the right side of his jaw. He gently touched the lump and vowed never to repeat that action.

I don't need this! he thought.

Milo was meeting with his web designer today—the first step in redoing his private detective persona. Unfortunately, his jaw had plans too. He dressed without brushing his teeth or shaving and resumed his shuffle, this time to the morning room.

Annie the cat did the tippy-toed-cat-spine-stretch as Milo approached her Gianna tree in the Lakesong Estate's Gallery. Sensing abnormal, she sat down and stared, but didn't descend. No bacon today. Lakesong's other cat, Jet, took his cue from Annie and went back to batting his fluffy cat toy through the gallery.

Sutherland McKnight, co-owner, with Milo, of Lakesong, a sprawling estate on the north shore of Lake Superior, wasn't as savvy as Annie and had no innate ability to know anything other than he liked to begin his day with his Wall Street Journal and a green smoothie.

Waving off Martha Gibbson, Lakesong's personal chef, Milo parked himself in his usual place. No breakfast. No coffee. Nothing.

"Are you okay?" Martha asked.

"Tooff," Milo said, pointing to his jaw.

The sandy haired Sutherland continued to peruse his paper. Milo reached over and slapped it down to the table. A startled Sutherland stared at a scruffy, unshaven Milo.

Milo pointed to his lumpy jaw. "Aysong..entas?"

"Are you saying, *dentist?*" Sutherland asked, "or are we playing strange charades this morning?"

Milo nodded. "Entas!"

"Estates don't have dentists, Milo, people do." Sutherland was having fun.

Milo was not.

Sutherland relented and called his dentist's office to make an emergency appointment for Milo. Setting his phone down, he said, "She has a cancellation. Go now! The old Medical Arts Building—Arnovitch. I'll text it to you."

Milo put on his coat and boots, and Milo apologized to Martha as best he could for not being able to eat the breakfast she had prepared.

"Not a problem, Mr. Rathkey. Don't forget I have those two ravenous young men who can easily down a repurposed scrambled egg sandwich as an after-school snack," Martha said, referring to Jamal and Darian, her wards—her two brothers who lived with her in a cottage on the estate.

Sutherland texted the info to Milo, finished off his smoothie, tapped his folded paper on the table then reopened his texting app. *I have a problem too. Need advice after your dental appointment.*

§

Duluth, Minnesota—known as the Christmas City of the North—was already decked out with red bows, holiday wreaths, and banners which hung from light poles up and down Superior Street. Milo was in survival mode, not festive mode. All the cheer was lost on him as he drove around the block four times looking for a parking space—an old habit from the lean days before he inherited half of Lakesong and millions of dollars.

Sutherland has good people. I'm going to go in, get a pill or a shot, and get on with my day, he thought, as he pulled into a parking spot being vacated by a white SUV with a blinking red nose and fuzzy antlers affixed to the hood.

Winter in Duluth had begun weeks ago. Busy plows had been pushing snow against the curbs until access points had to be cut through the shoulder-high drifts. Being in pain already, Milo opted not to climb the icy mounds and risk slipping and possibly falling. He trekked down the street until he found a break in the drift and hurried to the Medical Arts Building. Cold air and tooth pain were a bad combination.

Milo was greeted with a blast of steam heat, warm humid air—so characteristic of old buildings in Duluth—as he entered the lobby of the Medical Arts Building. Punching the elevator *up* button, he located Dr. Arnovitch on the directory and was ready with the floor number when the doors opened.

Stepping out of the elevator on the third floor, he found the dentist's office. As he pushed the office door open, Milo froze and patted his back pocket, relieved, that he had remembered his wallet with all the cards his financial advisor, Creedence Durant, had bestowed upon him. After handing most of his cards over to the friendly woman in her mid-fifties who sat behind glass, he received a clipboard with nine forms to fill out along with a plastic, daisy-topped pen.

Milo was not in a daisy mood. He doubted anyone needing an emergency dental appointment would ever be in a daisy mood. He found a chair in the corner of the small waiting room away from the pain-free clientele waiting for pedestrian teeth cleanings and started filling out the forms. *Why the hell do I have to put my birthday in here six times? Are they going to bake me a cake? Do I get a present?*

When he flipped to the second form asking for an emergency contact, he stopped. Since his divorce ten years ago, he had put Ilene of Ilene's Bakery, his landlord and friend as his contact. Now he was flummoxed. Should he put down Sutherland? Milo envisioned himself having a heart attack and the receptionist listening to Sutherland's mood music, waiting for him to come on the line. Milo shrugged and wrote, *Agnes Larson,* Sutherland's significant other and Milo's personal assistant. "She works for me. At least she would answer the phone," Milo argued to himself. The receptionist looked over to him not sure if his mutterings required a response.

When finished, Milo returned to the receptionist, and the exchange of forms for cards ensued. Holding out several cards, she said, "I didn't need your homeowners insurance card, your auto insurance card, or your health insurance card—just this dental insurance card, driver's license, and credit card, but thank you."

He sat back down in his corner chair and tried to fit all the cards back into his wallet. He waited another fifteen minutes staring at a kitchen renovation on TV.

"Mr. Rathkey," the receptionist called again.

Milo stood up and walked to the receptionist window, stopping to wince every time his jaw was hit by the electric shock of pain.

"They're ready for you now."

He was escorted into room three. The nurse, a young woman with a pleasant face and a welcoming smile, asked a few questions, performed a gentle preliminary examination of Milo's mouth, and then left to get the dentist.

Dr. Grace Arnovitch, a mature, tall, angular woman, introduced herself and asked Milo to open wide. After a bit of painful poking and prodding, she pronounced the need for x-rays, and Milo once again was left alone. The nurse came back to take the x-ray, all the while chattering on about her son's problems with reading. Milo wondered why she was telling him about her son but couldn't ask or answer because the awkward x-ray device filled his mouth. However, the chatter did keep his mind occupied which he guessed was its purpose—sort of like chatting up someone who was about to jump off a building.

Milo spent the next ten minutes counting the seconds between electrical shocks before Dr. Arnovitch returned. The shock interval decreased from ten seconds to three. The slight relief provided by the Excedrin earlier in the morning was wearing off.

"Your teeth need work, but the immediate problem is a cracked tooth that had a previous root canal." She pointed to the x-ray. Milo took her word for it. "There's no saving that tooth. It has to come out. I've gotten you an emergency appointment with Dr. Zackery. He's an oral surgeon in the building on the fourth floor. He will pull the tooth and put in an implant. You will be pain free in an hour."

Milo's visit to the dentist was getting complicated. "Not oo?"

"No, that tooth has issues. It's not a simple extraction. Also, you're going to want a replacement. It's in your smile area" she grinned awkwardly, pointing to her teeth. "You can talk all this over with Dr. Zackery."

Dr. Arnovitch rubbed a numbing agent on his gum, telling him it would ease the pain for the next half hour.

Leaving Dr. Arnovitch's office, Milo noticed both elevators were on the ground floor. Wanting this nightmare to be over as quickly as possible, he took the stairs.

The door to Dr. Zackery's office was a custom job—sleek, shiny, chrome, and glass—unlike all the other office doors in the building that were wooden with frosted glass installed in the sixties.

Milo was entering a new world. It wasn't just the doors that were different. Dr. Zackery's receptionist was different too—not mid-fifties friendly, but young and, Milo thought, attractive. She had long dark hair, and a smile that gave Milo the idea that he was her long-lost friend. She also wanted his cards. Having been schooled on which cards were necessary, he fished out the three required, and in return, she handed him an e-pad to fill out the same forms he had filled out downstairs—just no daisy pen. Milo looked at the pad. *Just shoot me now,* he thought.

In retaliation for having to fill out forms again, he thought about putting a different date down each time a form asked for his date of birth, but he knew that would only keep him there longer.

Before he found a comfortable spot to *epad* his forms, the receptionist explained that he would need someone to drive him home after the procedure. She had so much concern in her voice, Milo wondered if his life was teetering on the edge.

Milo sunk into an armless chair—no TV, just pleasant spa music. He called Agnes. She answered the phone immediately.

"Yes Mr. Rathkey?" Milo congratulated himself on his choice of an emergency contact.

Dr. Arnovitch's medicine was working; the pain had subsided. "Agnes, I'm at the dentist and they won't let me drive home. Could you come to Dr. Zackery's office in the Medical Arts Building and pick me up?"

"Mr. Rathkey, I work for you. I'm your assistant. Of course, I can pick you up."

"I don't know how long I'll be or what to do with my car," Milo said more to himself than to Agnes. "It might snow. I can't leave it on the street overnight. They'll tow it."

"Your car will be home before you are. I'm on my way," Agnes said, hanging up.

A tall, blond, lithe, ethereal cloud of comfort floated into the waiting room. "Mr. Rathkey?" the cloud asked. "I'm Faythe, I'll be your nurse. Please, come with me."

Milo rose from the chair and willingly followed. *She would never hurt me,* he thought. He entered a calming, baby-blue room, and eased himself down on an elongated chair. A cadre of beautiful female nurses glided around him. He liked Dr. Zackery already.

Faythe reclined the dental chair and checked on Milo's comfort as she explained the reason for an IV.

Dental surgeon? IV? Milo thought. "Am I having an operation?"

Faythe smiled. "We call it a procedure. Dr. Zackery will explain."

As if on cue, handsome, toothy, Dr. Andrew Zackery, clad in a pastel polo, strode into the room, introduced himself, and looked at Milo's x-rays on the computer. "Well, Mr. Rathkey, it looks as if you have an abscessed tooth."

Milo hoped he wasn't paying extra for that insightful analysis because the lump on his whiskered jaw this morning told him that.

Dr. Zackery continued explaining the *procedure* as Nurse Faythe organized a tray of dental tools. "Don't worry, it won't hurt. We are going to give you a drug that will put you in a dream like state, but not put you completely to sleep. I will extract your tooth, put in a post, and a temporary tooth. We'll send you home with a pain prescription, but most people just need Tylenol or nothing at all."

"What about Excedrin?" Milo asked.

"Not Excedrin," Dr. Zackery said. "It contains aspirin which thins the blood—not good if you are bleeding."

"I'm going to bleed?"

"Sometimes there is some minor bleeding."

Milo grimaced. Minor bleeding for Milo came with getting punched. That usually hurt.

Nurse Faythe inserted a syringe needle into the IV port. Milo knew something was happening but was soon feeling too good to be concerned. After what appeared to be only a few minutes the feel-good cloud dissipated, and Dr. Zackery told him the procedure went well. "Faythe will escort you to the recovery room."

Milo was handed off to another nurse—tall, curvy, with bright green eyes fringed with long, sweeping lashes—who introduced herself as nurse Monica. She sat him in a reclining chair and took his blood pressure. Another patient was escorted into the room forcing Milo to share Nurse Monica.

Remembering Nurse Faythe and enjoying Nurse Monica, Milo wondered who did the hiring in this office. He was thinking a medal of some sort was warranted.

Ten minutes later, Agnes was standing beside him, telling him it was time to go home. Reluctantly, Milo stood up and followed her out of the office.

§

"How are the neighbors in the condo next to you—the two young women?" Mary Alice Bonner asked her son, Richard.

"Friendly and busy. They are fostering a blind dog and two kittens, brother and sister. They had to bottle feed them. Mom abandoned them or something. I've taken a few shifts. They're really cute."

"The kittens or the roommates?"

Richard laughed, "Both."

Mary Alice enjoyed seeing her only child laughing. He had inherited her blond hair and soft features. Richard had been a gorgeous baby, a pretty little boy, and now people thought him handsome. He had lost the college handsome and had graduated to the young-professional-on-the-move handsome.

Mary Alice looked forward to these catch-up breakfasts with Richard. They afforded her a small glimpse of his personal life. She already knew how he was doing professionally. He worked for her in the real estate development company she was rebuilding from the gutter—scams and shady dealings had been her dead husband James' business model. When she asked about work, it was to get the details from Richard's point of view. He was the new generation and had new ideas.

"I received bad news from my contractor," Mary Alice said as her cook delivered their eggs benedict.

"A development project contractor, or your new hobby contractor—the guy who has been gutting this house for nine months?" Richard asked.

"I'm cutting you out of the will," Mary Alice joked.

Richard smiled.

"My new *hobby* contractor won't finish in time for my New Year's party."

Richard put down his fork. "Mother, he's been renovating two rooms. How long does that take?"

"They are two large rooms that set the tone for the whole house; besides, I haven't had time to focus. When I do focus, I change my mind on things. It's not his fault. He's patient. It's fine. What I really want to do is gut this whole house."

"Do you want me to take over this project, so the guy can finish?"

"No. This is my house. I'll do it my way. But that's not the point. The point is my New Year's Eve party. I need a place to hold it."

Richard moved a splash of egg yolk over his English muffin. "My twelve-hundred square foot condo has a nice view of the lake but it's a bit small," he joked.

"So are most restaurants or they're already booked."

"You told me Mrs. Worthington died this fall. If it's available, hold it at her place. After father's murder at the last New Year's Eve bash, you can carry on the death theme."

Mary Alice set her knife down and stared at Richard.

"Bad joke?" he asked.

"Bad joke maybe," Mary Alice said folding her hands in front of her, "but a brilliant idea!"

"What? A death theme?"

"No," Mary Alice said. "The Hawthorne Estate. Brilliant! I know the realtor handling the sale of the estate. I'll see if I can rent it for the party. Of course, adapting to a new venue complicates things. I'll see if I can borrow Agnes Larson."

"You told me Agnes works at Lakesong, and you already have a party planner."

"I do, and Peggy's great. I will just feel better if Agnes can oversee things. She knows me. I'm sure Milo will lend her to me."

"Milo Rathkey—I'm intrigued. What's the attraction?"

"Something different," she said, ending the topic.

§

"Are you in pain?" Agnes asked Milo as she guided him into her Mitsubishi Mirage.

"Excruciating! They only gave me a shot of whiskey and a bullet to bite down on," Milo said.

Agnes rolled her eyes as she walked around the front of the car to the driver's side. Sliding into the seat, she asked, "If you were biting on the bullet, how did they pull your tooth?"

Milo thought for a second. "Okay, I lied. How did you get a parking space in front of the building?"

Agnes shrugged. "It was here."

Before Agnes pulled away, Milo's ethereal cloud of comfort, Nurse Faythe, emerged from the building arm-in-arm with a tall, sturdy, young man. The nurse-patient bond is real. Milo shook off his disappointment at seeing her having interests outside of his comfort and took aim at her escort. “That guy outkicked his coverage,” he said, referring to the oft used football term when a guy isn’t quite as good looking as his partner.

Agnes immediately called up an image of Milo and Mary Alice. *You oughta know,* she thought.

Milo spent the ride to Lakesong trying to come up with a replacement for the whisky and bullet line.

2

Agnes made Milo comfortable in the library and rolled her eyes, once again, when he tried the same bullet joke with Martha who had brought him vanilla ice cream. It didn't work with her either.

On the way to her office, Agnes' phone began to ring. Looking at the caller ID, she thought, *Mary Alice? She's probably inquiring about Milo.*

"Milo's fine. Recuperating in the library with ice cream," Agnes said, not giving her usual hello.

"Recuperating? From what?"

"Oh, I thought that's why you were calling. He had dental surgery today."

"Who hit him this time?" Mary Alice joked.

"A bad root canal."

"Oh, I heard those can be painful. But I'm calling you because I need your help," Mary Alice said, launching into an explanation of her New Year's Eve party and the reasons for the venue change. "I cleared the use of the Hawthorne estate with the realtor. Could you meet me there tomorrow morning and look it over?"

Agnes was silent.

"I know James was…you know, last year, but it's not at my house so I'm hoping it's different for all of us. I will pay you extra of course. Agnes?"

"I thought my friend Peggy was your party planner," Agnes said, ignoring her stomach clench.

"She is, but the change of venue complicates everything. I talked with Peggy. She has no problem with you helping, and I would feel so much better."

Agnes was thinking.

"Agnes? You keep disappearing."

Agnes wasn't so sure she could even attend the party, much less plan it, after the events of last year. "I would have to clear it with Mr. Rathkey" she said, hoping that would provide a roadblock.

"I'll do that. He shouldn't be a problem."

Can I do this?

"Agnes? Are you there?"

"How many other parties do we have to work around?" Agnes asked, hoping that would be an obstacle.

"None. I rented the place through December. There are weddings in January, but they won't get in our way. So, is the answer yes?"

My therapist said I need to face the past. Okay, I'll face it. "Yes."

"I feel better already. What kind?"

"Sorry?"

"What kind of ice cream is Milo eating?"

"Martha gave him vanilla ice cream," Agnes said.

"I have Milo's power ice cream. I'll be right over. Open the garage door."

§

Faythe Cummings was having fun teasing Alex, her latest fiancé, keeping him in suspense with almost childish glee. "I have good news! I have good news!" she repeated in a singsong voice as she looked over the menu.

Alex sang along, rubbing his sore shoulder, "What's your good news? What's your good news?"

"Alex you are always so fun," Faythe giggled. Leaning into the table, her long blond hair fell across her face. "If we keep singing, will they throw us out?"

Alex looked around at the staring patrons. "Yeah, probably." Matching her lean and continuing to whisper, he asked, "What's your good news? Don't sing."

Faythe stuck out her lower lip and pouted. "Not as much fun, but okay. Well, you know how absolutely devastated I was after losing the garden restaurant for our wedding. I thought maybe it was a sign."

Alex sighed. "No, we talked about this. The restaurant lost its lease. You're being pervicacious."

Faythe held up both hands to stop him and sighed. "New word of the day? Just stop! I'm aware the restaurant lost its lease. I'm now calm and centered. I did a cleanse. My friend

Monica did the cleanse with me. We both feel great, and today I found out Monica has a mother who has a friend."

Alex wished they had ordered first because this conversation was classic Faythe, taking multiple side trips before getting to the point. He was hungry and fought not to look annoyed.

"Monica's mother's friend knows a dead woman who's selling one of those huge mansions by the lake."

"I'm confused." Alex said, salivating over food being delivered to a nearby table.

"Keep up, Alex. Monica's mother's friend knows a realtor who's selling the dead woman's home. Her name is...an *A* name...April or Anna or something. Anyway, I called her this morning. They are renting the mansion out for weddings. Now," Faythe took a deep breath, "this part is karma. January is completely booked except for January 18th—our wedding day! I booked it! We have a venue, and that's my good news! Lala good news! Lala good news!"

The waitress stood back waiting for Faythe to finish her *good news* song. Alex picked up his menu signaling they were ready to order. "I would like a chi bowl with tofu," Faythe sang, "and hibiscus tea."

Alex ordered a double grass-fed burger. He did not sing.

"You know, love of my life, you have only one protein," Faythe teased, "whereas I have two, edamame and tofu, but I love you anyway. Good news! Good news!" Faythe continued to sing and dance in her chair. Her phone lit up. Alex could see it was a call from Ike Granton, Faythe's ex-fiancé. She dismissed the call.

"I thought you took out a restraining order against him," Alex said.

"I did. He ignores it, but he's not part of our good news lunch. Away with the bad. Away with the bad." Faythe swished both hands in front of her face. "Sandalwood and sage. Sandalwood and sage."

"Okay. Staying with good news, good news," Alex made Faythe giggle again, "what does this place look like?"

"I don't know, but we can see when we tour it tomorrow afternoon."

"Tomorrow afternoon?" Alex took out his phone. "What time?"

"Three, but that's for the inside. Tonight, we're going to look at the outside."

"Tonight? Why? It's winter. It's cold, and it's dark! Who cares about the outside?"

"I do!" Faythe placed her hand on her chest. "For the wedding, we will rent heaters and the grounds will be lit." Faythe disappeared into her magical unicorn world. "Music will be playing. The fireworks will punctuate my unforgettable moment. The ceremony, then the party, and, as we leave, everyone steps out onto the balcony to be surrounded by starlight explosions."

Fireworks? How much do fireworks cost? Alex wondered. "Sounds wonderful. I'm glad you're so happy."

She refocused on Alex. "Oh, I am, and there's more good news. We need a caterer because it's not a restaurant like the last one. I thought that would be difficult because time is so short. But Monica's mother's other friend is a caterer and has agreed to do our wedding. We will meet her on Wednesday at six to set the menu."

Alex took out his phone again and entered that meeting into his calendar.

"Of course, it will add a little more to the cost." Faythe closed her eyes, shook her head, and drew a deep breath. "Centering, centering, sending all the negative away—positive in. Bad out. Good in. Bad out. Good..."

"You are efficient as well as beautiful," Alex interrupted Faythe's mantra, still not believing this beauty was going to be his wife.

"I am! Aren't you ecstatic?" she asked.

"Ecstatic is one word. Perhaps delirious, euphoric, rhapsodic, and athrilled," Alex proclaimed, wondering how much all those superlatives were going to cost. One more thing to talk to Fauchard about. He laughed to himself. *Fauchard,* he thought, *I know who you are. Getting my money back should be easier...maybe even getting a cut of the action.*

§

Mary Alice arrived at Lakesong in her black SUV. Agnes opened the gate and the garage door as instructed. By the time Agnes arrived in the garage, Mary Alice had backed in and opened the SUV's hatch.

"What's that?" Agnes asked, pointing at the large, brown, cylindrical container.

Mary Alice explained, "It's a tub of raspberry revel ice cream. I had a local dairy whip up a batch. I was going to

wait and surprise Milo at my New Year's party, but this is an emergency."

Agnes stared at the container. It wasn't going to move from the car up the steps by itself, and Mary Alice had disappeared into the house. Shaking her head, Agnes grabbed a dolly, parked it at the back of the hatch, and wrestled the twenty-five-pound, unmarked, commercial container of ice cream into place. Strapping it tightly, she walked backwards one step at a time pulling the cart up straining to prevent it from rushing back down. Once in the kitchen she found Mary Alice rifling around for an ice cream scoop.

Agnes was winded. "I didn't know dairies made ice cream on demand."

"Only if you buy it in quantity. This is not the only container. I have two more at my house. Where's Milo?"

"In the library."

"Please do something with this ice cream, so it doesn't melt," Mary Alice requested, as she left for the library with a bowl of Milo's *power* ice cream.

Agnes reminded herself that Mary Alice was the thoughtful one compared to her husband who dished out abuse on a daily basis. Agnes was glad this *favor* was part time, short term, and well paid.

Milo was reading in his favorite chair.

"I brought you ice cream," Mary Alice said, setting the bowl on his side table.

"Oh my God! Is this raspberry revel?" He took a spoonful. A look of pure joy spread across his face.

"It's raspberry revel and *me,*" Mary Alice complained, not used to coming in second to ice cream.

Milo started again. "Oh, Mary Alice! How nice of you to come over!"

Mary Alice nodded. "Much better."

"And what's this in the bowl?" Milo continued. "Why, it's raspberry revel ice cream! But how did you get this? No one makes it anymore."

Pleased to have made her point she countered, "I have superpowers."

"I believe it," Milo said, taking another bite.

"I need a favor." Mary Alice sat down in the chair opposite Milo.

"Oh sure, ply me with raspberry revel knowing you can now make me do anything."

Mary Alice smiled. "You understand so well. I need Agnes part time for the rest of December."

Still in the kitchen, Agnes looked at the two-foot-high container. *It won't fit into the kitchen freezer. I need Martha.* Agnes walked over to the intercom and pressed the *COTTAGE* button.

"Agnes?" Martha asked.

"Question. What do we do with a two-foot-high tub of raspberry revel ice cream?"

Long pause. "I'll be right over."

Five minutes later Martha came up from the basement tunnel. Agnes explained the presence of the ice cream.

"Let me put it in one of the basement kitchen freezers," Martha said.

"One of?" Agnes asked.

"There are two."

"Will it fit?"

“Those freezers will fit a battleship. We can use the elevator.”

§

Alex Sithens hated winter. Maneuvering in a bulky down jacket was difficult, but not nearly as challenging as chipping pieces of ice from the surface of Friendly Al’s Used Car Lot. Sithens’ air dancers needed to be level. Alex took off his gloves, blew in his hands, and plugged the blower into his extension cord. The last of his twenty-foot dancing pneumatic creatures came to life, rising like a maniac. Always the subject of ridicule, the air dancers got attention, and that was what Friendly Al Lerner, wanted.

Between the over-the-top reindeer, Santas, air dancers, banners, and signs, Friendly Al’s looked like a hallelujah circus in full parade. The visual assault of Friendly Al’s semiannual going-out-of-business sale couldn’t be missed.

Sithens, part owner of Sithens and Van Dyke Signs and Banners, surveyed the banners he hung last night, banners just the way Al wanted them, including the mistakes. He always had pointed out the mistakes when Al ordered them, but Al said they were part of his plan and insisted they be done the way he wanted. Sithens suspected that Lerner was a terrible speller but didn’t want to admit it. Alex fancied himself a wordsmith and was annoyed by the misspellings. He walked past the cars, each with the misspelled red, *CLEARENCE* sign on the window. Friendly Al’s semiannual going-out-of-business sales were grammatically distasteful jobs, but lucrative.

He glanced at the repair garage at the back of the lot. The shop was closed and dark. Alex was relieved. Friendly Al's mechanic, the muscular Ike Granton, was not happy about being cut out of Faythe's life. Ike usually didn't work Mondays, which is why Alex scheduled the set up for Sunday night and Monday.

Alex entered the sales building, walking directly to Al Lerner's office. The door was closed; the light was off. He retraced his steps and entered the office of Nancy Wickland, Al's bookkeeper. Wickland looked up. Taking off her glasses, and letting them hang from a beaded gold chain, she asked, "What can I do for you, Mr. Sithens?"

"Here's the invoice for the banners, car signs, and the tall boys. I just need my check," Alex said.

Wickland marched to the outer office and looked out at the lot. "I see you have the same mistakes on the banners."

Alex cringed inside. "You and I know that's the way Al orders them every year."

Wickland returned to her office and took out the checkbook. Alex thought Al may be the last of his customers to still pay by check.

"Where is Al?" he asked. "I need to talk to him."

Wickland removed her glasses for a second time. "I'm his bookkeeper not his mother, but if you must know he's with his realtor. Don't ask me why."

Alex put the check in his wallet and walked out of the office. He was almost to his car when a wrench wrapped in a greasy rag came out of nowhere and hit him in the head. Stunned, Alex was shoved against one of the used cars. An arm was thrust under his chin forcing his head up—choking him.

"You're a piece of crap!" Ike Granton shouted.

Gasping for breath, Sithens tried in vain to push Ike away.

"Faythe belongs to me or nobody!" Granton delivered a gut punch. Alex bent over in pain, trying to catch his breath, waiting for another blow. He knew the assault was over by the fading crunch of Granton's boots in the snow.

"Last warning, dirt bag!" Granton said over his shoulder.

Alex stood up, clutching his gut, struggling to breathe, watching his air dancers wave with glee.

§

At the end of the day, Faythe corralled Monica and some of the other nurses into the conference room to share her exciting news. "So, my life saver, Monica's mother, has a friend who knows a realtor who represents—are you ready for this—the Hawthorne Estate on London Road."

Crinkled noses, squinty eyes, and confused looks met her great news.

Faythe followed up, "Don't worry if you haven't heard about it yet. Nobody knows about this place, but it's going to be *the* wedding venue in Duluth! They had an open date and I snapped it up right away. Alex and I are going to see it tonight."

"You booked it sight unseen? What did Alex say?" one of the nurses asked.

"Oh, he is as excited as I am."

"Do you know anything about it?" another nurse asked.

"Nothing. It's like an early, unopened, Christmas present. We'll see the grounds tonight after work and the inside tomorrow," Faythe bubbled.

"Why at night?"

"Because we'll be able to see the grounds with all the lighting and everything. We're having a night wedding, and there will be…surprises outside," Faythe explained in her signature singsong.

Dr. Zachery cleared his throat and stepped into the conference room. The nurses looked up. It was a gentle reminder to disperse and set up for tomorrow.

Faythe was the last to leave the room. Dr. Zackery grabbed her by the upper arm and swung her around to face him. "So, you're really going to break my heart and go through with this wedding?"

"I am Dr. Z. You've been wasting my time." She reached up and peeled his fingers from her arm and freed herself from his grasp.

§

On these dark December nights, Sutherland was glad to return to the warmth of Lakesong. All the normal estate lights, made even more festive by the holiday decorations, elevated his mood. As he drove along the curved drive to the garage, he saw the Christmas tree lights twinkling through lead glass windows of the dining room. There were even five lighted wreaths on the garage doors. Last year, with the death of his father, Christmas had been forgotten.

"Hello Martha!" he bellowed, hanging up his jacket in the hallway.

"Good evening Mr. McKnight," Martha responded from the kitchen.

Sutherland joined her, purloined two pieces of celery, and asked about Milo.

"Agnes tells me he had a major dental day," Martha said. "The last I heard he was in the library."

"Is he hurting?"

Martha shrugged. "I haven't heard from him. Mrs. Bonner brought him some ice cream earlier, actually, enough to feed a small army if you would like some."

Sutherland wanted to join his biking group on their virtual trek along the Allegheny River Trail. He cut his conversation with Martha short, so he had time to stop by the library and check on Milo before exercising. He poked his head into the room expecting to see Milo dozing in his overstuffed leather chair. He saw Annie curled up by the hearth. Jet was batting one of the low hanging ornaments on the library Christmas tree, his yellow eyes complementing the amber glow of the fire. There was no Milo. A harsh white light coming from Milo's office clashed with the comforting light of the fire.

Sutherland followed the light. Jet left his activity to follow Sutherland. Annie twitched an ear but remained curled by the fire.

Milo was sitting at his computer.

"I've got ten minutes. How was it—the dentist," Sutherland asked.

Milo turned around. "I died in the chair. They took ten percent off the bill."

"You should have held out for twenty."

"I was dead. They weren't listening to me."

"I understand you had a tooth pulled."

Milo gave the thumbnail explanation of his visit to Sutherland's dentist and his subsequent trip to the fourth floor. "I had some great drugs and nurses. They coulda pulled all my teeth, I wouldn't have minded."

"You should be resting," Sutherland said, leaning in to get a better look at the screen.

"I did that this afternoon. It got boring. Right now, I'm searching for Lars—promised Jen I would find him," Milo explained.

Sutherland had come to accept that with Milo came the unusual, and Milo's agreeing to find his ex-wife's husband was certainly unusual. "How are you searching for him?"

"Jen said he took two-hundred dollars out of their checking account when he left. That's not much. I figure sooner or later he has to use his credit card. My software has been looking for it."

Milo's computer dinged. Both he and Sutherland looked at the screen. "His credit card was just used to buy gas in West Duluth."

"He's in Duluth!" Sutherland said.

"Maybe," Milo said, "This hit just means his credit card is in Duluth. Hope this gas station has cameras." Milo swung around in his chair to face Sutherland. "So, tell me the problem you texted me about this morning."

Sutherland shrugged. "The problem is I'm getting threats, yet threats may be too big a word. This situation started two weeks ago when we placed a bid on an old building up the shore—the old Kiner boat building. Mary Alice's company and mine formed a partnership for the project."

"Mary Alice hasn't mentioned threats."

"She's not getting them. I've taken the lead. I'm getting the threats."

"What do they say?"

"Basically, they're telling me to drop the bid or I'll be sorry."

"Who's sending them and how?"

"They're unsigned. Two came by messenger, three by text. I didn't get one today. Maybe they've given up."

"Who else wants that building?" Milo asked.

"Two other bidders that I know of—Sedow Development and Fencig Realty. I know Red Sedow. I don't think he would send me threats."

"What about Fencig?"

Sutherland nodded. "He used to work for James Bonner. He quit and went on his own when Mary Alice took over."

"Is he the sort of guy to threaten people?"

Sutherland paused briefly. "In a word, yes."

"Let me know if the threats start again. If this Fencig wants to play hardball, we can play hardball," Milo said.

"We?"

Milo smiled. "My former life. A little shake and bake."

Sutherland was not sure he wanted to know what that meant.

3

The soft, pleasant voice of Debbie, the GPS persona, informed Alex, "Your destination is on the right." All he could see was a long line of tall privets. "Unless we're getting married in a hedge, I think we have the wrong place."

"Wait," Faythe countered, "I thought I saw a small opening back there. Turn around and go back. I agree it's odd; it's so hidden. I expect an estate to have gates and be grand like a palace."

Alex managed to turn around on busy London Road and proceeded back to the point where he was—once again—informed he had reached his destination.

"Slow down! The opening is there!" Faythe exclaimed. "Turn left, now!"

Without thinking, Alex jerked the wheel and made an illegal turn in front of several northbound cars. Alex's risky move, punctuated by the sound of angry horns, plunged them onto a black, single-lane road surrounded by more tall hedges.

Staring at the hedgerow walls illuminated by headlights, Faythe said, "Isn't hawthorn a tree or something? It's called Hawthorne Estate. Maybe these bushes are hawthorns. That would be cool."

As Alex drove on, the hedges on the left gave way to a lighted, immense, snow-covered lawn, and the Hawthorne Estate manor. Dwarfed by some of the larger estates along the Lake Superior shore, this Tudor Revival manor stood in contrast to the ever-popular Jacobean Revival architecture.

"Oh," Faythe said, "not quite what I was expecting."

Alex's eyes moved from the decorative, half-timbered stonework to the large, round, stone turret on the left-hand side of the house. "Is it a large cottage or a small castle?" Alex asked.

"It's private. Unexpected. I think I like it," Faythe proclaimed. "It doesn't look like every other mansion. It's special, just like me." She batted her flirty eyes at him.

Alex knew he had to say something here. "So special, and anything you want, I want," he replied, hoping it was the right response. Judging from Faythe's light kiss on his end-of-the-day cheek scruff, it was. He was hungry and hurting from Granton's wrench to the head and gut punch. A reservation at the new brewery was waiting. Alex was in need of the numbing effect their new dark ale.

Faythe removed her knee-high, leather, fashion boots and put on practical snow boots. "That Audrey person, the realtor, warned me that the back lawn is snow covered."

"No problem here. I wear boots all the time. No telling where I'll be." Alex's phone rang. He looked at the caller ID. "I gotta take this call," he said, leaving the car.

"Hello?"

"Sithens! Small dividend last month. No dividend this month. I've waited like you said. No explanation. What's going on? Where's my money?" the man on the phone shouted.

Alex moved to the rear of the car and started walking back down the road into the darkness, out of earshot of Faythe. "I understand your concern, Mr. Quincy. I don't know what's happened. I'm in the same boat as you."

"The hell you are! You sold me this investment. In my book you're responsible!"

"I'm getting a meeting with the fund manager, Mr. Fauchard. Please have patience."

"If this crap is going south, you're the one I'm coming after Sithens. I will see you in court!" The phone went dead.

Alex began to tense up aggravating an earlier shoulder injury acquired two nights ago when another unhappy investor had pushed him in a bar. Alex could feel his heart racing as he paced the driveway. *What the hell? I'm the patsy.* He stopped and punched a hedge. *This will end!*

Faythe left the warmth of the car and ventured down the path closer to the estate house. With each step, more powerful lights illuminated the house walls, and lights hidden in the roof of the turret dramatized its cupola. The motion-activated lights more than met Faythe's flair for the dramatic.

The sudden up-lighting of the turret jerked Alex's attention away from his financial predicament. He looked toward the car. Faythe was not in sight. He jogged back, catching up with her on the walkway where she was beaming at the impressive nighttime light show of Hawthorne Estate. He grabbed her hand. The two strolled the shoveled walkway around the house. Alex moved his arm to encircle Fathye's waist to keep her balance. She wasn't watching the path. Her attention was on the magical display of lights.

Looking up at the balcony surrounding the top of a stone turret, Faythe envisioned wedding guests stepping out for a magnificent display of celebratory fireworks. The rest of the guests could *ooh* and *ahh* on the back veranda, or so Faythe thought as she circled the slumbering fountain, the centerpiece of the veranda.

"It's darker back here; be careful!" Alex cautioned as Faythe broke loose from him and glided to the steps. As her foot touched the first tread, twinkle lights erupted turning the back lawn into a fairyland, the white glow sparkling and glistening off the snow. Faythe froze. "Oh Alex! It's perfect!"

Alex stayed on the veranda watching Faythe float down the steps.

"How did they know this was my dream?" Faythe shouted as she danced on the snow-covered lawn. Alex smiled at his future bride twirling in her white coat across the sparkling ice crystals that had formed on the snow's crust. Even he was impressed.

Beyond the lawn, a thick stand of old pines, hardwoods, and manicured hawthorn bushes allowed only a slight, darkened glimpse of the water's edge. A shadow moved between the trees, hidden from the celebrating couple.

"We can walk out here hand in hand," Faythe said, holding out her hand, urging Alex to join her. He did as commanded. "Can you see it, Alex? This magical setting, me in my wedding dress and white furry bolero, you in your tux as we watch the sky explode in all the colors of the rainbow. It will be spectacular!"

The shadow moved again, closing to within ten yards of Alex and Faythe.

Faythe resumed twirling, bathed in lights. Her hand slipped from Alex's as he stood back to gaze at his blond angel dancing in white.

Covered in darkness, beyond the lights, the shadowy figure inched forward to the last stand of trees. An arrow was slipped from its quiver and nocked. There was a pause. Pulling the string back to the *let-off,* the hunter held the weapon at the ready pointing the lethal tip at the dancing prey.

Closing the distance, the blond beauty in white danced in the hunter's direction. The archer held tight. This was the plan; there was no going back. The arrow left the bow, flying through the air into Faythe's chest with the force of a bullet. She fell. Alex froze, his mind not comprehending what he had just seen. She must have slipped, fallen, but his eyes saw dark red blood spurting onto her white coat and pooling in the crystal snow.

In panic, Alex turned to escape up the veranda steps. He had to get help. A second arrow was set in motion. Alex cried out and stumbled, but kept moving forward, the arrow sticking out of his right shoulder blade. A third arrow ripped into his back before passing out the front of his body and into the snow. Alex fell forward, bouncing on the cold, hard steps.

From behind the trees, the frost-coated breath slowed. Neither prey moved. With care, tracks were brushed out as the hunter stepped back through the trees to the water's edge. Slipping into a kayak, the figure dug into the water with the oar, hugging the shore to a waiting car. The Hawthorne Estate once again had an open date in January.

4

Milo stretched his shoulders and neck before opening his eyes. He jutted his jaw from side to side, ran his tongue around the new tooth, took a deep breath, and smiled—no pain. He pushed the remote button that controlled his motorized drapes, expecting bright sunshine to stream through the windows into the room to match his no-pain mood. No luck. Low, gray clouds hung over the half-frozen lake. On the back lawn, pine trees were bending in the stiff wind. To Milo, the scene screamed bitter cold. The forecast last night mentioned possible blizzard conditions tomorrow, but the weather person doubted Duluth would see any of it.

Milo got out of bed, padded to the bathroom, and smiled as his bare feet savored the warmth of the heated tile. Checking his reflection in the mirror, Milo noticed he was fuzzy, needed a shave, and a haircut might be in order sometime this month. With all that insult to person yesterday, Milo expected his mouth to be a swollen mess. It wasn't. After a long, hot shower, and careful shave, Milo added one of his black Henley sweaters over his long sleeve, plaid shirt, put on his jeans, and began the procession to breakfast.

Annie the cat, sensing the house was back to normal, crawled down her tree, and took the lead, followed by Milo with Jet taking up the rear. Martha noticed the procession. "Morning Mr. Rathkey. How do you feel this morning?"

"Like nothing happened. I should have a fence post put in my mouth more often," Milo said as he made his way to the coffee urn.

"Fence post? Really?" Sutherland said, not moving from his paper. "I find it remarkable that you overplay the mundane dental procedure but underplay the extraordinary—getting shot at, beat up, and bleeding at inappropriate times."

"Part of my charm," Milo quipped, while eagerly accepting his breakfast from Martha. Annie demanded her tithe of bacon. Once sated, Annie sauntered to the hearth room. Jet knew he was the *next-up* cat. Milo sighed. "I give you bacon, Jet, and you ignore it."

Jet squeaked, which is what Jet did. Milo dropped a small piece of bacon on the floor. Jet sniffed it, left to get his small plastic ball, and returned to play soccer in and around Milo's feet.

"Why do you always give him bacon only to pick it up again?" Sutherland asked.

"It makes him part of the herd."

"He's not a cow."

"Well, group then."

Sutherland shook his head. "We've been over this. It's a clowder."

"Neither cat wants to be part of a clowder. They told me that last week. Besides, Jet may eat it someday—if he's hungry."

"Not with Darian feeding him!" Martha commented from the kitchen. Darian, Martha's youngest sibling, had the job of feeding the cats before school each morning.

Having eaten only ice cream yesterday, Milo concentrated on the complete destruction of Martha's full lumberjack breakfast—pancakes, along with eggs, bacon, and hash browns. Coming up for air, Milo announced, "Agnes is going to help Mary Alice with her New Year's Eve party."

"I assume Agnes is the Christmas Elf that set Lakesong ablaze in Christmas decorations," Sutherland joked.

"She works for me. I'm the Christmas Elf's boss."

"What does that make you?"

"Chief Elf."

"Tell Agnes to get you a name tag and a green elf hat."

"Us boss elves work undercover. No nametags and especially no hats. What do you think of her helping Mary Alice?" Milo asked.

Sutherland shrugged. "She works for you. I assume you approved."

"Mary Alice brought me raspberry revel ice cream, my favorite. So unfair."

Sutherland put down his paper. "So, if she didn't bring you ice cream, you would have refused?"

"We'll never know."

"Why does Mary Alice need Agnes?" Sutherland asked.

"Her house is a mess, so she is going to rent Jet's old house, the Hawthorne Estate," Milo explained. Jet squeaked his approval.

"That will be different," Sutherland said, getting up. "By the way, who's playing the part of the dead James Bonner this year?"

Milo was a bit shocked. "I think I'm a bad influence on you."

"You're right. I would have never made fun of Mary Alice's murdered husband before I met you. In fact, Mary Alice didn't have a murdered husband until I met you."

"I didn't kill him, but Gramm and I are still not so sure about you." Gramm was Lieutenant Ernie Gramm of Duluth homicide. "Speaking of Gramm, I need to get that gas station video."

"I'm going downtown to my office where I hope to feast on my goat-cheese-filled, honey-fig muffin leftover from yesterday's Monday morning meeting. No one else seems to like them."

"I am in shocked silence." Milo took out his phone and called Gramm.

"Milo?" Gramm asked

"I need a favor."

"Someone shoot at you again?"

"Not that I noticed, but I did get a tooth pulled yesterday."

"I can't arrest your dentist—tooth pulling is not a chargeable offense."

"That new Fast Mart in West Duluth, I need their surveillance video from yesterday afternoon."

"Ask them," Gramm suggested.

"My *Mister Consultant* doesn't carry as much weight as your *Lieutenant*."

"Not going to happen. I'll have Preston go ask them," Gramm said, referring to Officer Kate Preston who began working for homicide a few months ago. "Who are you looking for?"

"A guy named Lars Helvig," Milo said, offering no explanation.

"And Lars Helvig is?"

"He could be my ex-wife's husband," answered Milo.

"The dog catcher?" Gramm almost yelled.

"Animal control officer. Yeah, that's him."

"Kinda late in the game to go looking for revenge. She left you for him what, ten years ago?"

"A little more now, and I'm not getting revenge. He's missing, and Jen asked me to find him."

"Give me a second to process. You are trying to find the guy your wife left you for because your wife asked you to. Is that about right?"

"Yeah. Why? Do you think that's strange?"

"Yes," Gramm said. The phone went dead.

Jet squeaked again. His ball was caught under the coffee cart.

§

David Bonner, the brother of the murdered James Bonner, sat in his cell, wearing his civilian clothes for the first time in ten months, listening to his parole officer go through the terms of his release. "You will need a job or at least be looking for a job," the officer said.

Bonner hated cops—and this man had all the markings of a cop—but Bonner kept quiet, knowing any discussion with this guy could cause him, the volatile David Bonner, to erupt. Keeping quiet, not engaging anyone, had been his ticket out. Having served ten months on a two-year sentence, he didn't want to mess it up.

"I understand your brother James is deceased."

David continued to stare, while saying nothing.

"I hope you understand that you cannot return to your former life. No illegal activities whatsoever. Stay away from former friends, and especially stay away from anyone who testified against you at trial."

Bonner twitched slightly, rubbed his nose, and wiped his hands on his pants.

The man handed Bonner a paper which listed the points they had discussed. Bonner took it and followed the portly fellow out the door and down the steps. The parole officer, shivering in the cold, wished Bonner well, and hurried back inside.

Bonner waited until the man was out of sight before crumpling the paper up and throwing it into the bushes. He had decided to take a walk in the frigid sunshine when a car pulled up alongside of him. He recognized the vehicle. It was his black Bronco.

A young man in a single-breasted, beige overcoat with a Burberry plaid scarf, emerged from the vehicle and called, "Mr. Bonner? Mr. David Bonner?"

Bonner stopped. Too well-dressed for a cop. Bonner figured lawyer.

The young man came up to him, removed his black leather glove, and held out his hand. "I'm Chris Markovitch from the law offices of Haney, Jenson, Hamft." Bonner ignored the gesture.

"Why do you have my car?" Bonner growled.

"I'm bringing it to you per," Markovitch looked at a piece of paper, "Mrs. Mary Alice Bonner's instructions. She also wanted us to give you this." The young man handed Bonner a check book.

He grabbed the checkbook, looked at the balance, and smiled. "I want my keys."

"Yes, Mr. Bonner," the young Markovitch said, while stepping back, creating a more comfortable distance from the irritable Mr. Bonner. "One more thing, Mr. Bonner. Mrs. Bonner wanted us to remind you that there is to be no contact between you and her, or her son, Richard."

Bonner glared at the junior assistant lawyer. "My keys! Asshole!"

The young man thrust the keys at him.

Bonner shoved him aside, jumped into the driver's seat, and began pulling away.

"Wait!" Markovitch yelled. "My briefcase!"

The Bronco screeched to a halt. The passenger side window rolled down and the briefcase came flying out, hit the ground, and split open. Markovitch ran to pick up his papers and return them to the now damaged briefcase as Bonner drove away. Being a junior associate lawyer was the pits.

§

Mary Alice, with Agnes in tow, drove into the Hawthorne Estate through the tall, formal hedgerows, stopping in front of the parterre garden where tightly clipped evergreen bushes were laid out in a symmetrical pattern, the inlaid color gravel obscured by snow.

"Emma Worthington's pride and joy," Mary Alice said to Agnes. "I hope whoever buys this place keeps up the gardens. Emma believed English Tudor should be English Tudor and not Minnesota wilderness."

Agnes was looking at the manor house—a mixture of stone and stucco. Like so many houses of that ilk, it looked as though it had been designed by several different architects. She particularly liked the oversized turret on the north end. "Well, the circular driveway works—one way in, another way out."

Mary Alice was not in agreement. "Out to where? We have to park the cars. We can't put them on this perfect lawn. We're having a party, not holding a flea market."

Agnes laughed at the idea of Mary Alice holding a flea market. "Last summer, when we were preparing for the wedding we had at Lakesong, I had to go out onto the service road between Lakesong and Hawthorne. I noticed that like Lakesong, Hawthorne also had a side entrance to the road. The valets could drive the cars from Hawthorne across the access road to Lakesong. We have plenty of imperfect, flea-market lawn for parking there."

"I understand Lakesong is owned by two eccentric gentlemen. We will have to get their permission," Mary Alice joked.

"I doubt it will be a problem. We still have a large tub of raspberry revel ice cream."

"That takes care of Milo. I'll leave Sutherland to you."

Mary Alice's acknowledgement of her relationship with Sutherland made Agnes uncomfortable. Something to think about later.

Entering the circular driveway surrounding the parterre garden, Mary Alice found herself blocked by a red Kia and a white Lexus parked side by side. Mary Alice pulled behind the Kia. Realtor Arial Jenkins emerged from the Lexus. "Whose car this is?" she asked, nodding at the Kia. "Random people cannot just park here," Arial declared as if Mary Alice and Agnes were parking attendants.

Mary Alice ignored Arial's car problems, introduced Agnes, and said, "I will need an elongated, rounded awning in case it snows. I can't have people getting out of their cars in gowns and formal wear into bad weather."

Arial nodded. "Tudors don't do covered entrances. The awning will be a pleasant addition in case of bad weather. You cannot do anything permanent that will damage the house."

Agnes whispered, "Is she saying we can do the awning or can't do the awning?"

"The awning is a go," Mary Alice said. "You'll get used to Arial-speak."

Arial led them to the formidable, raised paneled, dark wood front door, unlocking it with an old skeleton key.

"The door is large and heavy. We'll need someone here to open it for guests," Agnes said, dictating oral notes on her phone.

"That note-taking phone thing, how does that work?" Arial asked. "I could use that in my business."

Agnes showed the phone to her. "It's a speech-to-text app. There are a number of them. I talk, it types out the note."

"Did you get the awning and the parking?" Mary Alice asked.

Agnes nodded.

The three entered the house.

Mary Alice looked around the dark-oak-dominated great room with its grandfather clock on the left nestled between two huge archways leading into the dining room. A long comfortable room on the right, featuring several seating areas, had been used by Emma Worthington for correspondence, and afternoons of sharing stories about the old days with people she thought might care. Mary Alice had been one of those people. She remarked that the room was as she remembered it. Even Emma's English bone china teacups and saucers waited for their mistress. "Did Emma's relatives take nothing?" she asked Arial.

"Almost nothing. They want to sell this place as is. I warned them, it would take some time. It really is authentic English Tudor," Arial said.

Turning to Agnes, Mary Alice said, "This tea room area will be for the coats."

"What's upstairs?" Agnes asked, looking up the dark oak staircase and the square paneled wall adjacent.

"Just bedrooms," Arial said.

"We'll cordon it off at the top—that will allow people to sit on the steps if they wish," Mary Alice advised Agnes. "Let's check out the dining room. I hope the table is still there; it's huge."

Huge is an understatement, Agnes thought as they entered the dining room. The table for twenty-two stretched between the two arches but did not take up even half of the room.

White plaster set off the exposed, dark oak ceiling beams which matched the oak of the table and chairs.

Arial went to the far wall and switched on the four, large, wrought-iron chandeliers. A warm, amber glow flooded the room.

"We can use these," Mary Alice said, placing her hands on one of the high-back, upholstered, Tudor chairs. "but we will need small tables along the walls. I want warm surroundings and comfortable conversation. That's my theme this year. No stark modernism and cold benches."

"Order twelve small tables for dining room," Agnes said into her phone. She turned to Mary Alice. "Should we check out the kitchen?"

"Oh, I've been in there before," Mary Alice said. "It's more than adequate for the caterers. You can check it on our way out. Our next stop is what Emma called the back room, but I always thought it should be the great room." Leaving the dining room, she proceeded to the closed pocket doors beyond the staircase. Sliding them open, Mary Alice stepped into the wood-and-wrought-iron-dominated room. Numerous seating arrangements stretched across the large metal lattice patterned windows that were serviced by heavy, velvet tapestry drapes. A large, carved stone fireplace, opposite the windows, was soot-stained from decades of use. Three red cut brocade couches surrounding the fireplace were set off by a gold, oriental rug.

"There's too much furniture in this room," Mary Alice said. "I want to use this room as a gathering place. We can put most of the bars in here."

"I can have some of the furniture moved to other rooms," Arial said. "That will be an extra cost."

Mary Alice looked at Arial as if she were speaking a foreign language. Arial was obviously not used to Mary Alice Bonner and her unlimited New Year's Eve party budget.

Agnes was admiring the woven tapestries that depicted knights, dragons, swords, and shields. "All we need is a gargoyle or two in here."

"The tapestries stay, I'm afraid," Arial said. "We might damage them if we took them down. Prospective buyers may love them." Arial rolled her eyes, not believing her own words.

Mary Alice nodded, "We'll live with them. Do those doors open?" She pointed to two doors which matched the latticed windows. "I want my guests to be able to step out and enjoy the fireworks."

"They do," Arial said.

"Good. Let's check the turret."

"I'm so pleased you are so familiar with the house. Since you seem to know what you're doing here, would it be all right if I left you to continue whatever it is you need to do? I need to call a tow truck for that Kia before my yoga class."

Mary Alice looked at Arial, thinking it odd leaving strangers unattended in a property.

Arial thought the look concerned yoga. "I used to go at night, but that didn't work out as well." Arial mumbled something about missing a murder. She left Mary Alice and Agnes to do ballroom turret inspection on their own.

Agnes followed Mary Alice who did indeed know the house. Walking past the dining room, Mary Alice turned right leading Agnes through a front room that featured cross-halberd pikes over a coat of arms tapestry.

"Was Mrs. Worthington British?" Agnes asked.

"No, but her house is." Mary Alice opened a rounded oak door at the end of the room and stepped into the turret.

"Oh my!" Agnes exclaimed. She looked up the three stories of stonework broken intermittently by leaded windows whose only function was to permit a small bit of prismed light to enter. "I don't know if this is a torture chamber or the most unique ballroom I've ever seen."

"The music will reverberate off the stone walls, and the soft light from the wall sconces will make everyone look lovely. This is perfect. Plus, if we go up those stairs," Mary Alice explained, pointing to the black, wrought-iron-railed steps that hugged the side of the rounded turret, "there is a viewing walkway that surrounds the turret. Dancers at this end of the house will be able to scurry up the steps to enjoy the fireworks. Let me show you."

Mary Alice dashed up the walnut stairs. Agnes caught up to her as they reached the top where double wooden doors blocked their exit out to the balcony. "I hope these aren't locked," Mary Alice said. She grabbed the black handle and pushed. The door creaked open.

A stiff wind blew Agnes' hair across her face as she stepped out into the cold December air, and tried to gaze out on the lake. "It's too bad the party is at night. This view would be gorgeous. It's a hundred-and-eighty-degree view of the lake and the grounds."

Mary Alice was silent.

Agnes turned and saw her temporary employer leaning over the stone wall, her face frozen.

"We have a problem," Mary Alice whispered.

"What?" Agnes questioned, thinking Mary Alice wanted another awning up here. Following Mary Alice's gaze, Agnes looked down and gasped. Two frozen figures lay on the ground—one face up in the snow, dyed red. The other was face down on the stone steps. "Are they real?" she asked Mary Alice.

"I don't know, but I think we should find out."

"You mean go down there?"

"I don't have binoculars."

"Maybe it's someone's idea of a practical joke," Agnes suggested.

"Let's hope."

5

"Please, don't tell Martha," Darian begged his older brother, Jamal. "It's scary up there, but I will be braver tonight. I promise. I'll stay up there in that room all night. It's scary."

"Dude, you're not a baby. My floor is hard. You need a bed, and you're not sleeping in mine." Jamal admired his brand-new double bed.

"I know. It's just last night I heard noises."

"It's the wind. You're at the top of the house. We're by a huge lake. There are trees. You're bound to hear stuff. I mean, it was your first night up there and you blew it."

Darian's big brown eyes began to water.

Jamal rolled his eyes but softened his tone. "Okay, okay, don't cry. Mr. Sutherland and Mr. Rathkey spent a lot of money fixing up that attic for you, so we could all have our own space. Use your headphones tonight. Do what you have to do."

Darian brightened. "That's a good idea! I can do that. Tonight, will be better."

"And no more sleeping on my floor. I almost tripped over you. I gotta game coming up. I can't pull a muscle tripping over my idiot brother."

§

Milo was enjoying some late morning reading, snoozing in the library, and looking forward to lunch with Gramm and Sgt. Robin White. He was hoping Preston had gotten the gas station surveillance video. Today was a Gustafson's day—meatloaf sandwich, mashed potatoes, and green beans that he never ate.

His reverie was broken by *Uptown Girl*—his ringtone for Mary Alice Bonner. He knew she and Agnes were spending most of the morning touring the next-door Hawthorne Estate. *Maybe Mary Alice wants to go to Gustafson's,* he thought.

§

Gramm was on the phone, so White picked up the incoming call before it went to voice mail. "Sgt. White, can I help you?"

"Sgt. White?"

White recognized the voice. She took a deep breath. "Ms. Larson. Please tell me this call doesn't involve murder."

"Ahh, I don't know. I'm at the Hawthorne Estate on London Road with Mary Alice. We're planning her New Year's Eve party. There are two forms on the back lawn. They look human. They could be store dummies. This could be a not-funny joke. I don't want to look."

"Okay. Two forms on the back lawn of the Hawthorne Estate. I assume they are not moving."

"No, they're not moving!"

"Do you see blood?"

"There's red in the snow. I have no idea if it's blood. Could you please send somebody? I would have called 911 but I figured calling you would be faster."

"Where is the Hawthorne Estate?"

"Just north of Lakesong. Next door."

White knew that next door meant acres away. "Please do not touch anything. When you say you're there with Mary Alice, do you mean Mary Alice Bonner?"

"Yes."

"Of course. We'll be right there," White said. Before heading into Gramm's office, she called the desk sergeant to dispatch uniforms.

Lt. Gramm had finished his phone call and was looking through a file.

"I just got a call from Agnes Larson," White said.

"Who died?" Gramm joked, then looked up and, from White's face, realized it might not be a joke.

§

"Hi. Hungry?" Milo asked Mary Alice.

"No! I think I discovered dead bodies. You're next door. I need you here, now!"

Milo thought if he was silent, he might get a further explanation. He was wrong.

"Did you hear me?"

"On my way," Milo said, hanging up.

Mary Alice shrugged, "What's the use in having a police consultant if you can't use him."

"I hear sirens," Agnes said. "I hope they're for us."

"It's cold out here. Let's go inside to meet them," Mary Alice suggested.

Agnes hadn't noticed the cold until it was mentioned. She followed Mary Alice inside, glad to leave the gruesome scene outside, below the turret. They made their way down the stairs and into the main house.

Milo arrived to find Mary Alice and Agnes sitting on the stairway in the foyer. Mary Alice watched as he removed his overshoes. "So, what's happening?" he asked.

"The police have just arrived and are in the back with whatever's back there," Mary Alice said.

Agnes stood up. "At any moment they are going to come back in here and accuse us of calling in a hoax."

Milo was going to ask for specifics when a uniformed policeman treaded into the house with a roll of yellow tape. He nodded at Milo and disappeared into the back room.

"Oh!" Mary Alice exclaimed. "I've lived with yellow tape before. I know what it means. Murder again! Happy New Year!"

Agnes looked at Milo who nodded, "They are marking off the scene. I don't think this is a hoax."

"Do you want to know what we saw?" Agnes asked.

"Not yet. I'll call Gramm. He'll go ballistic if he discovers you have already recounted the details."

"I already called him," Agnes said. "I got Sgt. White. I think they are on their way."

"Well, you two are a one stop shop, very efficient."

Gramm burst through the door, stamping the snow off his boots. Sgt. White followed. "So," Gramm said, "we meet again. Our own little murder group."

Agnes winced, and stared at the pattern in the oriental rug in the entryway, concentrating on her breathing—her go-to coping mechanism.

"Tell me what you saw, when you saw it, and why you're here," Gramm ordered.

"Which one of us?" Mary Alice asked.

Officer Preston joined the group, ready to take notes—her usual job in these situations. White asked if there was a better place to do the interviews, and Agnes suggested the dining room with its long table.

Once they were settled, Mary Alice told the story of their morning and the spying of the bodies from the balcony of the turret. "Being so far away we really didn't know if the scene was real or simply a bad joke. Shouldn't you be out there with the bodies?"

Gramm shook his head, "Our medical examiner and the forensics team aren't here yet. I have time and I need to know how this discovery took place."

"You're not suspecting me again are you?" Mary Alice asked, inspecting her perfectly manicured nails.

"Depends," White said.

"Depends on what?" Mary Alice demanded.

"Who the victims are."

"Mary Alice turned her attention to the crease in her slacks."

White thought it was a repeat performance of her husband's murder—same manicured nails, same detached attitude.

Doc Smith, the medical examiner, walked past the dining room. White got up and followed him.

Gramm's radio broke in. "Lieutenant?"

"Gramm here."

"We have a tow truck out front. The driver says he was called to tow a red Kia."

"What? Who called him?"

There was a pause as the officer talked to the tow truck driver. "Ah Lieutenant, the driver says they were called by an Arial Jenkins."

"Send him away," Gramm instructed. He turned to Milo. "How do I know that name, Arial Jenkins?"

Milo shrugged.

"She spoke at the Patsy Rand Memorial," Preston informed him. "She's the one who complained because she missed the murder—went to yoga, Pilates, or something."

Gramm was impressed with Preston's memory. "You're right, but why is she here? Why did she call a tow truck, and, most importantly, whose red Kia is that out in the driveway?"

Preston shrugged just as Arial stormed into the house. "Who sent my tow truck away?" she shouted. "Why are there police all over?"

Agnes got up and went into the foyer. "We're in the dining room, Arial. I think you need to come in here."

Arial followed Agnes sputtering about trusting them with the property and the expense of calling a tow truck for a second time.

"Don't worry, Ms. Jenkins," Gramm said, "we'll take care of it."

Arial threw her head back much like a peacock, her bright, red curls bounced with the movement. "And who are you?" she demanded. "You people shouldn't be in here, unless you're looking to buy." Noticing Preston for the first time, Arial moved back a step. "You're wearing a police uniform!"

Gramm produced his badge. "I'm Lt. Gramm, this is Officer Preston, and police consultant Milo Rathkey. I think you should sit down Ms. Jenkins this could take some time."

Two other officers came in the front door, paraded past the dining room, and disappeared into the back room.

"I can't have people traipsing through the house like this. These beautiful floors and priceless rugs need to be protected. What is going on? I go to yoga for an hour, and the next thing I know my property is being invaded!" Arial looked to Mary Alice as if she were to blame. "What did you do?"

"Arial, this is not your property," Mary Alice began. "You showed us a house with two dead bodies on the back lawn. Calm down."

"No, I didn't! I wouldn't." The peacock jerked back for a second time. "Dead bodies? Whose dead bodies?"

"There are two dead people on the back-lawn, Ms. Jenkins," Gramm explained. "We are only beginning our investigation. Ms. Bonner, and Ms. Larson saw them from the…"

"Turret balcony," Preston filled in the blank.

Arial leaned into Gramm, "I'll tell you one thing Lieutenant, I'm never going to yoga again!"

Gramm's radio came to life a second time. "Lieutenant, we traced the plates on the Kia. The car is registered to an Alexander Sithens, age thirty-one, from Duluth." Gramm looked up. "Does that name mean anything to you three?"

Mary Alice and Agnes shook their heads. Arial looked to be thinking.

"Ms. Jenkins?"

"The name doesn't mean anything, but I do know that a young couple was here last night to look at the grounds. They're planning a wedding for January…" She looked at her phone. "January 18th."

Gramm cued his radio. "Sgt. White."

"Whatcha need?" White answered.

"Describe the two victims."

"A young woman, blond. I would guess twenties. The man is face down, dark hair."

"Thank you." Gramm said as he looked at Arial.

"I don't know. I never saw them. She booked the place over the phone. She sounded young. That's all I can tell you."

"Do you have a name?" Gramm asked.

"Oh yes. Of course," Arial said, blinking rapidly.

Gramm waited. Arial fell silent. "Ms. Jenkins? The name?"

The peacock's red curls shook again. "Silly me." Looking at her phone, she said, "Faythe Cummings." Arial showed Gramm her phone and Preston copied down the number. "She transferred the deposit," Arial said as if the act of a digital money transfer saved one from being murdered.

Gramm stood up. "Thank you all. Ms. Jenkins, please give Officer Preston your contact information."

Preston looked confused. "Shouldn't I get *all* their phone numbers sir?"

Gramm growled, "I have Ms. Bonner and Ms. Larson on speed dial, but sure go ahead."

Preston looked to Milo for an explanation.

"I have no idea what the Lieutenant is talking about. I've never seen these two before in my life," Milo said.

Gramm rolled his eyes and grunted, "Come on Milo, we have a murder scene to investigate."

As they left the room, Agnes whispered to Mary Alice, "Milo just disavowed knowing us."

Mary Alice smiled. "Definitely different."

§

Doc Smith was on the terrace steps, bending over the body of the unidentified male, when Gramm and Rathkey arrived on the back patio. White and two forensics people were beyond the terraces on the lower back lawn looking at the body of the female victim.

Stooping under the yellow crime scene tape, Gramm and Rathkey joined Doc Smith on the steps.

"Whaddaya got?" Gramm asked.

Doc Smith looked up. "I've got two people with holes straight through them. Seeing as how this guy has an arrow stuck in his back, I suspect the other wounds were also caused by arrows—through and through."

"Nasty," Gramm said, seeing two forensic people poking at the snow. "What are they doing?"

"Looking."

"For arrows?" Milo asked.

Smith nodded, "You catch on fast. I can tell you one thing, she has a front entry wound, and he was hit in the back. That's all I know for now."

White walked up to Gramm. "The forensics people in the woods say somebody tried to rub out footprints. If the killer was standing in those woods, it looks to me as if she was the target. He hit her first and caught the guy as he was running away."

"He?" Gramm asked. "How do you know our killer is a *he*?"

"I stand corrected."

"I try and try to educate you young officers on your gender bias, but there is still work to do," Gramm snarked.

White didn't respond to the jibe, noticing that Preston was pausing behind the yellow tape. The young officer was surveying the scene, looking a little peaked. White walked up the terrace stairs and crossed the patio to her. "First murder scene?"

Preston nodded. "This…this…is horrific."

"Never gets easy. Concentrate on the job—take notes and take deep breaths. It's good we're outside. You'll be okay. Sit down on the step if you need to."

Preston followed White to the stairs, sat down, took out her tablet, and waited, eyes down, for someone to say something important.

"Do we know who they are?" White asked Gramm.

"They ran the plates on that Kia out front, it belongs to..." Gramm looked up at Preston.

"Alexander Sithens," Preston said, glad to be able to contribute.

"And that would be this gentleman," Doc Smith said holding up an evidence bag that held a wallet.

"The realtor said a Faythe Cummings was touring the grounds last night," Preston added.

Gramm looked at Doc Smith who said the female victim did not have an ID. White keyed her radio. "Whoever is at the red Kia, this is Sgt. White. Is there a purse in the car?"

"I don't see one," the radio answered back. "Forensics is opening the car now."

White keyed the radio again. "Tell them to look under the seat for a purse. We would like to ID the female victim."

Several minutes later the officer came back on the radio. "The drivers license in the purse says Faythe Cummings. Do you want the address?"

"Just have them bag it for now," White said. "Doc, do you have a time of death?"

Smith looked up. "It was cold last night, delayed decay. Right now, I can only give you sometime between six last night and six this morning."

Gramm looked out towards the woods. "So, anytime in the last twelve hours, a young couple comes here to check out a place for their wedding and both are killed. What the hell!"

"Faythe," Milo said, looking at the blond-haired body on the lawn. "Nurse Faythe?"

Everyone turned to look at Milo. "Got something to share?" Gramm asked.

"I may know her. I can't tell from back here, but she could have been my nurse—you know, at the dentist yesterday."

"Maybe she committed suicide," White said, "after having to be your nurse."

Preston closed her eyes, still unused to the grim humor.

One of the forensic people held up part of an arrow. "Found this in the snow. There's blood on it."

"It went through her?" Gramm asked. "Are we talking a crossbow?"

"Kinda fits the theme of the house," Milo observed.

"Looks like a regular hunting arrow," White explained. "Crossbow bolts are different."

"He or she would have to have a lot of strength to put an arrow through a person," Gramm said.

"Not if the killer was using a compound bow." Responding to Gramm's raised eyebrows, White explained, "I've gone bow hunting with my dad and brothers."

Doc Smith stood up and yelled at the two crime scene people moving through the snow. "Keep looking for arrows."

6

Gramm suggested the group leave the crime scene to Doc Smith and move on with the investigation. As they returned to the front of the estate where another forensics team was processing the Kia, Gramm asked Milo, "So, the Widow Bonner wants to use this place for her party?"

"That's her plan," Milo agreed.

White added, "She's not getting back in here for at least a week or two. Maybe you should tell her, Milo."

Milo furrowed his brow. "Thanks for that opportunity."

"We have two victims. We don't need four people at each place," Gramm said. "I suggest we split up. Milo, come with me. We'll go to the male victim's place..."

"Alexander Sithens," Preston added.

"Yeah, Sithens' place. Robin, you and Preston head for the female victim's house."

"Faythe Cummings," Preston again provided the name.

Milo smiled. "Good plan. Put the two people who can take notes together. We should know a lot about her place, and nothing about his."

Gramm looked at White. "Do you mind taking notes again now that you are a big-time investigator?" The reference was to White heading up the investigation into the death of blogger Patsy Rand a month or two ago.

"Well," White said, in an affected tone, "you have to clear it with my agent."

"Good. While we are working on that, let's get moving. Robin you come with me to Spiggins…"

"Sithens," Preston corrected.

Gramm sighed. "Preston you go with Milo to whatsher-name's. Don't tell me. I'll get it eventually."

§

"I need a drink," Mary Alice announced as she steered a course for the Lakesong family room bar.

Agnes agreed. "Still drinking vodka martinis?"

Mary Alice nodded and made herself at home on the couch. "Don't forget the extra olives."

Agnes began to mix the drinks.

Martha, hearing voices, came in from the kitchen. "So, how did the tour go? Will the venue accommodate a large event?"

"Yes, it would, and the tour went fine," Mary Alice said, "up until not one but two dead bodies popped up on the back lawn." She tucked her legs under her and closed her eyes.

Agnes looked at Martha, "It was horrible."

"What are you talking about?" Martha asked.

"We saw something in the snow and thought they were dummies or mannequins. We were wrong. They were real, and they were dead. We called the police and Mr. Rathkey," Agnes explained.

Mary Alice took a gulp of her drink, set it down then stood up and started pacing. "I can't plan a party with bodies on the lawn."

§

Alex Sithens lived in a side-by-side duplex in Duluth's Hunters Park neighborhood, north of the university district, a desirable area for young singles. Gramm knocked on the door. There was no answer. White tried the other side of the duplex with the same result.

"I'll get a locksmith down here," Gramm said.

"You do that," White said, while taking lock picking tools out of her coat pocket.

"That's a Milo trick. I've watched him do this before!" Gramm said.

"Not Milo. Learned this from my dad. Oh look! A black bear crossing the street," White said. She went to work on the lock.

Gramm shot a look back over his shoulder, but did not see a bear. "Where?" he asked as he looked back at the now open door.

"Oh look!" White exclaimed, "Lucky for us the door was unlocked."

"Yeah. Right," Gramm grumbled as they walked inside.

The apartment was a modern unit with an "open concept" as realtors called it. The living room featured a large leather couch, with two reclining sections. A sixty-inch television was attached to the opposite wall above a fireplace—a comfortable bachelor pad. A nearby end table held several framed pictures, one of Alex and Faythe skiing. Another picture showed a grinning Alex pointing to an air dancer in front of his shop.

"Who takes a picture of one of those annoying dancing creatures?" White mused.

Gramm agreed, but took a closer look at the picture. "He owns those things. He's standing in front of a store called *Sithens and Van Dyke Signs and Banners*. He has a partner. We need to talk to Van Dyke."

"Maybe he was killed by someone who didn't like those waving maniacs?"

"You'd be my first suspect." Gramm continued to look around the house while White called Sithens' office.

"Sithens and Van Dyke," a man answered.

"Who am I speaking to?" White asked.

"Van Dyke."

"I'm Sergeant Robin White of the Duluth Police Department. We need to speak to you."

"What about?"

"We'll be by this afternoon," White said. "We'll talk then."

A quick search of the bedroom closet revealed both men's and women's clothing and blue medical scrubs. "Either a woman is living here or Sithens is a cross dresser," White said.

"Nothing these days surprises me."

White held up a laptop that had been on a bedroom side table. Gramm nodded. The two went back to the living room. White opened the computer, swore when she was blocked by a password request, and started typing in her phone, trying to get a name for the waving creatures.

"What are you doing?" Gramm asked.

"He loves his waving creatures; I'm trying to figure out what they're called." She tried variations of possible passwords: *tube man, sky dancer, and air dancer.* No luck. "One more," she said, typing in *tall boy.* "I'm in!"

Gramm sat next to her as she went through his email. "He has some emails that are encrypted. We'll let the forensic people worry about those," White said. "He also has the electronic version of the New York Times crossword puzzle. I'm impressed."

She moved on to Sithens' small business software. "He seems to be doing okay financially," White said. Gramm agreed.

Checking his contacts, White said, "Here's a phone number for his mother."

Gramm who had stopped looking at the computer, questioned how she knew that.

"It's a phone number under the word, *Mother.*"

Gramm sighed and looked at the number. "Not local. I'll call." Gramm hated this part of the job—calling next of kin. He and White stepped out onto the porch. White secured the door as Gramm made the call.

§

"I knew some people who lived in these apartments," Preston said to Rathkey as they stood outside the Hilltop Apartments off Arrowhead Road. The complex, in an area known as Duluth Heights, held seven three-story apartment buildings, each with a different façade. Building Three was brick.

"None of these buildings were here when I moved from Brainerd ten years ago," Rathkey said. "I probably couldn't have afforded them anyway."

"So, sometime between then and now, your fortunes seem to have improved. I mean gauging from the size of your current house."

Rathkey shrugged. "The door to Lakesong was open, and I just walked in. The place is so big no one noticed me there for six months."

Preston let it slide, figuring she would get the story eventually. Her phone buzzed. It was a text. A forensics team would join them at Cummings' apartment within a half hour.

Rathkey knew Cummings lived in apartment seven, but as he scanned the intercom panel and found apartment seven it was listed to a Marla Maslowski. He pushed the button.

"Yes?" a voice answered after a brief delay.

"I am looking for Faythe Cummings' apartment."

"She's not home."

"My name is Milo Rathkey. I'm with the Duluth Police Department. We need to talk to you."

"Really? Why?"

"Could you let us in please," Rathkey insisted.

The door buzzer sounded, and Preston pulled it open. The apartment was on the second floor. There was no elevator.

Rathkey knocked on the apartment door. It opened a crack still held by a chain. "Show me some identification."

Preston was eager to show her official badge, proof that she was part of the homicide division.

"Who's he?" The voice asked.

"He's a police consultant—homicide," Preston said.

The door closed. They heard the chain being removed. The door flung opened revealing a stocky woman in her late twenties with one hand on the doorknob, the other hand holding a five-pound barbell on her hip. "What has Faythe done now?"

"Now?" Preston questioned. "What has she done before?"

It wasn't quite how Rathkey would have opened, but he was willing to let Preston take the lead and see where it went.

The woman took a step back. "What's this about?"

Rathkey dialed back Preston's aggressive opening. "We have some bad news about your roommate. Could we come in please?"

Without a word, the woman turned her back to both Rathkey and Preston, walked into the living room, paused her television workout, dropped her five-pound weight on the floor, and plopped on the yellow-and-blue-striped love seat.

Rathkey and Preston sat down on the adjoining chairs. "The intercom said this apartment belongs to Marla Maslowski. Is that you?" Rathkey asked.

"I'm Marla. This is my apartment. Faythe pays me rent." Her eyes darted from Preston to Rathkey. "What's the bad news?"

"I'm afraid that Ms. Cummings was killed last night," Preston said.

"What? How? Was it a car accident?"

"No, but we aren't at liberty to discuss the details," Rathkey said. "When was the last time you saw her?"

Marla ran her fingers through her short brown hair and looked down at the carpet. "Oh gees, not today, not yesterday, I think it was last week. She comes and goes, but I expected her last night. The rent was due."

"Were you concerned that she didn't come home last night?" Rathkey asked.

"I was concerned she didn't Venmo me the rent. Where she sleeps is none of my business."

"Do you know of anyone who wanted to harm her?" Rathkey asked.

Marla sat back. "Harm her? No! So, you're saying someone killed her? Should I be here? In this apartment I mean?"

"We are just beginning our investigation, but you seem to have good security," Preston said.

"Tell us what you know about Faythe," Rathkey urged.

"Not much really. She's lived here for about a year. We're both dental nurses. She works for that hoity toity practice—Dr. Zackery. He pays well. She's always been on time with the rent until this month."

"Hoity toity? I take it you don't work there," Preston said.

"I wish, but I didn't pass the physical. You have to look like Faythe to work there. I'm a bohunk from the Range—Hibbing. I can lift these stupid barbells and stretch until I'm dead, and I would still be a chunk." Patting her thighs, she added, "Dr. Zack doesn't hire chunks. He likes tall and gorgeous."

"Define *likes,*" Preston asked.

Marla cocked her head to one side. "There are rumors."

"Did Faythe ever talk about it?"

"Not in so many words, but she did refer to him as Andy."

"We need to talk to Faythe's family," Rathkey said. "Any idea how we can reach them?"

"I know she has parents, but I have no idea who they are or where they live."

"Can we see her bedroom?" Rathkey asked.

"Can you do that, go into somebody's bedroom without a warrant and all?"

"I was only being polite," Rathkey said. "We are going to look at her bedroom."

Marla got up and led them down a short hall to Faythe's bedroom. "That's it. Hope you have a key, 'cause I don't."

"She locks it?" Rathkey asked.

"Yup. Don't know why."

Rathkey took out his lock pick tools and opened the door, telling Preston he learned that skill from White's dad. "We worked together a couple of times when I was in Brainerd. Knowledgeable man."

"Slick," Marla said.

Inside they were surprised to find photography lights, a tripod supporting a digital camera, a green screen, a small day bed, and side table.

"What's with this green paper?" Milo asked. "Is that her favorite color?"

Preston shook her head. "It's what's called a green screen. If you take a picture in front of it, any background can be keyed in behind you."

"How do you know that?"

"Two courses of television production," Preston explained as she opened the closet and rifled through the few outfits hanging there. Rathkey checked out a small table near the bed. A plastic holder held makeup brushes. He went through several cloth bags and found eye shadow, liners, and foundation.

Looking around Preston said, "This is not right."

"Don't you have a photography studio in your bedroom? I do. So does my cat," Rathkey said.

"Okay, that's odd, but it's what isn't here that bothers me," Preston explained.

"Enlighten me."

"The clothes aren't right. Too much skimpy swimwear, no casual kick around clothes. No regular go-to-work clothes. And the underwear is for show."

"Meaning?"

"She wasn't living here."

"Curious," Rathkey said. "Let's have another chat with the roommate."

Marla was back at her workout when Rathkey and Preston emerged from the bedroom. Once again, she paused the television.

Preston spoke first. "We didn't find a lot of clothes."

"We're dental nurses. We wear scrubs all day—don't need many clothes," Marla explained.

"There were no scrubs in the closet, and she wasn't wearing scrubs when she died," Rathkey said.

"She was wearing skinny jeans," Preston said. "And she would need nonexotic underwear of some kind."

Marla scrunched up her face. "Eww. I didn't keep track of her underwear."

"What's with the lights and camera?" Rathkey asked.

"Oh, that. She was an Instagram Influencer on the side."

"A what?"

Preston took out her phone and, in a few seconds, pulled up Fathye's Instagram page and showed it to Rathkey. Picture after picture showed Faythe in various skimpy attire with some pictures showing no clothes at all but revealing nothing.

Rathkey thumbed through it. "I see where she is telling people to shop at certain stores and meet her at local bars. Is she paid for this?"

"Look at her. Do you think she'd do that for free?" Marla laughed.

As Rathkey and Preston prepared to leave, Marla asked, "I need her rent money. How do I get that?"

"I don't know," Rathkey said, "but no one can go into that room. Forensics is almost here now. They'll tape it off."

"Are you kidding me? I need that rent money! This doesn't happen to people like me in real life," Marla complained.

The intercom buzzed.

"That would be real life at your door—forensics," Preston said.

7

Vincent Rembrandt Van Dyke was born into a family of artists who had expected great things from him. He was sitting behind the counter of his banner and sign shop, contemplating the end of days, when he heard banging on the door. He put his elbows on the counter, and his hands over his ears. His long, red, corkscrewed curls fell in front of his eyes. The banging persisted. With great effort Van Dyke pushed back his stool, swung his body around, mumbled an invective toward humanity in general, and trudged his way to the door.

"We're closed!"

Lt. Gramm banged again and pressed his badge against the glass door. "Duluth Police. We called you earlier."

The deadbolt clicked open, but the door remained closed. Vincent returned to his seat behind the counter. Gramm and White looked at each other.

"That's different," White said.

Gramm pushed the door open. They approached the man who was staring at the wooden counter with his head in his long-fingered, ink-stained hands.

"I spoke to you earlier," White said.

Vincent nodded. "It's Tuesday. I don't like Tuesdays."

"We can't reveal all the details," Gramm said, "but we're sorry to tell you, Alex Sithens is deceased."

Van Dyke looked up at Gramm. "Deceased?"

"Murdered."

"Murdered?" Vincent didn't move. "Of course. Why not? That's about right." He put his head down on the table and covered it with his arms.

"Are you all right?" White asked. "Should we call someone?"

Vincent straightened up. "Someone? Yes, I need someone. Alex was someone, my partner, but now he's no one." Vincent reached in his pocket, took out a small bottle, shook out a pill, and swallowed it without benefit of a liquid chaser.

"What did you just take?" White demanded.

Vincent showed her the bottle. "Prescription from my doctor."

Gramm took the bottle; the drug was used to treat depression. "We're trying to get an idea of Alex's life. You say you and Sithens were partners. How did that work? Any problems?"

"No. Alex and I made a good team. Alex was the salesman. He was good with people—all kinds of people. People bother me. I created and printed the signs and banners."

"Did Sithens have any enemies?"

Vincent put his hands out on the table in front of him and started tapping his little fingers. "Alex? No. Everyone loved Alex—well, except for that guy at the car lot yesterday. He punched Alex in the stomach."

"Why?"

"Alex stole his girlfriend." Vincent paused the finger taping. "I'd like a girlfriend."

"Got a name for this guy?" White continued the interrogation.

"No. He's a mechanic at Friendly Al's Used Cars, down the street. Friendly Al is a good client. He has two going-out-of-business sales every year." The pinky taping began again.

"Was there anyone else who threatened Alex?" Gramm asked.

"No. Everyone loved Alex. Except for that mechanic I mentioned and the crazy girl."

"What crazy girl?"

"A couple of weeks ago she came in yelling at Alex. She had a knife! Threatened to cut him! Pretty edgy. I liked her. I think Alex dumped her."

"So, everybody loved Alex except for the mechanic who punched him, and an ex-girlfriend who threatened him with a knife. Anyone else?" White asked.

Vincent began to tap his thumbs.

Neither White nor Gramm knew if the change in tapping digits was significant.

"Anyone else?" Vincent thought for a second. "Some members of our investment club. Well, it wasn't mine or his, but he was fronting it for someone. I invested. I lose again," Vincent sighed.

Gramm prodded him for more details.

"The club was paying good dividends for a while, but not a dime since September. Alex complained about getting nasty emails, and one investor attacked him over at the Tip Top Tavern."

"So," White said, "everybody loved Alex except the people who attacked him. Got a name for the investor?"

Van Dyke shrugged.

"Did you lose money?" Gramm asked.

"I guess. Alex said it was only temporary."

"Who inherits Alex's share of the business?" White asked.

"Me, I guess?"

"How's the business doing?"

"Okay. I'm working all the time."

"Are you making money?"

"We both get paid every week. Is that what you mean?"

Gramm got up. "Thank you, Mr. Van Dyke. I'm going to have our forensic people go over your books if that's okay."

Vincent nodded.

"Have you ever gone bow hunting?" Gramm asked.

He shook his head. "I don't hunt." Vincent stood up and headed for the back room. He stopped and turned around. "I don't want people coming in. I gotta lock the door when you leave."

§

David Bonner was free and had money in his pocket after obtaining a temporary ATM card and withdrawing two hundred dollars. He made an illegal left turn out of the bank parking lot.

Next on his list was Bud Budack at the Tip Top Tavern. Bonner worked for Bud when he wasn't working for his brother, James. Bud ran a little loan sharking out of the tavern. David collected for him.

The Tip Top's busy time was after seven when there was a band and dancing. Only a few customers occupied the vast space this afternoon. A thickset woman stopped wiping down the bar, recognized Bonner, and nodded.

"I need to see Bud," Bonner said.

"Can't. He's in Florida. I'm his niece Darlene. I bought him out six months ago and I don't do money lending."

"Crap!" Bonner slapped his hand on the bar.

Darlene didn't flinch.

"I need a job—even a pretend job."

"Ahh, a pretend job. That's right. You went to jail. I guess you're on parole—right?"

Bonner nodded.

Darlene looked around the bar. "I gotta proposition for you. I need a bar back and bouncer."

"What the hell is a bar back?"

"The guy who lifts the heavy cases and keeps the bar stocked when we're busy. Do I have to explain bouncer to you?"

"I get the bouncer part."

"Last week some guy came in causing trouble and it took three of us to throw him out."

Bonner nodded.

"I know your reputation. I don't want you hurting anyone."

"I'll only dent them a little."

"I can't pay much," Darlene said.

"I don't need money. I need a job and a place to stay."

"I got a place upstairs. I could let you have it cheap. It has a bedroom, a living room, and a kitchen. Oh, and a bathroom of course."

"I'll take it."

"Don't you want to see it first?"

"Does it have windows?"

"Of course."

"I'll take it and a beer."

§

Milo ran his tongue around his temporary tooth as he and Preston walked into Dr. Zackery's dental office. "I just had a tooth pulled here," he told Preston. The same pretty, brunette receptionist looked up. "Mr. Rathkey? I hope everything is all right."

Milo was impressed she remembered his name. "Today I'm here in an official capacity," he said, showing his police consultant card. The receptionist looked past him at Officer Preston in full uniform.

"Oh!"

"We need to see Doctor Zackery," Milo said.

The receptionist stood up, turned to read the schedule, and turned back. "He's in surgery right now."

"We can wait," Milo said intending to go into the spa music waiting room.

Thinking that cops in the lobby was a bad look, the receptionist said, "No! Come through. You and the officer can wait in our conference room." She led them into the small, white walled conference room with an oval table and six semi-padded chairs. A green counter with a sink, small fridge, a water cooler, and a Keurig coffee dispenser took up the rest of the room.

Along the long wall were twelve pictures of Dr. Zackery shaking hands with politicians and sports stars. There were a few of him hunting and fishing. Preston noticed eleven of the pictures had light blue frames, but one frame was dark blue and smaller than the rest. "This guy sure likes pictures of himself," she said. "Why is this one different?"

"That would have driven Jen crazy," Milo said to himself, wondering why he remembered that.

Fifteen minutes later, Dr. Zackery walked in. He smiled. "I hope your procedure wasn't so bad that you've brought a policewoman to arrest me."

Dental humor, Milo thought. "I'm afraid this is official business, doctor. I'm a police consultant and this is Officer Preston. We are here to inform you of the death of one of your staff."

Dr. Zackery's face morphed from a conversational grin to brow-furrowed, grave concern. "Oh my God." Zackery said, pulling out one of the chairs and sitting down. "Who?"

"Faythe Cummings."

Zackery stared at Milo and began blinking rapidly.

"We are treating her death as suspicious. Was she supposed to be here today?"

Zackery stood up. "I don't know." He walked to the door, opened it, and said, "Give me a second."

He came back with a white notebook labeled *Schedules.* "She had today and tomorrow off."

"Is that usual?" Preston asked.

"No, but she's getting *married*. It probably had something to do with that."

The way he said *married* made Milo think Dr. Zackery was not pleased with his nurse's upcoming nuptials. "Do you know if she had any enemies?" Milo asked. "Anyone who would want to hurt her?"

"Hurt Faythe? She was a sweetheart, so easy to work with." Dr. Zackery went to the water cooler, filled a paper cup, and sat down. "There was one incident a while ago. A woman came in shouting, demanding to see Faythe. We threatened to call the police and the woman left."

"So, she was threatening Faythe?"

"From what I was told, yes."

"Do you have a name?"

"One of my nurses might."

"Is there one particular nurse that Faythe was close to?" Milo asked.

"Monica and Faythe were scheduled together as a team. They work well together."

"Monica?" Preston asked.

"Sandlan. Monica Sandlan." Dr. Zackery finished his water and stood. "I'm sorry, I have a patient I need to get to."

Milo nodded. "Do you have Faythe's emergency contacts?"

"We must. See the receptionist."

"Could you send Ms. Sandlan in please?" Milo requested.

"She's working recovery today. I'll see if she has a few minutes," Dr. Zackery said, leaving. "This is terrible."

Nurse Sandlan, dressed in baby blue scrubs, glided into the conference room about ten minutes later. "I'm Monica Sandlan. Dr. Z informed me about Faythe. I can't believe it."

Milo recognized her from his time in recovery. "Please have a seat; We have a few questions."

She sat down opposite Milo.

"We need to know as much as we can about Faythe Cummings," Milo said. "How long did you work with her?"

"We've worked together for about three years. Weren't you a patient here recently?"

"I was. Do you know of any reason someone would want to harm her?"

Sandlan paused, looking up at the ceiling, choosing her words. "You have to understand about Faythe. She was all about fun."

"Meaning?" Preston asked.

"She was *social* with *many* people, and some of those people took it the wrong way. They thought she was serious."

"By people, you mean men? Right?" Preston asked.

"Yeah. And some of the men—well—they caused her some trouble. Faythe often didn't cut it off in time."

"Cut what off?" Preston persisted.

"Relationships they would make up in their heads."

"Do you have any names?"

"Eddy somebody or other. He came in here asking for Faythe. Dr. Z doesn't like it when our personal life interferes with work. He insists on an atmosphere of calm for his patients."

Milo could agree with Nurse Sandlan on that.

"I know Faythe complained about him once or twice. I know she told him to stop coming to the office. He was getting too serious."

"What about her fiancé, Alex Sithens?"

Monica shrugged. "What about him?"

"She seemed to be getting serious with him," Preston continued.

"Well, let me just say it, Faythe liked to get engaged."

Milo sat up. "Was she engaged to Eddy?"

"Oh yeah—pretty ring."

"She still had it?" Milo asked.

"I think so."

"When did she break it off with Eddy?" Preston asked.

"That's something Faythe had trouble doing. I don't know if she ever did."

Milo looked at Preston.

"So, this Eddy person might think he's still engaged to her?" Preston continued.

"Probably. There may have been one or two others."

Milo was disillusioned. His ethereal beauty collected fiancés. "Did Faythe tell anyone where she was going Monday night?"

"She told us Monday afternoon. She had just booked some big estate for her wedding."

"Who's us?"

"All the nurses working Monday. She was telling us this estate was going to be the next *it* place when Dr. Zackery came in and shooed us back to work."

"Did he hear what Faythe was saying?" Milo asked.

Sandlan shrugged. "Maybe. I know he talked to her privately for a little bit."

"Do you know anything about her Instagram page?" Preston asked.

"Oh yes," Monica beamed. "She was teaching me. I was going to take over her local appearances. She wanted to stop doing that."

"I'm out of the Instagram loop;" Milo confessed. "Explain it to me,"

Monica smiled. "She has thousands of followers. She posts she is going to be at some bar at a certain time and day, and her followers show up. These places pay her to bring in customers. Now they're going to pay me."

"Why did she want to give it up?" Preston asked.

"I think the latest fiancé asked her to. I don't think he was too happy about her pictures either, but she wasn't going to lose the lingerie revenue. She wears it, plugs it, makes money from it."

"I understand an angry woman came in here looking for Faythe," Milo said.

"I heard about that, but I was off that day. Come to think of it, so was Faythe."

"Did she mention the incident?" Preston asked.

"No, we never talked about it. I think Faythe apologized to Dr. Zackery." Monica looked at her watch. "I have to go. My patient is due in recovery."

On their way out, Preston retrieved the names and number of Faythe's parents. Milo told Preston to call Gramm.

Gramm took the information and said he'd make the call. Preston was relieved.

"Why did you play dumb about Instagram?" Preston asked Milo when they got into the car. "I explained it to you in the apartment."

"I wanted to hear Nurse Monica's version. Point of view. Now we know that Monica was going to get into the business."

"Right. Our victim was coaching her to take over the personal appearances," Preston said.

"Or so she says. How do we know she wasn't planning to be a rival?"

"I have to get much more cynical," Preston said, looking up Monica Sandlan on Instagram. "Well, well, I *do* have to get more cynical." Preston showed her phone to Milo. Sandlan had a page with pictures similar to Faythe's and one appearance two weeks ago.

"It doesn't disprove what she said, but she made us think she was just learning how to do it."

"She's a fast learner," Preston said, texting the Instagram information to Sgt. White.

Milo smiled and started the Honda. "It pays to play dumb."

§

Gramm ended his call to Faythe's parents and sighed. "I hate this part of the job."

"Why not make me do it, or Preston?" White asked. "Not that I'm eager."

Gramm turned to her. "When I'm retired and you're in charge, always make these calls. As awful as it is, you need to hear reactions. They may tell you something you need to know."

"So, what did you hear?"

"Shock. Hysteria. Disbelief. We need to add the parents to our interview list."

"It's getting late, and you already explained what happened."

Gramm started the car. "It's one of those things you learn when you make the call."

"What's that?" White asked.

"When I mentioned the wedding, I got disbelief. They didn't know."

§

On Milo's way to the police station to drop off Preston, he asked if she had been successful in getting the surveillance video from the Fast Mart in West Duluth.

"Oh yeah. Piece of cake," Preston said. "I have it on a thumb drive on my desk. This is a new gas station with a state-of-the-art system, so the video is in the cloud."

"Did you have to get a tall ladder?"

Preston glanced at Milo to see if he was serious.

"Come on, I'm not that out of it," Milo protested.

"I never know with you. That playing dumb thing has me confused."

"I'm an enigma."

Preston looked at him again, wondering which of the many Milos was real.

"Scary, isn't it?" Milo smiled as he pulled into the police parking lot.

§

Most days, Friendly Al's used car lot was forgettable—a small, blue roofed, white hut in the middle of a cracked blacktop lot. Today, between the Souza band playing holiday favorites, Gumby-like dancing men, and a purple-balloon-encrusted hot dog stand, it could not be missed. Large, garish signs near the street advertised a going-out-of- business sale.

"Looks like a fun party," White said as Gramm pulled into the lot and parked in front of the building.

"They should put their money into selling decent cars. Bought one car here for my daughter. Never again," Gramm said.

"Bad?"

"A real lemon, and Friendly Al became less friendly."

Gramm made his way through the signs, banners, and balloons to the office. White walked to the end of the parking lot and took a picture on her phone.

"What was that about?" Gramm asked as she returned to him.

"This is great. Look at the signs. *Clearence Sale Every Thing Must Go*! Clearance is misspelled. I even took a video to get the oompah-pah version of Silver Bells. Christmas meets Oktoberfest. So funny.

A tall, thin man wearing a bright red ski cap, and matching down filled jacket decorated with holly came out to meet them. His hands were shoved into the pockets of his jacket, so he bobbed his head in greeting as he asked what he could do for the couple.

Gramm said, "I'm Lt. Gramm, Duluth police. This is Sgt. White."

Friendly Al's smile disappeared. "I remember you. Your kid junked up a great car. He thought he was a mechanic."

"My kid was a her, and she didn't do anything to the car, but that's in the past. We're here about Alex Sithens. Do you have somewhere we can talk?"

Gramm and White followed Lerner into the building to a small office in the back, past the main room staged with the obligatory coffee pot on a side table. White noticed that a companion office was occupied by a woman who was also wearing red. She had tight-permed, mousy-brown-hair and wire rim glasses with a gold chain attached that looked like a necklace.

Al sat down behind his desk; Gramm and White occupied the two folding chairs facing the desk. "So, what about Alex Sithens?"

"How many mechanics do you employ?" White asked.

"Why?"

"Just answer the question."

"One."

"Name?"

"Granton. Ike Granton."

"We understand he attacked Sithens on your lot yesterday," Gramm said.

"First I've heard about it."

"He punched him."

Al shrugged. "Shouldn't you be talking to Granton? Is Sithens filing charges?"

"Sithens was murdered last night," Gramm said.

"So, you think Ike did it just because he popped Sithens one?"

"Is Ike here today?" Gramm asked, ignoring Lerner's jibe.

"Nope. He's off today." Al smiled.

"How convenient." Gramm stood up to leave.

White did the same. "Did you know *clearance* is misspelled on those banners?" White asked.

"Marketing. Makes me look stupid. People think they'll buffalo me into a good deal."

8

Gramm was cranky. The winter sun had set; it was only four-thirty; he was hungry, and all he had was one of White's protein bars. "They would have to live out of town—Proctor," Gramm grumbled as they exited the Duluth city limits.

"It could be Cloquet," White countered, "much farther."

Fifteen minutes later they arrived at a prewar gray-sided house with an oversized brown dormer added with little thought given to blending it into the existing house. Gramm stared at the unshoveled sidewalk. "Doesn't look like the front of the house is used much in winter," Gramm said. "Let's try around back."

"I'm already halfway there," White said, plodding through a foot of snow.

Gramm watched as his partner trudged up to the three-season porch, pulled open the screen door, and walked up to the interior front door, stomping her feet to loosen the packed snow on her boots.

Gramm reluctantly followed.

Not finding a doorbell, White knocked.

A pleasant looking woman with wavy, salt-and-pepper hair answered the door. “Yes?” she asked.

White showed her badge. “I’m Sgt. White, Duluth police.” She turned to introduce her partner. “This is Lt. Gramm. Are you Hope Cummings? We spoke on the phone.”

“Oh no,” the woman said. “I’m Bea from next door. Our minister called, told me what happened. I’m here to help and comfort. It’s such a tragedy. Please come in.”

Graham removed his galoshes.

“Bea-from-next-door” guided Gramm and White into a cluttered living room filled with multi-colored depression glass, porcelain dolls, and pictures of Faythe. Hope Cummings and her husband Bobby huddled together on a small, green-plaid couch. Hope had been crying. White thought they looked too old to be Faythe’s parents.

Gramm introduced himself and Sgt. White and the two sat down on kitchen chairs brought in by Bea. Gramm hated the phrase, ‘sorry for your loss,’ and refused to use it. “I know this is a hard time, but we have to gather as much information as we can if we’re going to find out who did this to your daughter.”

Bobby nodded.

“We understand, Lieutenant,” Hope said.

“As I said on the phone, we think Faythe and her fiancé were looking at wedding venues when they were attacked,” Gramm said.

Hope's face broke into a sad smile. "You're wrong, Lieutenant. Our Faith didn't have a fiancé. She barely dated. We urged her to get to know some of the nice young men at the church, but she never seemed interested—too busy with her work."

"Who was she…who was she with? Was he hurt too?" Bobby Cummings asked.

"Yes. He was also killed. Alex Sithens. Have you ever heard her mention him?"

Hope looked at her husband. They shook their heads in unison.

Looking around the room at the pictures of Faythe at various stages in her life, White asked, "Was Faythe your only child?"

"Yes," Hope said. "She came late in our lives—a gift. That's why we named her Faith."

White's eye caught a high school picture of Faythe labeled *Faith Cummings. Miss Proctor Speedway 2009.* "I'm a little confused, Mrs. Cummings," White said. "Did your daughter spell her name F-a-i-t-h, or F-a-y-t-h-e?"

Hope sat back as if she had been punched. "F-a-i-t-h of course. Where did you get that other spelling?"

White ignored the question. "Did your daughter do much social media?"

"I don't know what you mean?" Bobby said.

"Twitter, Instagram, Facebook, Snapchat?"

The stares were reminiscent of a deer in headlights. "I'm sorry, dear. I don't know what you're saying," Hope said.

"When was the last time you talked with Faythe?" Gramm asked.

"She calls every Sunday after church," Hope said as she started to cry. "She will never call us again!"

Gramm stood up. It was time to go. "We've intruded long enough. We may need to come back if we have more questions."

Bobby nodded. "How did she die?"

"She didn't suffer. We are sure of that," Gramm said offering no further explanation.

Back in the car, White asked, "Are we sure she didn't suffer?"

"We are always sure they didn't suffer," Gramm said as he steered the car back to Duluth.

§

Milo returned home planning to check out the Fast Mart surveillance video, but he was ambushed by Mary Alice, Agnes, and Sutherland who were gathered in the family room. "We've been waiting for you," Sutherland said.

"We need an update," Mary Alice added. She was sitting on the couch with Agnes. Sutherland had pulled a straight-backed chair out from the table and was sitting on it sideways.

"An update? An update on what?" Milo asked.

"My grandmother's cribbage game," Sutherland snarked. "What do you think we want an update on?"

"Granny was a cribbage shark," Milo teased, knowing he was avoiding Mary Alice's questions.

"Milo!" Mary Alice challenged. "Stop being yourself."

Milo made a vodka gimlet. After a pause to sip his drink, he explained as much about the case as he was allowed. It wasn't much. "Two dead. Suspicious circumstances. No suspects."

After Milo sat down on an over-stuffed chair opposite the couch, Jet jumped in his lap and sat staring at him. Starting with chin scratches, Milo's hands slid down the soft fur of Jet's back. Jet began to purr and laid down.

"I think Milo's a cat therapist," Sutherland said.

"I may need a therapist if I can't get into Hawthorne house soon," Mary Alice replied.

Milo was surprised. "Two people died."

"Oh, I realize that. You missed our earlier discussion about how horrible it was, and how young those poor people were. Now the discussion has moved on to the party venue."

"Don't you remember last year?" Milo asked. "Parts of your house were cordoned off for several weeks. The first police wave looks for physical evidence, but as the police investigate, they may learn something more and have to go back. That's why it takes so long."

Mary Alice groaned and looked at Agnes who said, "That won't work. We have to have access."

"We have an *in* with the police," Mary Alice said, "Maybe that Milo guy could cut us some slack."

"Sorry," Milo said. "Not my call."

Mary Alice put her cocktail down on the coffee table and crossed her arms. "I can't find another venue of the size I need at this late date. Getting the Hawthorne place was a fluke." She sighed and looked up at the ceiling. "This year my party will not happen."

Sutherland jerked up, proclaiming he needed another scotch. “Milo? Another gimlet?”

“Still working on this one, thanks,” Milo said.

“No, with the day you’ve had, you need another.” Sutherland began to make a second gimlet.

Milo grimaced and shot up, “That’s not how you do it! You’re disrespecting the Rose’s Lime Juice.”

“Then get over here and make your own!” Sutherland demanded.

Mary Alice and Agnes were busy discussing how to disinvite a hundred and twenty people. Neither noticed Sutherland and Milo having a confab at the bar.

Sutherland took his scotch and sat down in one of the other comfortable chairs opposite the sectional. “Mary Alice, it’s too bad that you don’t know anyone who has a large estate.”

“Yeah,” Milo said, standing beside his chair. “A large estate, you know, on Lake Superior.”

“Oh right, on the lake,” Sutherland continued, “with plenty of room, and a large catering kitchen in the basement,”

Milo sighed. “Really. It’s too bad you don’t know anyone who has anything like that.”

“Tragedy,” Sutherland mocked.

Mary Alice had been following this ping pong discussion with her eyes as a gradual smile reached her lips. “Are you two serious?”

“Serious about what?” Milo asked.

“About holding my party here.”

“Oh!” Milo exclaimed. “I never thought of that. But she’s right! We have a big house by the lake!”

Sutherland chimed in. "With a catering kitchen and lots of room."

"If you two have finished, can I ask a question?"

"Question away," Sutherland said.

"Are you sure? It will mean a lot of disruption to your monk-like lifestyle here at Lakesong," Mary Alice said.

Sutherland smirked. "Sure, it could cut into our vespers time, but we've already held a wedding for Morrie Wolf's granddaughter, and life went on."

"Delayed by someone looking for dead bodies on the back lawn!" Agnes said.

Mary Alice laughed. "When you put it that way, this simple party could be a piece of cake."

"Unless Sutherland wants to do GZP under the floorboards," Milo needled.

"GPR," Sutherland corrected. "Ground penetrating radar. I admit, not my finest hour."

Mary Alice looked at Agnes. "I think we have a new venue."

"Convenient for me," Agnes nodded. "I already have an office here."

§

Martha, having served dinner for four, retired to her cottage and her two siblings, Jamal, and Darian.

"Evening boys," she said as she arrived via the tunnel.

She found Darian watching television and Jamal doing his homework. She didn't fuss at Darian. She was sure he had already finished his homework. Jamal on the other hand was a B minus student, and an A minus athlete. The basketball team was good for him. The coach demanded good grades; hence Jamal was doing his homework.

Jamal pulled out one ear bud and grunted. If Darian said anything, it was drowned out by the soundtrack of the *Black Panther* movie. Martha, ever vigilant, picked up the ear bud to listen to what Jamal thought was cool.

"Toosie Slide?" Martha questioned. "Since when are you a Drake fan?"

Jamal yanked his remaining ear bud out. "Kelly likes it."

Kelly likes it? "Kelly?" Martha inquired.

"She's just a girl," Jamal explained.

"Oh, just a girl," Martha mocked. "What a shame. Tell me more about this *just a girl*."

"Don't make a big deal out of this. She's just a girl I know. She's one of the basketball cheerleaders."

"Do you like this *just a girl*?"

Jamal shrugged. "She's cute, and she's into me,"

Martha held her tongue but had a new task when she went to his next game–ID Kelly, *just a girl*.

Continuing into the living room, she saw Darian fighting for the fate of Wakanda.

"I'm going to be like Black Panther in this movie," Darian proclaimed.

Martha sat down and watched Wakanda being saved. "How did you sleep last night in your penthouse apartment?"

"Oh, it was great!" he lied.

"Good." She sat back and watched the rest of the movie with him.

§

After dinner, Mary Alice and Agnes said their good-byes, leaving Sutherland and Milo in the gallery enjoying an after-dinner drink. "So, who really killed those two people over at Hawthorne?" Sutherland asked.

"Don't know. It's still early," Milo said.

"Why arrows?"

"I'm thinking a perp without a gun permit."

"Yeah, because when I want to murder two people, getting nailed for no gun permit is on my mind," Sutherland quipped.

Milo looked at him. "Do you want to murder two people often?"

"Only on a full moon," Sutherland said, looking through the gallery windows at the bright night sky. "Oh look, a full moon tonight. Where did I put my quiver?"

"I worry about a man who can't find his quiver," Milo said, taking a sip of his gimlet.

"Moving forward," Sutherland joked, using his business lingo, "what's new on the Lars front?"

"Oh crap!" Milo exclaimed. "I almost forgot." He reached in his pocket and pulled out Preston's thumb drive. "I have surveillance video from the Fast Mart I gotta watch."

Sutherland followed Milo into his father's former office, now Milo's. "I didn't get a chance before, but I wanted to compliment you on your arty addition to the wall," Sutherland said, referring to a portion of Milo's old office door, now framed and hanging on the wall. "It's primitive intarsia."

"Are you calling my intarsia, primitive?" Milo questioned.

"Quite. That elegantly framed piece of wood on the wall with the raised letters spelling *RAT KEY.* Does that go back to your days of making keys for rodents?"

Milo sighed. "Those were my salad days, and the rats were appreciative."

"*Salad Days?* How Shakespearian of you."

"I didn't know it was Shakespeare. I just thought it was when I had no money, and a head of lettuce was supper—for the week," Milo said as he plugged the thumb drive into the computer.

"You told me a while ago that you lost your fork," Sutherland said. "How did you eat the lettuce?"

"Like an apple. It was sad." The video began to play. "I asked for the whole day, so this could take a while."

Milo went fast forward, stopping every time he saw a male pumping gas. Sutherland made a quick trip to the billiard room to grab a poker chair. After fifteen minutes, Sutherland suggested that, in the future, Milo prescreen these little movies to get to the good parts. "Not that this isn't drop dead fascinating," he said.

"My bad," Milo apologized. "Next time, I'll provide popcorn."

"That would help."

Seconds later, one of the gas pumping males looked familiar. Milo checked the picture Jen had sent him. "That, my bored friend, is Lars, friend to the furry," Milo said.

Sutherland moved in closer, "I hate to say it, but he doesn't look like a wife-stealing ogre."

"Unfortunately, I think he's an okay guy. Now the question is why did this okay guy go off the rails?"

"He looks kind of scruffy," Sutherland said, leaning back. "By the way, I thought these videos were all black and white, and of horrible quality. This is in color, like we're watching a movie."

"New gas station, new system according to Preston. Lars does look like he's been living out of the car."

"So, what do you do now, stake out the gas station?" Not waiting for Milo's answer, Sutherland began forming his own plan. "I'm thinking—he's driving a Toyota Rav 4. So, assuming he just filled up, and assuming that the Rav gets about thirty miles to the gallon..."

Milo looked at him in disbelief.

"Okay. Let's say he does about thirty miles a day and the Rav has a fifteen-gallon tank...he should be back at Fast Mart in...um..."

Milo shook his head. "You're at it again!"

"What?"

"Maybe, just maybe—stay with me here—he fills up somewhere else."

"He can't do that! It will mess up my calculations!"

"When I find him, I'll tell him," Milo said, letting Sutherland be Sutherland. "I, however, have a different plan I'll put out a few feelers in the west end. Someone will spot him again."

"So, you're like Sherlock Homes. You have a cadre of street urchins who do your spying?"

"Street urchins?"

"Arthur Conan Doyle calls his informants *street urchins*."

"I call them people. I give them each five bucks and the guy who spots Lars gets an extra ten," Milo explained.

"Ten? Kinda cheap don't you think?" Sutherland chided.

"Well, that's the way it worked before, but now I could raise it to twenty."

"Make it a hundred. You're rich."

"Not for long if I listen to you," Milo said, taking his phone from his pocket. "Right now, I have to call Jen and tell her Lars has been spotted."

She answered on the first ring, "Is this good news, Milo?"

"I think so. I have video of Lars pumping gas in west Duluth a day ago. He's here."

"I wish I knew what was going on with him. I'm coming up," Jen said. She paused. "Do you know of a cheap, safe motel."

"You can stay here," Milo offered.

"It's a little awkward."

"It's a lot awkward, but the place is big—so big you have to make an appointment to see anybody."

Jen didn't laugh. "I could sleep on your couch. I won't be a bother."

"Well, see, that would be a bother because we'd have to figure out which couch. On the other hand, we have at least seven unused bedrooms upstairs. I think we can spare one."

Not caring about the details, she thanked Milo and told him she would leave tomorrow morning and arrive by noon.

"If I'm not home, Agnes will let you in."

"Is Agnes the lovely lady I saw you with when I barged in on your dinner party?" Jen asked.

"No, that was Mary Alice. Agnes is my assistant. She is also lovely, I guess, to Sutherland…it's complicated."

"Who's Sutherland?"

"He owns half this place. It's complicated too."

"See you tomorrow," Jen said. "And Milo,"

"Yes?"

"Thank you."

9

"Morning Annie, Milo, and Jet," Martha said as the parade entered the hearth room before taking a sharp right turn into the morning room. Annie gave a silent meow. Milo said, "Morning Martha." And Jet squeaked.

Only Milo said good morning to Sutherland, who was sipping his smoothie while reading his Wall Street Journal. Sutherland mumbled a perfunctory "Morning," from behind his paper.

Unfocused, Milo filled his coffee and sat down, waiting for Martha to bring his breakfast. Annie sat patiently at his feet.

"Here you go, Mr. Rathkey," Martha said. "I made you watery poached eggs, and some healthy bran cereal."

Milo startled.

"Just wanted to see if you were awake yet. Here's your scrambled eggs, bacon, and hash browns."

Milo smiled as he broke off a few small pieces of bacon for Annie. "There are some things we don't kid about?"

"I doubt that," Martha said sarcastically. "By the way, notice the latest cat tricks."

Sutherland looked up. "Do they spin plates?"

"No. Annie has left one piece of her bacon on the floor for Jet."

"Jet doesn't eat bacon," Milo said. "I think he's Jewish… very religious."

"Could be Muslim," Sutherland countered, without looking up.

"He's a cat!" Martha said. "Jet doesn't eat the bacon. He's playing hockey with it. Watch."

Annie left the one piece, walked toward the hearth room, and turned around to watch Jet move in and start batting the bacon around the floor.

"I think she bets on the outcome," Martha said.

"With whom? There's only one player," said Sutherland.

"It's probably a cat thing," Milo mused. "Need-to-know basis, and we don't need to know."

Jet was now pretending the bacon was prey, but he squeaked before pouncing which, to Sutherland's mind, was an ineffective way to capture anything. He voiced that concern. Jet ignored him.

"By the way, I have invited Jen to stay here while we look for Lars," Milo announced.

"So, you've invited your ex-wife to stay at Lakesong while you look for her current husband."

Milo thought for a second. "Yeah. That sums it up. Good job."

And I thought the cats were unusual, Martha thought. "When will she arrive and what are her dietary preferences?"

"Today, and I don't have a clue."

Sutherland shook his head. "You were married to her and you don't know what she eats?"

"Ten years ago, when we were married, she ate food. Now she may eat gluten-free library paste. I don't know."

"I don't think they make gluten-free library paste—it's not cost effective."

Martha left the morning room and returned to the kitchen. "I'll ask her when she arrives," she said to herself.

Jet, who had played his bacon puck into the kitchen, squeaked his agreement.

§

Gramm's and White's first order of business was a meeting with Doc Smith at the morgue. They were both relieved that the bodies were not on the autopsy tables. The room itself was bad enough, with its stark, white walls and bleachy smell.

"Like we thought, the arrows killed them," Doc Smith said, clicking his magnetic glasses together. Gramm smiled knowing that the good doctor bought the glasses long ago after he saw a medical examiner use them in a television show.

"I've done a lot of research on bows and arrows in the past twenty-four hours. I haven't seen this type of weapon used before, at least not in a murder."

"So, what do we have?" Gramm asked.

Smith held up the intact arrow that was taken from Sithens' back. "You are looking at an Easton full metal jacket arrow with red-and-white fletching. These particular arrows are 30 inches."

"And we care about that, why?" Gramm asked.

"Means the killer has long arms."

"Arrows come in different lengths?" Gramm asked.

"It's called the draw. There is a correlation between the length of the archer's arms and the length of the arrow. Short arms—short arrow, long arms—long arrow."

"And a 30-inch arrow is long?" Gramm asked.

"Yes. Long arrow. Long arms. Tall guy."

"Or tall woman," White added.

Smith nodded.

"How tall?" Gramm asked.

"Six feet or over."

"You mentioned something was red and white."

"The fletching," Smith said. "The feathers are vanes, and a group of vanes is a fletching."

"Hunters tend to use the same color feathers," White said. "At least my brothers do."

"I've researched that. The technique of attaching the fletching is somewhat unique. We could match these arrows to their unused cousins, if you find them, but it wouldn't be absolute."

"So, this isn't like a bullet, where we can trace the striations and all to a particular gun."

"No, but fletchings tend to be different from one another; arrow length is different; and then there is the blade." Smith showed Gramm.

The lieutenant touched the tip. "This is nasty,"

"It's a three-blade fixed broadhead," Smith explained. "These are used by experienced hunters."

"Fixed as opposed to?" Gramm asked.

"Expandable," Smith said. "Expandable gets less penetration but is easier to aim. This tip is designed to cut through veins and arteries causing severe hemorrhaging. Death occurs within seconds."

Gramm shook his head. "So, this arrow could go right through a person?"

"From my research," Doc Smith said, "if the arrow doesn't hit bone, it can easily pass through a body."

"Okay, could this have been a hunting accident?" Gramm asked.

"Poacher?" White questioned. "The property owner is dead—good time to hunt there. Deer migrate toward the lake in the winter because snow depths are less."

Doc Smith clicked his glasses together, folded his arms, and stared at White and Gramm.

"What?" Gramm demanded.

"I have work to do. I need to follow logic and common sense."

"How is a poacher not common sense?" White asked.

"The victims were on the lighted lawn, fully visible. Since when does a blond woman in a white coat in full light get mistaken for a deer? I think the female victim was the target. She was shot through the heart from the front. The male victim appears to have been leaving the area—shot in the back, twice. The archer was in the woods. And, given the accuracy, this guy…person…was an experienced bow hunter."

Gramm summed up. "So, you're saying: not an accident, premeditated murder, and we're looking for experienced, tall, bow hunter with long arms, who hunts with red and white fletchers."

"Fletchings," Smith corrected.

§

Sutherland brought his coffee into his office and sat down. First order of business was finalizing tomorrow's Kiner site inspection with his environmental and structural engineering contractors. That task being accomplished he sat back to enjoy his coffee when he heard the ding alerting him to a new email. Sutherland froze. A new missive had arrived with the heading *THIS IS YOUR LAST WARNING.* Sutherland hesitated, and then opened it. There was no message, just the headline, but he knew from past threats what it was about. These threats were not going away. He had to tell his project partner, Mary Alice.

She answered on the first ring. "Sutherland. Not a problem with my new venue I hope."

"No, Lakesong is fine. Our project up the shore is causing concern, however."

"How so?"

"I've been getting threats, mostly by email. 'Drop your bid or else.' That sort of thing. I didn't know if I should take them seriously because they stopped for a while, but I just got another one moments ago."

Mary Alice didn't hesitate to name the perpetrator. "It's that bastard Fencig. He's just like James, thinks he can bully his way to what he wants. We are not dropping our bid, but don't go to the property alone."

"Well, Richard and I are meeting the engineering and environmental consultants out there."

"A crowd is good. I'll alert Richard to the threats. Oh, and tell Milo."

"I mentioned the previous threats to him. He said we needed to do a little shake and bake, whatever that is."

"Tell him it's shake and bake time." Mary Alice said as she hung up.

Sutherland called Milo. It went to voice mail. He left a message about the latest threat.

§

"I'm gonna tell Martha," Jamal informed Darian. "You can't keep sleeping in my room."

"Why not?" Darian asked. "We've had the same room for five years."

"You have a bedroom. Stay in it."

"It's scary even with earphones. It's too quiet. I'm up there all alone."

"She's gonna figure it out, dude," Jamal said, "and then I'll be in trouble for not telling her."

"The room is not happy. It doesn't want me there."

"Make friends with the room. Don't be stupid. I'll give you a day."

§

Sgt. White knocked on Gramm's doorframe. "We know more."

Gramm told her and Officer Preston to sit down. "Let's go through it."

"We've looked through both victim's phones," White said. "Sithens was getting interesting texts from a woman named Kayla Maki—angry and threatening."

"Threatening how?"

"Her words: 'I'll stick you and your bitch!"

"Knife? Arrow?"

"Certainly, something sharp," White said.

"Could this be the angry woman mentioned by Van Dyke?"

"And Nurse Sandlan," Preston added.

White nodded. "We're looking to find the right Kayla Maki. There are a number of them."

"What about the female victim's phone?" Gramm asked.

"Here's another interesting bit—she was also getting threatening emails from this Kayla Maki."

"Along with a lot of others," Preston added. "I don't know why she even opened up some of these emails."

"Who from?" Gramm asked.

Preston looked at her notes. "An Eddy Peterson wonders why she's ghosting him when they're engaged. His words border on threatening."

Gramm sat up. "Ghosting?"

Preston didn't get it. "I don't understand sir?"

"Think generational confusion," White said. "He knows we're not talking about ghosts, but he doesn't know what ghosting means."

"Oh, sorry," Preston apologized. "She had stopped answering him. When Milo and I talked with the nurse, Monica Sandlan, she indicated that the victim was engaged to an Eddy. Didn't know the last name."

"Another series of threats comes from—drum roll please—Ike Granton," White said. "He also thinks he's engaged to her. He doesn't care about ghosting. He's just plain threatening her because he saw her out with another man. If the other man is Alex Sithens, jealousy could be a motive for killing her or both of them."

Gramm sat back. "Mom and Dad say our victim didn't date. A nurse she works with says she likes to get engaged, and, so far, we have two guys who think they're going to marry her, and neither is the guy she died with. Who was she?"

Milo walked in, rolling a desk chair. White and Preston moved over.

"You're late! Again!" Gramm admonished.

"My ex-wife is coming to stay at Lakesong. I had to make arrangements," Milo said, without apology.

Gramm stared at him, in silence, for at least ten seconds. "I'm going to stop trying to make sense of anything you say. It hurts my head."

Preston laughed and said, "Just ghost him."

§

"I got a problem," Martha said to Agnes as they chatted over coffee.

"What?" Agnes asked.

“Darian’s not sleeping in his room. I think he’s coming down at night and sleeping in Jamal’s room.”

“What gives you that idea?”

“I heard him last night. Little footsteps came down the stairs but didn’t go back up,” Martha said.

“Maybe he had to go to the bathroom, and you just didn’t hear him go up,” Agnes suggested.

“He has a shiny new bathroom upstairs.”

“Oh, right. I forgot.”

“Breanna is coming home tonight to study for finals. I’ll ask her to investigate,” Martha said, referring to her oldest sibling who was living in a college dorm on the Duluth campus of The University of Minnesota.

“Why not ask Darian?”

“He would be embarrassed.”

“Jamal?”

“That would force him to violate the ‘bro code.’ I think the solution is a non-testosterone person—Breanna.”

“Smart move.”

§

Friendly Al Lerner waited for Nancy Wickland to leave for the day so he wouldn’t be overheard. Pressing Ike Granton’s home number, he waited for his mechanic to pick up.

“Yeah?” Granton answered.

“The cops were in today looking for you!”

“Me? Why?”

“Because you punched the sign guy!”

“The sign guy? Oh, yeah. He’s an asshole.”

"Not smart, Ike. Not smart at all."

"So, the wimp went to the cops. Big deal."

"The *wimp* is dead. Murdered!"

"Tough break for him."

Friendly Al scowled. "I don't need this, Ike."

Granton didn't react.

"I think the cops are gonna pay you a visit," Lerner said as he ended the call.

I'm out in the country. They're not coming out here, Ike thought. He put his phone down, stretched out on his couch, and fell asleep.

10

With so many interviews to conduct and so much information to share, Gramm requested that the troops eat in rather than spending precious hours watching Milo harass restaurant owners and their staff. White and Preston convinced Gramm to avoid the vending machines, and get soup and sandwiches delivered from Mike's House of Soup. Milo bucked the trend and followed his taste buds to two vending machine burritos and a Diet Coke.

Bad luck. Herman from bunco was hunkered in front of Milo's favorite machine. Milo spotted his burritos inch by as Herman rotated the food trays. Finding nothing to his liking on the first complete go around, Herman began the crawling rotation for a second time. Milo thought a Taser might help Herman decide. After watching eight columns of sandwiches, burritos, chicken fingers, and oranges go by a second time, Herman gave up and went to another machine.

Credit card in hand, Milo pressed the rotation button six times until the burritos arrived. One burrito later, he repeated the action a second time. While the industrial strength microwave melded the burrito beans, cheese, and preservatives inside the soft, floured tortilla, Milo rushed to the soda machine and selected his go-to soda, Diet Coke. Milo, food and drink successfully acquired, returned triumphantly to Gramm's office.

Gramm was already in a grumpy mood, and watching Milo savoring the burritos didn't help. Milo finished burrito one and started in on burrito two, declaring it more delicious than the first.

"Floodwood!" Gramm erupted, causing his companions to jump. "Why does Ike Granton have to live out in Floodwood?"

White turned to Preston. "You would think if someone were going to be a suspect in a murder, they would have the courtesy to live inside the city limits."

Preston laughed. "Suspects can be so uncaring these days."

Gramm's eyebrows knitted together. "Glad we're all in agreement." After several seconds of silence, Gramm barked, "Milo!"

Milo looked up. "What?"

"Get me one of those burritos or I'll shoot you and steal yours!"

"Don't want to wait for the House of Soup?"

"Burrito! Now!" Gramm could be even grumpier when he was hungry.

Milo repeated his vending machine trip—minus the Diet Coke—and returned, setting two perfectly melded burritos in front of Gramm.

Gramm devoured his vending machine fare, while White brought Rathkey and Preston up to date on the discussion with Doc Smith about the arrows and bow involved in the killing.

"Whoever did this, left the scene by boat," Gramm added. "He or she," Gramm nodded to White, "tried to erase his or her tracks but left a trail that led to the lake. There is still open water for a boat to be maneuvered close to shore."

"This wasn't just planned," Milo said, "it was produced."

"What's the difference?" Preston asked.

"If you wanted me dead, and knew I was going to be at Hawthorne, how would you do it?" Milo asked.

Preston thought for a second and said, "Well, the easy way is to follow you to Hawthorne and shoot you. Then drive away."

White jumped in, "You could be heard driving up, or be seen by a random jogger. Coming from the back, by boat, you avoid detection. I just checked. That night the wind was blowing out of the west, toward the lake. If I were the hunter that's where I would approach, downwind from the prey—you know, so the deer couldn't smell me."

"But these are people. People don't smell people," Preston said.

"No," White agreed, "but it's just habit if you hunt."

Milo finished his second burrito. "Who knew our victims were going to be at the Hawthorne Estate? Nurse Sandlan told us she knew."

Preston waved her phone. "Everybody who looked at her Instagram page knew." She read from Faythe's page. "Tonight's destination Hawthorne Estate planning for the most magnificent wedding ever! #superweddingplan."

"How friggin' convenient," Gramm muttered.

"Don't forget the realtor, Arial Jenkins," Milo said.

"Why would a realtor kill them?" Preston asked.

"Don't have a clue."

"What about talcum powder?" White blurted.

Gramm stared at her before picking up the forensics report he received that morning.

"Before I go hunting, I bathe in corn starch," Milo said. "It makes me feel fresh."

Gramm, still looking at the report, said, "If anyone has a weapon, please shoot Milo."

"I don't know if I'm up or down wind," Preston joked.

"Son of a gun!" Gramm exclaimed. "Traces of talcum powder were found on two trees." He looked up at White. "Care to explain?"

"Wind direction. When I hunted, I always carried a puffer of talcum powder to check on wind direction. Even though the killer came up from the lake, he or she was checking on which side of the trees was optimum."

"That cements it. Our killer was an experienced bow hunter," Gramm said, standing up. "Piece of cake. There are probably only thousands in this area alone." Stretching out his back, he added, "I guess White and I are off to Floodwood to interview Ike Granton. What do you propose to do, Milo?"

"I thought Preston and I would go to the Arrowhead Archery Range. I need to see these compound bows for myself."

"Why?" Gramm asked.

"Well, for one thing, I don't know anything about them. Listening to Robin, our killer could be a woman." Milo said.

"Absolutely!" White agreed. "Extreme strength is not necessary for extreme results with modern compound bows."

"Preston will be my model," Milo said, "I want to see her use one of these bows."

Preston smiled. "I never thought of myself as a model. Can I put it on my Instagram page?"

§

"Martha, I'm home early!" Breanna yelled as she walked into the cottage.

Martha greeted her in the kitchen. "Welcome home, college person!" she said, enfolding her sister in a hug before Breanna broke away and reached for the cookie jar.

Two oatmeal-chocolate-chip cookies in hand—one being munched on—she informed Martha, "I finished my last class and I have to study for finals. My room will be quieter than the dorm."

Martha watched Breanna blink. "Not quite used to your new contacts?"

"Today they are uncomfortable for some reason. I've got the drops in my purse. They'll be fine." She lugged her bags into her room.

"Are you hungry for more than cookies?" Martha shouted.

"Always," Breanna shouted back.

"I'll heat up some beef stew."

"I'll eat after I throw in a load of laundry."

§

The drive from the Duluth Police Department to Floodwood, Minnesota took about an hour. Gramm complained the entire time. "O'Dell is investigating the death of a woman on Arrowhead Road. There were three people in the house the night she died. In the house! All the suspects live in the same house! After the autopsy, it's probably natural causes. We catch a murder-by-arrow that has us all over the place—up to Proctor and now out to Floodwood."

"O'Dell lives right," White said.

"Maybe you should partner with him," Gramm kidded.

"And miss these quaint drives in the country? Never!"

The GPS told Gramm to turn left onto a narrow, two-lane country road, made narrower by snowdrifts. After crunching through packed snow for about a mile, the GPS declared that they had arrived at their destination. Gramm stopped and looked at the two giant snowbanks on either side of the car.

"Unless he lives in the snowbank, I think this is not it," White said.

"This was a lot easier when the county used fire numbers," Gramm complained. He traveled a little farther and spotted a mailbox, almost buried in snow, next to a rutted, poorly plowed lane. Turning in, he stopped in front of a brown farmhouse with a green shutter hanging down from an upstairs window, and a porch rail leaning too far right to be trusted.

Gramm and White got out of the car and walked up the warped steps, testing each one before committing their entire weight to it. Gramm knocked. There was no answer. He knocked again. Nothing.

Ike Granton, still asleep on the couch, bolted up, checked his doorbell camera, and saw what he thought were two cops. "Crap!" Slamming on his boots, and grabbing his leather jacket, he ran out the back door to the barn.

"I think we're on camera," White said, pointing to the doorbell.

"Why would you need that out here?" Gramm wondered out loud.

The Harley gas tank is full, Ike thought.

White tilted her head, "I hear something around back,"

Granton looked around at all the *merchandise* waiting to be moved. *I'm in no mood and they need a search warrant.*

Gramm and White left the porch, and trudged around the house to a weathered, red barn also in need of repair. As they approached the double doors, they heard an engine start up seconds before one of the barn doors flew open and a motorcycle roared out of the building. White jumped out of the way, hit the ground hard, and rolled. The motorcycle screamed past, narrowly missing her leg. Gramm took a step back and shouted at the retreating rider who held up a middle finger before turning left, onto the road.

White stood up. "Asshole!" she shouted.

"You okay?" Gramm asked.

"Yeah. Do we think that was Granton?"

"Yeah, I do. It's his place and he was anxious to get away."

"Let's check out the barn, since it's open," White said, brushing snow off her coat as she walked through the doors.

Gramm joined her. They moved with caution through the barn to make sure the runaway cyclist didn't have an accomplice. There were no people, but they found a white panel van, stacks of televisions, game systems, phones, a canoe, and two kayaks.

"This may be why our motorcyclist was in such a hurry to leave," White said. "Stolen property or a large Christmas list?"

"Not our problem," Gramm countered, calling the St. Louis County Sheriff's department. "However, I'll put out a BOLO on Granton."

"Look at that." White pointed to a round target hanging from a bale of hay in the back of the barn. Two arrows with black and white fletchings were imbedded near the center. White pulled them out and looked at the tip. "Target arrows," she pronounced, "not hunting arrows."

"Still, somebody's a pretty good shot," Gramm added.

"Should we get a warrant to look in the house?" White asked.

"Let's wait for the sheriff. This is county jurisdiction. He has probable cause. We'll tag along—saves on paperwork."

§

Jen Helvig arrived at the Lakesong gates with questions, but with more hope than her initial visit a week ago. Then, she was desperately looking for her vanished husband. She didn't know anything. Now, thanks to Milo, she knew Lars was alive and maybe living somewhere in Duluth. She just didn't know why he disappeared. As the gates opened inward Jen took in the majesty of Lakesong in the daylight. "Milo, how is this your house?" she asked out loud.

Workers were placing Christmas wreaths, lights, and ribbons on the house and the surrounding trees. Jen drove around two trucks to the front steps and watched the decorations being arranged. *Cranes and trucks! My Christmas comes with a ladder and a cardboard box,* she thought.

Agnes had been alerted to Jen's presence by the intercom and met her at the front door. "Welcome back," Agnes said, having seen Jen when she arrived unexpectedly during the dinner party last week.

"Thank you," Jen said, pulling her suitcase up the front steps.

"I'm Agnes, by the way. I'm Milo's assistant. Anything you need, just let me know. Your room is ready. Let's get you settled, and then, if you like, I'll give you a tour of the house."

Jen followed Agnes who took the suitcase and headed up the double staircase. "Martha wanted me to ask you if you have any food allergies or preferences."

"Who's Martha?" Jen asked.

"Lakesong's chef. You'll meet her when you come down," Agnes said as they arrived at the bedroom. "I picked this one because it's my favorite." Agnes tossed a welcoming smile in Jen's direction as she placed her suitcase on the bed. "You have an en suite, and a view of the lake."

Jen smiled as she took in the dusty-rose carpeting, pink-flowered wallpaper, and the dark, carved, four-poster-bed with matching nightstands. "This is beautiful. And a fireplace! Does it work?"

"All the bedrooms have working fireplaces," Agnes explained.

Agnes noticed Jen absently reordering the little Chinese porcelain vases on the mantle by height, with the tallest one in the middle.

"I'm going back to my office. When you're ready to come down, I'm right off the front door. Or you can just wander in the gallery—our indoor park. Say hello to Annie the cat. She will be up in her tree. And be careful not to trip over our black cat, Jet, who loves to walk in front of people and stop. We don't know why."

Jen walked over to the pink-and-white-striped chair by the window, and watched the cold, gray clouds hang over Lake Superior.

§

Milo's idea of just dropping in on the Arrowhead Archery Range was nixed by Preston who called ahead and made an appointment to see the director. "What if nobody is there that can help us?" she had argued.

"What if these two deaths were part of an Arrowhead Archery Range conspiracy. Now you've given them time to bury the arrows in a neighbor's garden," Milo protested.

"It's not easy living in your brain, is it?"

"I simply point out the obvious," Milo said as he pulled into the archery range's parking lot. Next door, at the tire store, a front loader was digging up a portion of that parking lot. Milo immediately pointed to the activity. "See. I was right, they're burying arrows as we speak."

"You'd think they'd be a little less obvious," Preston joked.

"Hiding in plain sight. They're diabolical."

As Preston got out of the car she added, "Let's go back to the difficulty of living in your brain."

Milo wondered about the ice machine out front and then he saw the smaller, faded sign under the main archery range sign that read, and Bait Shop. "Great. We can pick up some nightcrawlers. You can't have too many nightcrawlers in December."

"Archery Range and Bait Shop?" Preston questioned. "Kinda odd pairing isn't it?"

"It's Duluth," Milo said. "Every store has a bait shop. My chiropractor has a bait shop. Crack your back, get a free minnow."

Preston started laughing.

"Let's maintain a little decorum," Milo said, straight faced as he entered the one-story, corrugated-metal building with a dark-green-painted wood façade.

Bubblers from several minnow tanks provided a background noise, but not enough to drown out the thumps coming from the six-person range. A large floor fan failed to rid the place of a fishy, musty smell.

Milo waited in line at the counter that serviced both archers and fishermen. Two people bought bait, and one person paid for an archery lane. "Isn't it kinda late in the season for fishing?" Milo asked the two bait people

"Naw. Ice fishing up at Leech Lake. Going up for pan fish," one said, showing his recently purchased maggots and minnows. "But if a walleye wants to hit my jigging spoon, I wouldn't throw him back."

"Ice fishing?" Milo asked. "Is the ice thick enough?"

"Oh yeah," the other man said. "On the inland lakes, but no ATV's yet. You're gonna go through."

"Yeah, some poor guy went through the ice over in Wisconsin last weekend. You gotta be safe."

"Well, good luck," Milo said.

"Oh yeah," they said in unison and left.

"Do you fish?" Preston asked Milo.

"Nope; hate it," Milo said.

"Then why ask them all those questions?"

"Who knows—the next murderer could use a jigging spoon. Now I'm ahead of the game."

"Whacha need?" the tall, thick, bearded man behind the counter questioned, looking at Preston's uniform.

"We are here to see Eero Maki," Preston said.

The man yelled, "Hey Eero, you got a lady cop here."

"Send her back," a voice yelled in reply.

The man pointed to a door on the left. "He's in the shop."

Milo motioned for Preston to go ahead. "Lady cops go first."

Preston rolled her eyes. The guy behind the desk didn't appear to catch Milo's sarcasm.

Milo stopped to watch a woman fire an arrow in the bullseye. "She's good," Milo said, then realized that he was alone. Preston had already left. He caught up, entering the shop—a building within a building.

"Milo, this is Mr. Maki," Preston said, introducing a short-cropped, white-haired, stubble-bearded man with glasses sliding down his nose. The room was cluttered with bows of various types, and arrows lined up on a table next to a machine that attached new feathers.

After completing a couple of feather attachments, Maki looked up, shook Milo's hand, and introduced himself.

"So, the feathers are just glued on?" Milo asked.

"Yeah, with the help of my jigging machine. Whaddaya need?" Maki asked.

"We need to see a compound bow—part of an investigation," Milo said.

"Those two people there on the shore? I read about them." Maki turned to a wall of bows and pulled one down. It was black with a thick center and two thinner arms jutting off to cams that seemed to hold a number of cables. Three arrows were affixed to a bow-mounted quiver.

Milo stared at it for almost a minute. "What type of engineering degree do you need to use this thing?"

Maki nodded. "It's complicated to design, but not to use."

Milo looked again at the cams, cables, and collection of bolts, sights, and knobs. "Can you show it to us—in action I mean."

"Sure. This particular bow pulled down an 800-pound elk with only fourteen pounds of force. There's a picture of the elk there on my wall. This little lady here could do it."

Preston took a deep breath and let the *little lady* remark pass. "Let's do this."

Maki led them to the florescent-lighted archery range. Preston took off her uniform jacket. Her draw was measured to determine the arrow length. Maki gave her a brief training session, and she stepped up to the firing line. Preston nocked the arrow, pulled it back, aimed, and fired. The arrow buried itself into the top ring of the target.

"This is not hard at all!" Preston said, nocking another arrow. Her second attempt hit closer to the center of the target.

Milo declined an offer to give it a try, asking instead about the arrows. "I see the feathers are red and yellow. I noticed one of the people out there was using red and white feathers. What's the difference?"

"Preference," Maki said. "The color doesn't matter, but the composition of the vanes or feathers does make a difference, along with size, placement, and patterns. Different fletchings, or group of feathers, for different wind conditions. Oh, and as color goes, most fletchings have one odd color—two red, one white for instance."

Eero was a guy who knew his stuff and could go on for hours explaining it. Milo had enough. He didn't care why one arrow was a different color, only that it was normal. After Preston had shot a few more arrows, they proceeded back to the shop where Maki proudly pointed to the elk picture. Milo noticed that, below the picture of the elk takedown, there were several pictures of a young, pony-tailed girl standing next to Eero. In each picture, the young lady was holding a competition medal and a compound bow. Seeing the pictures of the girl had caught Milo's attention, Eero explained, "My daughter. She's good."

§

While the sheriff deputies were going through the stolen goods in Ike Granton's barn and house, Gramm and White discovered several bows and hunting arrows in the barn loft. After grabbing and tagging them as evidence Gramm suggested there was still time left in the day to interview Kayla Maki.

Through a series of phone calls, White had learned that *a* Kayla Maki, who fit the age of *their* Kayla Maki, leased a small booth in a cooperative in Hermantown where she sold homemade candles, soaps, and essential oils. After complaining about having to go to yet another small town outside of Duluth, Gramm pulled up to the garish, yellow building with a painted, blue sign that read, "Mini Mall."

The mall consisted of a long hallway with doors on either side, some open, some closed. As Gramm and White walked down the hall, they passed a t-shirt shop, a tattoo parlor, several jewelry shops, and a natural-fabric clothing store. White stepped into the clothing store. A young woman wearing a tie-dyed shirt came over to assist.

"I'm looking for the candle shop. A friend told me it was here," White said, "but I can't find it."

"That's Kayla. She's got a kiosk in the big mall area. It's in the back," the woman said.

White complimented the store owner on how attractive her merchandise was and thanked her for the information.

"You aren't buying anything?" Gramm asked.

"Not at those prices."

Passing several more shops, the two walked into a large mall area with numerous booths set up as a market. Gramm spotted a kiosk with candles and soaps and pointed it out to White. A blond, twentyish woman glanced up from her phone and took off running toward a back door.

Gramm shook his head. "Another runner? Why?"

White took off after her. Several customers and kiosk owners stared at the unusual activity, moving out of the way as White streaked past. Kayla had a good head start, and by the time White slammed open the outside backdoor, her prey had disappeared. She came back in and shook her head.

Gramm nodded. “Why is everyone so anxious to get away? We don’t even know if she’s the right Kayla Maki.” He called in another BOLO. “We now have time to talk to Eddy Peterson. His office brings us back to Duluth closer to dinnertime. Let’s see if he wants to run too.”

“At least she didn’t try to run me over,” White added, noticing another shop person putting away Kayla’s merchandise and cash box. “You look as though you have done this before.”

The woman looked up. “Kayla has her moments. We look out for each other.”

11

"This is delicious!" Jen said, sampling a Martha-made-tuna-avocado salad. She was relaxing at the gallery patio table, enjoying a late lunch with Agnes and Martha.

"This is so nice of you," Jen said, cutting the avocado into smaller, bite-sized pieces then placing the knife at the top of her salad bowl. "I hope I didn't put you to any trouble." Jen's attention went back to her knife. She slid it slightly to the left, centering it.

Martha smiled. "Being a personal chef, I tailor my food to my client's tastes."

"This must be an awkward situation for you," Jen acknowledged. "Do you know why I'm here?"

"We excel in awkward situations," Agnes admitted.

"Especially since Mr. Rathkey came to live here," Martha added.

"He always did attract interesting situations and characters," Jen said. "I guess now, I'm one of those characters."

"I was one of his characters a year ago," Agnes said. "That's how I came to work here."

Jen waited for further explanation, but there wasn't any.

"I have to ask this. I've been staring at your hair since you arrived," Agnes said. "I love your short, feathery, pixie bob. I wanted to go with a short, sophisticated do for my reunion a few months ago—something to age this baby face. Martha and I thought my cut was pretty good, but yours is better. It's youthful and fun, spiky yet smooth. Where did you get that done?"

"Oh, thank you. My cousin thanks you. She does hair in one of those edgy salons in the cities and does mine for half price in my kitchen in Brainerd."

"I get to the cities now and then," Agnes said. "I'd love her contact information."

Jen brought up her cousin's contact information and slid her phone over to Agnes. Finishing her salad while looking around the park-like gallery, she mused, "The last time I heard, Milo was living in an apartment over a bakery downtown. This place does not look like it's above a bakery."

"Milo lived above Ilene's Bakery for years before he inherited half of this place," Agnes explained.

"Oh gosh," Jen exclaimed, catching sight of Annie in the Guiana chestnut tree. "That's a real cat."

A squeak under Agnes' chair complained about the singular reference. Jen looked down at two blinking, yellow eyes. "Oh, I guess this is the other one."

"Annie and Jet," Agnes said. "They live here. We just work here."

Jen sat back. "To talk about hairstyles and cats is wonderful. I have been so hyper-focused on Lars. I was so worried—still am."

Jet crawled out from under the chair and rubbed up against Jen's legs. She reached down to pet him and he rolled on his back exposing his tummy.

"Oh, well, he's relaxed. A good role model," Jen said, petting Jet's soft, black fur.

"He has picked up the vibe of Lakesong," Agnes said. "Mellow."

§

The Peterson Insurance Agency occupied a small corner of a strip mall on the Miller Trunk Highway. As Gramm and White left their car, Gramm wondered if they should have backup at the rear door. "Two runners already. Three strikes and we're out."

White nodded. "I'll go around the back. *Covering our bases* as long as we're doing out-of-season baseball analogies."

Gramm waited a couple of minutes before entering. The small yellow office featured a receptionist's desk and two small glass enclosed cubicles. The receptionist, a middle-aged woman with sharp, piercing eyes yet a soft voice, welcomed him to the Peterson Agency.

He showed his badge and asked to see Eddy Peterson. "He knows we're coming."

She looked behind her at the man in one of the cubicles. "He's not on the phone so go on in."

As Gramm moved toward Peterson's cubicle, he was joined by White who entered through the back door. "If he ran," White said, "I missed him."

The cubicle door was open. Gramm couldn't see any other means of escape. He knocked on the door frame. "Mr. Peterson?"

The tall man with a receding hairline looked up. His round, hazel, watery eyes moved from Gramm to White. He cleared his throat and tried to stand up, but only succeeded in moving up in his chair. "Yes?"

"I'm Lieutenant Gramm, and this is Sergeant White. We would like to ask you a few questions."

"Of course. Sit down."

Gramm and White complied. White took out her pad as she looked around at the various *Agency of the Year* plaques that insurance companies seemed to hand out to all their agents.

Gramm went right to the point. "I understand you knew Faythe Cummings."

Peterson took a drink from his fast-food cup and blinked several times, staring at them. He smiled but said nothing.

White knew from Peterson's glassy eyes that he was drinking something stronger than pop.

"Mr. Peterson?" Gramm asked with agitation. "I asked you a question."

Peterson started, "Sorry. Didn't I answer?"

"No, you did not," Gramm insisted.

"What was the question?"

"What was your relationship with Faythe Cummings?"

"Faythe and I are engaged to be married."

White glanced at a picture on the back credenza of Peterson, a woman—not Faythe—and two children. "From that photo behind you, I would guess you are already married."

Peterson tried to swing around but almost lost his balance on the chair. Righting himself, he explained, "My wife and I are in the process of getting divorced. I think."

"You think?" Gramm asked. "You don't know?"

"Well," he took another drink from his Chicken Delicious cup. White stood, reached over, removed Peterson's cup from his shaking hand, and handed it to Gramm. Peterson looked surprised, "That's mine!"

"I'll get you coffee," White said, getting up and going to the receptionist.

Gramm sniffed the Chicken Delicious cup and jerked back. "When did Chicken Delicious add whiskey to its menu?"

"This has not been a good week."

White caught the receptionist's attention. "Could I get a cup of coffee for Mr. Peterson?" she asked.

"Good luck with that. I've been trying to get him away from those Chicken Delicious cocktails for at least a week. Clients have been walking out. I'm going to be out of a job." She pointed to the coffee cart. White poured a cup of black coffee and took it into Peterson's office.

Peterson stared at the cup in bewilderment.

"It's either coffee, or you can come to our office to sober up," Gramm said.

Peterson took a sip. He sat back, hunched over, and mumbled, "My life's a mess."

"Because of Ms. Cummings?" White asked.

Peterson stared at her. "Faythe. My lovely Faythe. Why?"

"Why what?" Gramm was confused.

He looked up at Gramm. "We were going to get married then she disappeared—wouldn't return my calls or texts. Why? I tried to see her. I'm a nice guy."

White looked again at the Peterson family picture, *Nice guy? Yeah, right, buddy.*

"Did you know she was marrying another man?" Gramm asked.

"No!" Peterson erupted, struggling to stand. "She's mine! She belongs to me! I belong to her!" He slumped back down in the chair.

"Are you a bow hunter?" Gramm asked.

Peterson seemed confused, "Yeah. I golf too. I've got a fifteen handicap. Not bad for a duffer." A smile crossed his mouth then disappeared. "Why are we talking about golf?"

"We're not. You are. We're talking about bow hunting," Gramm challenged, wondering how a drunk man remembers his golf handicap.

"Drink the coffee," White urged.

Peterson took another sip, set the cup down, and shoved it toward White. "I really enjoy hunting. My group goes. We fly." Peterson waved his hands in mock flight as if Gramm and White didn't understand what flying meant. "Montana. Good times."

Gramm wondered if this was a drunk act or the real thing. "So, what do you do in Montana, golf or bow hunt?"

Peterson giggled. "Who would go to Montana to golf?"

"Where were you on Monday night?" White asked.

Peterson squinted at the Chicken Delicious cup across the desk. "My kids. I love my kids—watch them all the time."

"Where were you Monday night?" White repeated.

"Watching my kids."

"Do you know why we're here?" White asked.

"Faythe's mad at me…with my emails. She won't talk to me. It's a game we play. I say mean things. I say I'm sorry. She forgives me. She says okay. All is good."

Gramm looked at White. "Mr. Peterson," he began, "Faythe Cummings was murdered Monday night."

Peterson looked from Gramm to White back to Gramm, his eyes blinking. He snorted. "No. She's just mad…so beautiful!"

White asked where he was living and noted that he had a room at the Extended Stay Hotel on Lake Avenue. Peterson attempted to recapture his Chicken Delicious cup from across his desk but knocked it over, spilling the contents. "Oops." He laughed.

White stood up and demanded Peterson's car keys. Reluctantly, he handed them to her. On the way out, White gave them to the receptionist. "Call him a cab when he's ready to go home."

The receptionist put the keys in her top drawer and locked it. "Thank you. You saved me the trouble."

Gramm made an unusual request of White. "He bow hunts and is estranged from his wife and our victim. We need to talk to him again when he sobers up. Check to see if Mr. Peterson has acting experience."

§

Breanna walked into the gallery looking for her sister. Seeing that Martha was in a conversation with Agnes and a woman Breanna had never seen before, she excused herself, and was about to leave when Martha stopped her. She introduced Breanna to Jen before asking what her sister needed.

"I wanted to see Darian's new room, but I can't find it," Breanna said.

Agnes and Martha laughed. Jen looked puzzled. "You lost a room?"

"It's a secret room," Martha explained.

"First you put on Jamal's old going-to-church shoes," Agnes said, "then walk fifteen paces from the kitchen and kick the baseboard on the right side. All will be revealed."

"You're kidding!" Breanna exclaimed. "A normal stairway up to the attic would be too much to ask?"

"This is Lakesong," Martha said.

"After we found that secret door, I found another in the main house connecting the upstairs and downstairs libraries though a secret staircase," Agnes said.

Martha collected the dishes and said to Breanna, "Let's go to the cottage. I'll watch you try to find it."

"Would you mind if I came?" Jen asked. "I've never seen a secret staircase."

"Certainly," Martha said. "Let's all go."

"Where is the cottage?" Jen asked.

"It's toward the back of the estate," Martha explained.

Jen nodded, "I'll get my coat,"

Agnes laughed. "Coats are not necessary. We have tunnels."

As Martha led the way to the basement. Breanna said, "We also have an elevator that nobody knew about except Mr. Rathkey."

Jen turned around on the stairs and looked at her. "You lost an elevator?"

"And a kitchen," Martha added. "We've had many discoveries since Mr. Rathkey returned to Lakesong."

"Returned? Oh, wait a minute! This is the house Milo always talked about. This is where he grew up. Now it makes sense," Jen exclaimed. "Well, hello Lakesong. I feel I know you."

"We live in the caretaker's cottage. Maybe you know about that too," Martha said.

Jen nodded. "Oh, the telescope on the roof! Milo talked about that a couple of times."

"Telescope!" Breanna exploded. "We have a telescope? Martha?"

"Oops. Did I say too much?" Jen apologized.

"It's fine—for Breanna," Martha said. "I don't want Darian or Jamal to know about it yet."

Agnes led the way through the tunnel to the cottage. Jen kept asking if the tunnel was safe. Agnes assured her it was maintained by one of Sutherland McKnight's guys.

"Who's Sutherland McKnight?" Jen asked.

"Milo's brother from a different mother and father," Agnes cracked. "Mr. Rathkey and Mr. McKnight co-own this estate."

"Ah, Milo talked about a different McKnight—John, I think. All these pieces are coming together."

Once in the cottage, Agnes insisted that Breanna wear Jamal's shoes. Laughing, Breanna put on Jamal's oversized shoes with balled-up socks in the toes and counted out fifteen steps from the kitchen: "…fourteen…fifteen."

"Now kick—hard!" Martha instructed.

Breanna looked at her. "Really? Kick the woodwork? Really?"

"You want to see the room? Start kicking," Martha said.

Jen hung back, watching to see what was going to happen. Breanna gave the woodwork her best soccer-forward kick. The panel in front of Breanna opened. "Oh my!" she exclaimed.

"Breanna, Lakesong. Lakesong, Breanna," Agnes said, explaining that people get introduced to the house when they discover one of its secrets. It was a tradition she was starting.

Martha flipped on the new light switch and the troop ascended the bright stairway into the newly constructed bedroom, with its light gray walls, white trim, and recessed lighting.

"This is nice!" Breanna said. "What's in here?" she asked as she went into the bathroom. "Darian has his own bathroom? Why?"

"What a great room!" Jen said, looking around.

"Well, you would think so, however Darian is a young nine. He has always slept in the same room as his brother. Since getting this room, he's coming down at night and sleeping on the floor next to Jamal's bed. I think being by himself scares him. I'm not sure what I'm going to do."

Breanna came out of the bathroom and touched Martha's shoulder. "I do. Let's talk."

§

Gramm and White arrived at the station having interviewed only one of their three suspects. They hit the vending machines one more time and headed to Gramm's office.

Gramm sat back in his chair and opened his peanuts with a sigh. "I really wanted Cheetos, but, after thirty years of marriage, Amy has had a detrimental effect on me. Peanuts are healthier, she says."

"Good for Amy," White said, opening her package of crackers. Seeing Gramm's envious look, she added, "I need the carbs. I'm going to the gym after work."

"So," Gramm began, emptying his peanuts on his desk, "tomorrow we need to talk to Peterson's wife—check his alibi."

Before White could react, Gramm's phone rang. He picked it up, hit speaker, and said, "Gramm."

"Yeah, this is Sergeant Zimmerman up in Hibbing. We got your boy."

"Ike Granton?"

"Yup. Are you looking for someone else?"

"We are, but she's a she. We got a lot of runners today. Thanks for grabbing Granton."

"I'd like to take credit for him, but he was racing through town, hit a pothole, and rammed his bike into a car. When we ran his name, up popped your BOLO. He's okay, but the bike is a wreck. It came up stolen."

"Yeah, Ike has a stolen goods problem with county, but we want to talk to him about murder. The sheriff and I agreed—murder before theft."

"He's a real pain in the ass. We'll bring him to you. I assume our trip will be reimbursed by the Duluth PD," Zimmerman added.

"Certainly." Gramm thanked Zimmerman one more time and transferred him to the desk Sergeant to work out the details.

"Change in plans," White said, almost to herself. "Tomorrow, we interview Ike Granton. Let's send Preston to talk to Peterson's wife."

§

"Has Jen arrived?" Milo asked Sutherland as the latter came into the family room for dinner.

Sutherland shrugged. "I haven't seen her. Did you lose her again?"

Milo had finished his vodka gimlet by the time Sutherland mixed and shook his martini and poured it into a glass. They both took their seats at the table.

Jen walked in. Sutherland stood. Milo followed his lead. "Hello," Sutherland said, "I'm Sutherland McKnight. Welcome to Lakesong. I hope you have settled in comfortably."

"Everyone has been so helpful and gracious."

"Can I get you something to drink?"

"If you have the ingredients, I would enjoy a cranberry juice spritzer," Jen said.

"Remind me again, what goes into one of those?"

"Cranberry juice, honey, seltzer, ice cubes and a slice of orange."

Taking a few minutes to look over the well-stocked bar, Sutherland said, "We're missing a few ingredients."

"Like the cranberry juice, honey, and orange?" Milo questioned.

Jen shrugged. "Oh, that's okay…"

Martha interrupted coming in from the kitchen, handing Jen her drink. "Try this."

Jen sipped the spritzer. "Oh, this is good!"

Sutherland pulled out the chair next to him for Jen to sit down. Milo introduced himself, "Hi, I'm Milo Rathkey. We were married a long time ago."

Jen looked at him, cocking her head to one side. "Rathkey?" she said slowly and then repeated, "Rathkey? Nope—doesn't ring any bells."

Sutherland laughed. "She out Miloed you!"

Milo shrugged. "It could be I'm not that memorable."

"I think we can all agree on that," Sutherland raised his glass, "and drink to it."

Jen moved the bottle of wine to the center of the table, saying, "Now you have out Miloed, Milo."

"Thank you. I've been working on it for the past year," Sutherland said.

"Hello. I'm here you know, sitting at the table," Milo complained.

Martha entered with salads. "I have roasted vegetable salad with maple-curry vinaigrette for Mr. Sutherland and Ms. Helvig," she said, placing them in front of Sutherland and Jen. "Mr. Rathkey you have…"

"Iceberg lettuce with blue cheese dressing," Jen said, moving her plate an inch and a half to the right, straightening her already straight silverware.

Martha placed Milo's salad in front of him.

"Sometimes I marvel at my consistency," Milo said.

"So, he has been eating the same salad for a long time, I take it," Sutherland said.

"And cutting it with his fork," Jen added.

"We discovered that he learned that from my Father."

Martha returned and announced that the evening meal would be Wellingtons—beef for Milo and Sutherland, and mushroom for Ms. Helvig per her request.

"Oh, you shouldn't have gone to any trouble for me," Jen protested.

"I enjoyed making it."

"I like my Wellington beefy these days," Milo joked.

"You always did, especially when it was the April special at McDonalds," Jen joked back.

"Again," Sutherland said, "Jens McWellington out Milos, Milo."

"Stop keeping score," Milo chided. As they ate their salads, Jen asked if there was any news about Lars.

"Oh yeah, I almost forgot," Milo said. "I got a call from one of my people. He was spotted again today in West Duluth. I think we've narrowed down where's he's living. I've got a PI buddy of mine actively looking for him."

"What do we do now?" Jen asked.

"Eat dinner and wait," Milo said.

§

Gramm kicked off his work shoes, dropped them next to his galoshes, and stuffed his feet into his work-is-over, black, lace-up winter boots. Grumbling about the bother of winter, he stood up, grabbed his overcoat, and joined White in the bullpen area. "I'm heading home," he said, putting on the coat.

White was at her computer. She turned around and said, "I just got word from forensics. The arrows we found in Ike Granton's barn loft match the arrows in our victims."

"Thirty-inch arrows, red and white …um..."

"Fletching. Yes. The broadheads also match. You know, the blades—the business end of the arrow."

"Can I hope this murder is going to solve itself and the guilty party is already in custody?" Gramm asked.

12

A light, cleansing snow fall was dusting the back lawn of Lakesong as Sutherland sat in the morning room, staring out at the lake rather than his Wall Street Journal. He had had an unusually fitful night. Another threat had been delivered to Lakesong late last night by messenger. Real estate was a business. These people were making it personal by delivering threats to his home.

When it arrived, Sutherland found Milo reading in the library and showed him the threat: *We're gonna break your legs,* spelled out in childish letters cut from a newspaper. Milo took the paper and envelope into his office and slipped them into a manila mailer to have them dusted for prints.

This morning Sutherland avoided any talk about the threats as Jen was also having breakfast. Richard Bonner buzzed the gate intercom. Sutherland excused himself and met Richard at the front door and led him into the breakfast room.

"Are you hungry?" he asked Richard, after introducing him to Martha and Jen, and reintroducing him to Milo.

"Already ate, thanks." Richard said.

"We're going up the shore to look at a property," Sutherland explained.

"Are you going to be near Betty's Pies?" Milo asked.

"I could."

"Pick up three or four cherry pies. I think they could come in handy."

"Handy for what?"

"Something I'm working on," Milo said.

Sutherland agreed he would purchase the pies, and he and Richard left.

"You know, Milo, this is just like old times," Jen said. "Me, you, breakfast served by a personal chef, an eight-hundred room mansion."

Milo laughed. "I knew it felt familiar."

"I assume Richard Bonner is a relation to Mary Alice."

"Son. Sutherland and Mary Alice have formed a partnership to do something with an old building up the shore."

"What are you doing today?"

"Consulting. We're working on a murder case."

§

Gramm set his coffee cup down stretched his neck to the right then to the left before sitting down at the interview table across from Ike Granton who sat bleary eyed, and unshaven.

"Bad night?" Gramm asked.

Granton, dressed in jailhouse orange, grunted.

"You tried to run me over," White charged.

Granton sniffed, slid down in his chair, stretched out his legs, and crossed his arms. "You got in my way. I was late, and I don't know how that stuff got in my barn."

Gramm pinched his shoulder blades together trying to loosen up. "That's not why you're here, Granton. The sheriff will talk to you about the stuff in your barn. You're here with us to chat about murder."

Granton sat up. "Whoa! Not me! Not my style!"

"Don't you want to know who was murdered?" Gramm asked.

"Don't matter—didn't do it," Granton said, rubbing his thigh. "I cracked up my bike. My leg hurts. I need medical attention."

"It wasn't your bike," Gramm said.

"And the Hibbing police already took you to the emergency room," White added. "You're fine."

"Doesn't mean I don't hurt. Don't yah have a pill or somethin'?"

"You're confusing us with a pharmacy," Gramm snapped.

White opened her folder. "How long did you know Faythe Cummings?"

Granton stopped rubbing his leg. "Faythe baby? What's she got to do with anything?"

"Answer the question," Gramm demanded.

Granton scratched his beard stubble. "Sweet chick. We met about a year ago."

"When did you see her last?"

"Why?" Granton asked.

"She's dead–murdered," White said.

"Crap! I guess we're not engaged anymore. Can I get my ring back now?"

"We tell you your fiancée is dead, and your first worry is the ring?" White asked.

"Yeah, it was a sweet ring. Somebody around here could steal it!"

"A lot of that going around," Gramm said, doubting Granton would get the sarcasm. "So, answer the question. When did you see her last?"

"Long time. Maybe a month. She kept blowing me off—pissed me off."

"Did you know she was about to marry someone else?" White asked.

Granton leaned over the table and pointed at White. "That's bullshit."

Unfazed, White continued, "Where were you Monday night?"

Returning to his slouched position, Granton mumbled, "At the farm."

"Can anyone corroborate that?"

"Whaddaya mean?"

"Was someone with you?"

Granton raised his eyebrows. "What do you think, babe?"

"Answer the question," White demanded.

"Nope. I like my privacy at the farm."

"You served three months for poaching—hunting deer out of season."

"Poaching my ass. I was on my own goddamn property! I get hungry. Why are we talkin' about deer hunting?"

White pulled a photo from her file and slid it over to Granton. "We found these hunting arrows along with a compound bow in your barn. Faythe Cummings was shot with an arrow identical to these."

Granton went silent.

"Did you kill her?" Gramm asked.

"No!"

"How do you explain the arrows?"

"I was robbed. Five of my arrows went missing. I was pissed. They're expensive."

Gramm gave Granton his hard, cold stare. "Don't bullshit us Ike. You want us to believe that a killer drove out to your barn, stole your arrows, and then killed Ms. Cummings. I have a simpler solution, you killed her with your arrows not realizing we could trace them."

"Why would I kill her? Faythe was a babe."

White slid another paper Granton's way. "Your last text—*Your gonna hurt babe.*"

Granton rubbed his left leg again. "How'd you get that? It's private!"

"She's dead. Nothing is private anymore."

"We know about your attack on her real boyfriend, Alex Sithens. By the way, he's also dead," Gramm said.

Granton pounded the table with his fists. "It was one punch. He stole Faythe! I don't like when what's mine is stolen!"

"Yet, he's still dead and you're in this up to your neck."

"I want a lawyer. I don't know what's goin' on here."

Gramm and White stood up. White motioned for the attending officer to come in and told him to take Granton back to his cell.

"What do you think?" Gramm asked as he and White headed back to his office.

"The guy's a Neanderthal with a temper," White said.

"We need something that puts him at the scene. Let's have forensics look for that talc stuff on his clothes."

Checking a text, she stopped. "We have another guest this morning," White said. "A Kayla Maki walked into the station about fifteen minutes ago. Told the desk sergeant we're looking for her."

Gramm nodded, "Runner number two? Maybe she wants to confess, and my holiday season can be peaceful again."

"And I want a pony with rainbows," White joked as she and Gramm turned around and walked back to the interview room. Kayla Maki was escorted to the room moments later. An officer handed a jack knife to White.

"What's this?" White asked Maki.

"It's mine. They took it away. I want it back."

White opened the knife and looked at the sharp three-inch blade. "This is no toy."

"It's for self-defense," Maki said.

"Is someone threatening you?"

Maki sneered. "Yeah, you."

"Have a seat," Gramm pointed Maki to the chair opposite to him and White. Noticing the red full lips and stringy blond hair, White wondered if Kayla was going for a retro forties look.

Kayla sat down, hands in the pockets of her oversized, barn style, jean jacket, "I heard you're lookin' for me."

"We were looking for you yesterday and you ran from us." Gramm said.

Kayla stared at him.

"Do you know why we want to talk to you?" Gramm asked.

Kayla shrugged and shoved her hands deeper into her jacket pockets.

"Why did you run?" White asked.

"Thought you were bill collectors."

White began pushing her hard to see her reaction. "Yesterday we wanted to talk about emails. Today, we're here to charge you with the murder of Faythe Cummings and her fiancé, Alex Sithens."

Kayla jumped back in her chair. "What the hell are you talkin' about?"

Gramm picked up on White's lead. "We're talking about cold-blooded murder, Miss Maki. This past Monday night you killed both your former boyfriend and his fiancée."

"We know you attacked him with a knife and threatened her on numerous occasions," White added, pulling a paper from her file. "Let me read this text to you: *Leave Alex alone or I'll kill you!* That was one of the mild ones."

Maki slapped her hands on the table and screamed, "I threaten people who hurt me. That's what I do. I don't murder them."

"That knife seems to disagree," White said. "Some self-defense."

Kayla stood up, hands balled into fists.

Both White and Gramm jumped to their feet. "Calm yourself Miss Maki," White directed, "or we will put you in restraints."

Kayla flopped down in the chair, grabbed her upper arms, closed her eyes, and lowered her head. "I wanted to cut him so he'd remember me! I wasn't going to kill him!"

White and Gramm sat back down. Their suspect looked up. "Sorry," she whispered. "I do that—get angry."

Gramm resumed the questioning. "Where were you this past Monday night?"

"What time?"

"Seven o'clock on."

"I was home. I live over my dad's garage. I eat out of his fridge. If there's food gone, he knows I was there."

"Not exactly airtight," Gramm said.

"Do you bow hunt?" White asked.

"No."

She could be lying, White thought. *Hard to tell.*

"Let me ask again," Gramm said. "Why did you run?"

Kayla ran her fingers through her stringy blond hair. "This is messed up. I might have threatened a customer who told me my stuff was crap. I ran because I thought you were going to arrest me for that."

"So, why come in?" White asked.

"I told my dad the cops came looking for me, and I ran. He said I had to deal with it. He's usually right."

§

Sutherland and Richard had been on the Kiner site for several hours talking to the engineering and environmental folks. The old Kiner site had been a winter boat storage facility and boat repair shop. Several buildings on the site had fallen down after years of nonuse, but the main building still stood. An inspection by the engineers found it to be structurally sound.

The environmental people pointed out several areas that had become contaminated by marine petroleum products, but they didn't feel that the cleanup would be prohibitive. "The cost of doing business," Sutherland proclaimed.

Sutherland and Richard left the engineers to continue their work and walked down to the lake. "I am thinking about a dock, a big one, with a restaurant along with a marina. Eventually, we could recreate the winter boat storage building."

Engrossed in discussing plans, costs, and timelines, neither of them realized that the engineers had finished their work and had left the site until Sutherland and Richard completed their discussion and started back up the hill. Sutherland looked up to see a black Mini Cooper with a red racing stripe pull up behind his Porsche.

"Who's this?" Richard asked.

"I don't know," Sutherland answered. "Where are the engineers?"

Two husky men wearing ski jackets, unfolded from the car, and walked down to where Sutherland and Richard were standing.

"Morning," Sutherland said.

The men were not friendly. "You don't listen so good, McKnight,"

Sutherland folded his arms. "This is private property. Leave before I call the cops."

One of the men, the one with a nasty looking scar on his cheek, smiled and stepped into Sutherland slugging him in the stomach. Richard came to his defense only to be shoved down by the other man and kicked in the ribs.

Sutherland was dazed by the punch, on his knees trying to find his breath. The first man grabbed Sutherland by his collar, forcing him to look up at a switchblade in front of his face. Sutherland stared at the menacing six-inch blade. "You see my pretty face, McKnight? Keep screwing around, and I'll give you a scar like mine."

"Or maybe we should do it to your pretty girlfriend," the other joked as his partner threw Sutherland into a snow drift.

Not fearing any retaliation, the two trudged back up to their car leaving a deep scratch in the side of the Porsche.

Sutherland and Richard watched them leave. "Are you okay?" Sutherland asked.

Richard nodded.

Sutherland called Milo, explaining what had transpired.

"Did you recognize the men?"

"No, but one had a long, nasty scar on the left side of his face."

"What were they driving?"

"A black Mini Cooper with a red racing stripe."

Milo laughed. "So, you were attacked by two guys in a clown car?"

"Milo, it's not funny. They also threatened Agnes."

"Okay, call the Two Harbor's Police, fill out a report, and buy four cherry pies at Betty's Pies."

"Again, with the pies? Why?"

"Very important."

§

"No Gustafson's. No Chinese Dragon. If we want a peaceful lunch, without Milo's antics, let's go somewhere new," White insisted, referring to Milo's annoying proclivity to ask a million questions and then settle for his usual order.

"What you got in mind?" Gramm asked.

"The Yellow Scooter Café," White said. "Burgers, salads, and I'm sure nobody knows Milo." White was somewhat disappointed when she called Milo to tell him about the change in restaurants. She expected a rant about something called the Yellow Scooter Café. Milo just said he would meet them there.

Gramm, White, and Preston arrived several minutes before Milo. A smiling waiter named Faizan welcomed them, led them to a table, and handed them menus. He introduced himself and turned to see who had just entered the establishment.

"Milo!" he waved. "Where have you been?"

White placed her hand on her forehead, closed her eyes, and shook her head in disbelief.

"Good plan you had here," Gramm said, laughing.

Milo shook the waiter's hand. "Good to see you, Faizan. I've been eating at the reasonably priced places," Milo explained.

"And here we go," White mumbled

Gramm looked at the menu. "You're right, this place is kinda pricy, and yet Milo seems to know it well."

Milo sat down at the four top table and asked Preston why she was laughing.

"Robin told a funny joke," she lied.

Faizan did not give Milo a menu. "Are you all Milo's associates?"

White and Gramm simultaneously shouted an emphatic, "No!"

Faizan cleared his throat. "Milo, should I have the chef prepare your usual?"

"Oh my God!" White exclaimed, looking at Milo. "You have a "usual" here too?"

"I have no idea what you're talking about." Turning to the waiter Milo asked to see the menu. "What kind of mushrooms does the mushroom Swiss burger have?"

"Poisonous," Faizan said. "Are you ready to order the Frisco Melt. You know you will."

"I noticed one burger is called The Hawk. You cook hawks?"

"Yes. Eagles and bunnies too."

"I also noticed, since I was here last, you have added a craisin chicken salad. Are you sure you didn't mean raisin?"

"Very sure," Faizan said.

"Is the Greek salad really Greek?" Milo asked.

Faizan wrote on his pad, "One Frisco melt, onion rings, and a Diet Pepsi." Looking at White, he asked for her order.

"Diet Coke," Milo corrected.

Faizan sighed. "We only have Pepsi, but I'll put it in a glass and call it Diet Coke."

"Thank you."

White ordered the craisin chicken salad.

"I'll go with Milo's Frisco melt," Preston said, "but sweet potato fries for a side."

Gramm ordered the walleye sandwich with a side salad. "I can tell Amy I had a salad for lunch."

White looked at Milo. "I want a list of restaurants you haven't been to–ever!"

"I wouldn't know if I haven't been to them. I could give you a list of restaurants I have been to. The list is long."

"If I'm not mistaken, I asked one of you to shoot Milo earlier this week," Gramm said.

"What did I do?" Milo asked with perfected innocence.

White ignored Milo and launched into a description of the suspects she and Gramm had interviewed. Summing up, she said, "Granton is high on my list. He's an angry crook who threatened our victim and was arrested for poaching with a bow and arrow. Eddy Peterson…"

"Oh, wait," Preston said. "I called his wife who said she's about to be his ex-wife, and she denied that Peterson was with the kids Monday night. She said he could have been stalking them—sitting outside the house. He does that a lot despite her restraining order. So creepy."

"Good to know," White said. "So, Eddy Peterson lied, and, at this point has no alibi. He's an alcoholic, a womanizer, and a bow hunter."

Gramm shook his head. "Alcoholic, or actor? Preston, did you ask her about Eddy's drinking?"

"No. She enumerated her husband's many flaws but didn't mention an alcohol problem."

Gramm raised his hands in self-congratulations. "I'm so clued into my fellow man."

Faizan returned with their orders. Preston took a bite of her Frisco melt and declared that she was going to follow Milo's restaurant suggestions from now on. "The cheese and bacon…yum!"

"If you ask a million questions, like Milo," White said, "you'll eat alone."

"I want to make sure I have this right," Milo said. "Both of these guys hunt, and both of them think they're engaged to the victim. What about Sithen's former girlfriend?"

"Kayla Maki visited us this morning after doing an Ike Granton-like runner yesterday. She has anger—maybe a violence problem—but she denied bow hunting experience."

"Maki?" Milo questioned.

"Yeah, Kayla Maki. What about it?" Gramm asked.

Preston jumped in, "The owner of the archery center is named Maki—Eero Maki."

White stopped eating her salad. "Look, Milo, you lucked out with the name Carlson on our last case. I refuse to let you do the same thing with Maki."

Gramm looked at Preston, "Quick, how many Makis are there in Minnesota?"

"Six billion," Preston said, with no hesitation.

"Eero had several pictures of a young girl winning archery awards with a compound bow. Did you take a picture of Kayla?" Milo asked.

"I did. As I said, she did a runner, so I took a picture of her when she came to the station just in case she runs again," White said, looking at her phone.

Milo waited for the picture of Kayla Maki to show up on White's phone. Instead, a video of a circus came up.

"What's this?" Milo asked.

White leaned over to look at her phone. "It's my video of Friendly Al's Used Cars. I thought it was funny. I sent it to my family. They thought it was funny too. You know, the oompah band, the waving men, the misspelled banners. And don't miss the holiday hot dogs and purple balloons." Parodying Milo, White said, "I think this entire case revolves around this video. Also, everyone working on the lot had a red jacket or sweater. No one went up a hill, and the oompah band was off key. I found all to be extremely suspicious."

"You're mocking me, aren't you?" Milo charged.

"He's so sensitive," Gramm said.

White found the picture of Kayla Maki and showed it to Milo and Preston.

Milo looked at Preston. "Whaddaya think?"

Preston nodded. "Skinny, long blond hair, could be an older version of the girl on Eero's wall."

"Kayla told us she didn't hunt. I thought she was lying," White grumbled.

Milo interceded. "She may not hunt; maybe just competes for medals."

"Oh, come on," Gramm said. "She knew what we were asking."

"Technically she didn't lie."

"Someone has to do a follow up," Gramm crabbed.

"I'll wear my running shoes," White said, looking at her phone. "Oh, our forensics people say Ike called Friendly Al's Used Car Lot while he was on the run."

Gramm's eyebrow raised. "He's running from us, and he calls his boss?"

White shook her head. "Was the phone call about the murder? There's no connection there."

"How do you know he called to talk to Lerner?" Milo asked. "He called the lot."

Faizan came with the check. “Give it to Milo,” Gramm said. “We, once again, had to put up with his silly questions.”

“I don’t ask silly questions,” Milo said. “I probe.”

Gramm looked at the waiter. “Double the bill. Call it an abuse tax.”

13

The last thing Gramm needed was a summons to a long, drawn-out meeting in the middle of a murder investigation. But there was the email from Deputy Chief Sanders. Sanders was normally a call-on-the-phone guy, reserving emails for notices of the dreaded meetings. Fearing the worst, Gramm clicked on the email. It was short and to the point: *Revised forecast. Duluth is now directly in the path of the blizzard. Sleet, snow, and high wind. Send all nonessential personnel home ASAP. Breakout the snowmobiles. Let the games begin.*

Gramm looked up at the three people sitting opposite his desk. "Guess what's on the way."

"Santa?" Milo guessed.

"Those of you who have reached adulthood take a guess."

Looking at a recent text, White said, "Alex Sithens' encrypted emails. IT unencrypted them."

Gramm's eyebrows shot up. "That may beat the blizzard."

"You mean the blizzard that's going to miss us?" Milo asked.

"Catch up, Milo. We're in for sleet, snow, and heavy winds hitting us late afternoon. Don't you get weather forecasts at Lakesong? Nonessential personnel are being sent home immediately. We're quasi-essential, but I suggest we not linger."

"I've never been a quasi. Do we get t-shirts?"

"Let me rephrase that," Gramm said. "We, except for Milo, are quasi-essential."

White and Preston hurried to the bullpen to copy the emails to thumb drives and a server, leaving Milo and Gramm alone. "Well, Milo, any gems bubbling up?"

"Not so far. Lots to follow up. If we survive this storm, you and Amy are going to get an invitation to Mary Alice's New Year's party."

"That's practical on her part. I can be on hand for the next murder. Let's see, last time it was her husband," Gramm teased. "I wonder who it would be now?"

"Oh my God. Do you think the cats are in danger?"

Gramm laughed.

"We just think Amy would be a great addition to the party…even though she comes with you."

§

Jamal and Darian arrived back at the cottage two hours early. "They called off school and bussed us home," Darian complained. "I missed science class. Bummer."

"What's going on?" Martha asked.

"There's a big storm coming," Jamal explained. "They called off our b-ball game against Superior tonight. Now *that's* a bummer."

Breanna emerged from her room. "I'm glad you're all here. I want to call a family meeting."

Jamal rolled his eyes. "I know, I left my towel on the floor in the bathroom."

Breanna smiled. "For years I've had to share a bathroom with you two. Towels on the bathroom floor don't even begin to talk about the horrors I've witnessed."

"Cut the drama," Martha said. "Family meeting time. We're all here, let's do it. The kitchen table awaits."

Martha, Breanna, and the boys sat down. "Your meeting, Breanna," Martha said.

"I want that attic bedroom! Darian can have my room." Breanna said.

"Breanna, that room was promised to Darian," Martha objected. "Besides, you are gone most of the time."

Breanna cleared her throat and clasped her hands in front of her. "Those are two valid points, but here's my argument: I was never consulted. Am I no longer a part of this family?" She locked eyes with each of her siblings.

Nice dramatic effect, Martha thought.

"Also, that room has a bathroom! I wouldn't have to share. My last point is…" Breanna paused again. Martha hoped she wasn't overplaying her hand. "It's quiet! I can study."

Martha was about to object again when Darian burst in. "Breanna's right! She wasn't consulted. She's the oldest. I'll take her room."

Martha pretended shock and amazement. "You would give up that fabulous room?"

Darian shrugged. "She's right. Everything she said is true."

"It is." Breanna agreed. "Thank you, Darian." Breanna jumped up and wrapped her arms around the back of Darian's shoulders. "Let's go and make this happen." The two went off to move items up and down the stairs leaving Martha and Jamal sitting alone in the kitchen.

A smirking Jamal stared at Martha. "I get what you two did here. You knew, didn't you?"

"I have no idea what you're talking about," Martha lied as she folded her arms.

"Nice," Jamal said.

"Good. I'm glad you approve. Now take the beds apart and carry them up and down. Watch your head."

"Aw shoot."

"Look at the bright side. You won't have a Darian throw rug anymore."

§

Gramm glanced out of his office window at the solid gray sky, and the trees bending to the ever-growing wind. The half-empty parking lot was still dry. He had time.

Gramm called to get Ike Granton transferred across the road from the jail to the police station. The transfer—which usually took thirty minutes—only took five. People wanted to get home.

Ike Granton sat in the interview room, shackled wrists folded in front of him. A lone police guard stood by the door. Gramm sat down, stared at Ike, but said nothing.

"Get on with it!" Ike demanded. "I don't want to get stuck here."

Gramm looked around at the industrial gray walls. "This place is worse than jail?"

Ike said nothing.

Gramm opened his folder and said, "Yesterday, you assaulted Sergeant White with a stolen motorcycle. Then you called Friendly Al's Used Cars. I'm curious. You're fleeing the police and you call the car lot? To say what? You won't be in today?"

"It was a butt dial," Granton smiled.

Gramm again consulted his file. "A fifty-two second butt dial."

"My butt likes to talk."

Gramm stood up. "It would be in your best interest to start cooperating. You're still number one on our suspect list. You have motive, opportunity, and means."

"I'll keep that in mind. Thanks for the advice," Granton sneered.

Gramm turned to the guard. "Take him back."

In the bullpen, White finished copying Sithens' emails to thumb drives for her and Preston to read at home. Gramm joined them.

White looked up. "We're leaving. Milo has already departed."

"Good," Gramm nodded. "I'm right behind you. We won't be bothered unless there's another homicide."

"How do we respond in a blizzard?" Preston asked.

"When you leave the station, you'll see the emergency prep arriving. I checked the radar," Gramm said. "This is going to be doozy."

White and Preston turned off their computers, took the flash drives, bundled up in coats, hats, scarves, and gloves, and headed out the door together.

"Oh!" Preston said as they stepped outside. Four-wheel-drive vehicles were arriving, each pulling a trailer of four snowmobiles.

"Before my last promotion, I got duty in the snowmobile patrol," White said. "It was fun at first, but the novelty wore off after the first few hours."

"If we have to use these, I don't have a snowmobile suit," Preston said.

"One will be delivered, along with boots and gloves. It may not be an exact fit, but you won't freeze. This is not the Duluth PD's first blizzard."

§

Milo and pelting sleet arrived at Lakesong about the same time. He drove his Honda into the garage, parking in his spot between the Bentley and the Rolls. Sutherland's Porsche was already there along with Agnes' Mirage and Jen's Camry. *Full house,* Milo thought.

"Hello Martha," he said as he walked past the kitchen.

"Good evening, Mr. Rathkey," Martha returned the greeting. "Everyone is gathered in the gallery."

Milo stopped in the family room to mix his gimlet before joining Agnes, Jen, and assorted cats in the gallery. The humans had picked one of the seating arrangements away from the windows, not wanting to compete with the noise of the sleet slapping against glass. Annie was down from her tree and lying under the couch by Agnes' feet, a sure sign of bad weather. Jet was on Jen's lap.

"Sutherland suggested I stay," Agnes said to Milo.

"Good idea. Where is Sutherland?" Milo asked.

"He's between Spain and France on his virtual bike ride,"

"Ride is over. I arrived safely in France. Well, virtual France. Much better weather there," Sutherland said, joining the group.

"Sutherland got Milo on a real bike this past summer," Agnes told Jen.

"I was ambushed by trees," Milo complained. "They have no respect for beginners."

"Do you have pictures?" Jen asked. "I would love to see Milo on a bike."

"I wasn't quick enough to get any pictures. Milo was up then he was down, and then he gave the bike to someone who could make better use of it," Sutherland said.

The wind was growing in strength. Jet squeaked his displeasure, jumped down, and ran toward the billiard room. Annie joined him.

"Are those cats playing pool these days?" Sutherland asked.

"The billiard room doesn't have windows," Agnes explained.

Even though they moved away from the windows, the sleet beating on the glass dome of the gallery was still making conversation difficult. Sutherland, with raised voice, suggested his fellow humans move to the family room. "Dinner should be ready soon, and we won't have to shout."

Darian was setting the table, not one of his usual chores, but glad to be with his big sister during the storm. "Mr. McKnight, Martha said to set the table in here but, if you want to move to the dining room, she says I'd be happy to set the table in there."

"This will be fine. Thank you, Darian," Sutherland said.

Martha came in from the kitchen just as the lights flickered and failed. There was confusion and murmurs from Agnes and Jen.

"Let's count to three everybody," Milo said.

On the joint count of three, the lights returned. Jen looked at the group for an explanation.

"Generator," Sutherland answered.

As the adults took their places around the table, Sutherland suggested that Darian join them having picked up on the young man's insecurity. Darian looked at his sister.

"Okay," Martha nodded.

"Look, Darian," Milo kidded, "let's not have that four-martini episode like last time."

Darian looked at Martha who said, "It's Mr. Rathkey's humor, Darian."

"Don't worry," Jen said, "I often didn't get it either."

As Martha served the salads, Sutherland asked Darian what nine-year-old boys were doing these days.

"I let Breanna have my room in the attic," Darian said. "She really wanted it because it has its own bathroom."

"Quite noble of you," Sutherland said.

Darian seemed pleased.

"It seems to me," Milo said, "with all that snow coming down, you, Darian, are now old enough to partake in a long standing Lakesong tradition."

The table was puzzled.

Darian got it. His face lit up. "Goliath?" he whispered.

Martha rolled her eyes.

"What is Goliath?" Jen asked.

"It's a monster that lives in the maintenance shed," Sutherland said.

"It awakes only after a snowstorm," Milo added.

Jen looked to Agnes for an adult explanation. "I am told it's an old army-surplus halftrack with a snowplow."

Darian ate his salad and listened to the on-going conversation. He looked around the room and blurted, "The house is happy!"

Conversation stopped and all eyes turned to Darian. "What do you mean?" Sutherland asked.

"When we moved here, we were sad, and this house was sad. Last year, the house was even sadder. Now it's happy. The house likes people," Darian said, returning to his salad.

"Maybe that's why she is showing us her secrets," Sutherland suggested. "Secret tunnels…"

"Secret staircases," Agnes added.

"What will she show us next," Milo mused.

Sutherland sat straight up. "I just had a memory flash. I know what she will show us next. When I was a little kid, I think I found another hidden room, but I didn't know what it was."

"Where?" Agnes asked.

"Follow me," Sutherland urged.

The group, Darian included, left the dinner table, and followed Sutherland to the double staircase.

"I don't know why I thought of this, but I was riding my tricycle…"

"In the house?" Agnes questioned.

"Of course; it was winter. This whole gallery area was designed by my mother to be a park, an escape for the three of us during the dark, cold, months. The marble floors are perfect for bike riding, ball bouncing, fun. My mother would read, and I was a trike terror. I remember ramming into the wall here, under the staircases, and it cracked open. I thought I broke it, so I got off my trike and pushed it back. I fixed it. I was so proud." Walking over to the wall, Sutherland kicked where he remembered his tricycle had struck so many years ago. The panel opened as it did back then.

"I love this house!" Agnes exclaimed.

Pulling the panel open, Sutherland used his phone flashlight to find a light switch. The group stepped inside the long, curved room that wound its way under the staircase. A small bar anchored the center of the curve with a few tables and chairs at each end. "What is this?" Sutherland asked.

"It looks like a prohibition room," Jen said. "A place for illegal alcohol parties in the twenties."

"How do you know that?" Milo asked.

"We had one in our house in St. Paul where I grew up. Not as fancy, but why else have a hidden bar in the house?"

Agnes looked around the room. "I think Mary Alice is going to love this."

Outside, the wind picked up the driving snow and slammed it against the house which stood tall and strong against the weather. With the possibility of a party in the no-longer-secret prohibition room, Lakesong was indeed happy.

14

Agnes woke up in an unfamiliar, deep-shadowed room. She could hear the wind howling. It took a minute for her mind to recalibrate. Last night, she and Sutherland had gone upstairs to his suite of rooms. He gave her the tour. They sat on the couch, drank a wonderful Merlot, and listened to the storm.

I must have fallen asleep, she thought. It was a delightful, romantic evening. *Where is Sutherland?* As she stood up to stretch, the shades, that completely covered the windows, began to rise. Agnes blinked as daylight flooded the room. "Did I do that?" she asked out loud. The shades refused to answer.

Agnes checked her phone for the time. "Oh, 8:30. I slept late." She had one message. It was from Sutherland: *Good morning sleepyhead. I have gone downstairs to breakfast. By the way, the shades will open on your movement.*

Agnes laughed. “Kinda late on that shade thing, Sutherland.” Between her gym backpack and her purse, she was hoping she had enough to get herself cleaned up before descending to meet the world.

§

The slamming shards of sleet late Thursday had given way to a wind-driven snowstorm in the middle of the night with blizzard conditions continuing into the early morning. Wet snow pelted the windows of the morning room as last night’s dinner group gathered for breakfast. Milo was the last to arrive. Darian, sitting on the hearth petting Annie, was waiting for him.

“Mr. Rathkey is it time for Goliath yet?” he asked eagerly.

“Darian let Mr. Rathkey have his breakfast in peace,” Martha called from the kitchen.

Milo looked beyond the morning-room table at the wet snow slapping against windows. “That weather could hurt us.”

“But not Goliath,” Darian insisted.

“True but look out there. We couldn’t see anything in front of us. We might plow over important things like Martha’s garden. Then you and I would have to move.”

“Far, far away,” Martha insisted, passing Milo and Darian on her way to the morning room.

“Jamal said he got to drive it last year,” Darian disclosed.

Martha turned back to look at Milo with mild shock.

“I passed out in the driver’s seat. Luckily, Jamal was able to throw me in the back and steer Goliath on a safe path until I came to. Very dramatic,” Milo said.

"Very dramatic indeed," Martha mocked. "Darian will not be driving Goliath."

"Oh, certainly not," Milo agreed, following Martha and his breakfast into the morning room. "The doc said I probably won't have another one of those fainting spells until Darian is at least twelve or thirteen." Checking Martha's face, he amended, "Maybe fifteen or sixteen?"

"My room is so cozy," Jen said, taking a bite of her French toast. "I lit a fire and listened to the wind until I fell asleep. I hope Lars is somewhere safe and warm."

Agnes was working her way through a fruit smoothie, a counterpoint to Sutherland's vegetable smoothie. Still uncomfortable being a guest around her friend Martha, she offered to help.

"Do I offer to help you do whatever you do for Milo?" Martha asked.

Agnes sighed.

"Drink your smoothie," Martha said. "Later you can praise my blender skills." She placed Milo's eggs, toast, hash browns, and bacon on the table.

Milo looked at the floor. "Where's Annie?"

Sutherland laughed. "Annie is still by the fire and she's not moving."

A loud meow from the hearth room told Milo he could deliver the bacon to her. He got up and gave her two small pieces.

"I can't believe that!" Sutherland said. "She's a cat. She has cat food. You deliver bacon to a cat?"

Jen smiled. "Our dog always had him trained. Pets know Milo is trainable." Her smile faded. "How is this storm going to affect finding Lars?" she asked as Milo returned from his food delivery.

"I had hoped to find him this weekend, but he's not going anywhere either."

"None of us are," Agnes offered. "I left my book at my house. This would have been a perfect day for reading."

"We need to run past your house to make sure it's okay," Sutherland offered. "You may have lost power. You can pick up your book while we're there. Also, we should let the water run a little bit to keep your pipes from freezing."

Milo laughed. "Are you gonna take Goliath. I'm not sure he's street ready."

"We have the twins," Sutherland said. "Chip and Dale."

"What are the twins?" Milo asked.

"Snowmobiles. They're in the maintenance shed behind Goliath."

"Snowmobiles?" Agnes questioned. "I'm in."

"I thought you could ride on the back of mine," Sutherland said.

"No way! I'm practically a sled head. I love snowmobiles!"

"Sled head?" Milo mumbled to himself. Before he could get clarification, his phone chirped the Ernie Gramm *da dunk* from "Law and Order."

Milo excused himself, going back to the hearth room to take the call. Annie was upset he didn't bring more bacon and told him so. "Ernie, I'm not coming to work today," he joked.

"Either am I," Ernie said. "But White and Preston want to fill us in on those emails. We will have a Zoom call in a couple hours."

"Okay."

"Milo?"

"Yeah?"

"Do you know what a Zoom call is?"

"Not a clue, but Ed Patupick put something called Zoom on my laptop. I'll ask Agnes to do whatever needs to be done. How are *you* going to Zoom?"

"I got Amy."

§

Agnes kept Martha company in the kitchen after breakfast. "Can I ask you something about Darian?" she asked.

"Sure," Martha said, "What'd he do?"

"During dinner last night he said this house was happy. It was almost as if he and the house talked."

Martha paused long enough to think about how to explain. "He gets like that sometimes. I don't know if it reflects how he is feeling or if it's a sensitivity. My mother used to tell me her mother was sensitive like that. Maybe it skipped a generation and landed on Darian. I go with it. If he says the house is happy, the house is happy."

"Well, the happy house certainly had an effect on Sutherland's remembering that room under the stairs," Agnes said. "He was almost giddy. Not square-corner-Sutherland at all. That reminds me, I need to call Mary Alice and tell her about that room."

"For the party?"

"Yes. All the guests won't fit in that room at one time, but people could come and go. Maybe we get a bartender that looks nineteen-twentyish."

"I figured the sibs might be old enough to contribute—take coats, hand out appetizers."

"I think Breanna is a guest," Agnes said.

"Why would Mary Alice invite Breanna?" Martha asked.

"Well, it's not completely Mary Alice's party. Because it's at Lakesong, Sutherland feels compelled to invite some of his clients and friends."

"Back to my original question. Why would Mary Alice or Sutherland invite Breanna?"

"They might not, but the wild card would."

"Milo?"

"Milo. I asked for his preliminary guest list. Ed Patupick, Ilene, Dr. Bixby, Breanna, you, and Ron Bello—so far. He leaves me sticky notes with names on them. I assume it's for the guest list and not a gangland hit."

"Oh my! Is Morrie Wolf on the list?" Martha was prepared to be shocked.

"Funny you should mention Mr. Wolf. He is on the list—a guest of Mrs. Bonner. I recently realized Morrie was always on Mary Alice's list. I just didn't know who he was. Each year he would thank her but decline. An eclectic party to be sure. Is it noon yet?"

"Eleven-thirty."

"Good, I have time to get Mr. Rathkey on Zoom."

§

Agnes read the Zoom email from Robin and connected Milo's office computer to the call. She noticed that Ed Patupick had included random backgrounds. She mischievously enabled that feature, hoping none of the backgrounds were inappropriate.

Milo and Robin were the first to join, followed quickly by Kate Preston, and finally by Ernie. Gramm was saying something, but no one could hear him. Amy came into the picture and pressed something on his computer. "Unmute yourself," Amy was saying.

"I didn't know I had a microphone. Where's the microphone?" Gramm asked, looking around.

"It's magic!" Amy shouted as she left the room.

"Okay, we're all here," Robin said. "Lt. Gramm has a magic microphone and Milo is visiting Paris. Why did I think this call would be normal?"

"I'm in my office," Milo insisted.

"Look at your picture," Robin said. "You're in Paris. Oh, wait, now you're in Venice."

Milo noticed that his background was not his office. "It's something Patupick did. I don't know how to turn it off."

"Okay, let's just roll with it," White said. "These unencrypted emails show that our victim, Alex Sithens, was fronting the investment club mentioned by his partner, Van Dyke."

"How did it work?" Gramm asked.

White continued. "From the emails, the members pooled their money, and one guy, a Mr. Fauchard, invested it. As Van Dyke said, this investment club was doing well until several months ago when dividend payments stopped. There are a number of emails to Sithens asking what was going on. A couple of the emails were angry and bordered on threatening."

"Why Sithens?" Milo asked. "Why not this Fauchard guy?"

"Sithens was the point person. We don't think investors could contact Fauchard. But Milo you're now on the moon!" White complained.

"I can't control it. I told you that."

"Goddamnit, Milo!" Gramm shouted. Somehow Patupick had gotten the program to reduce Milo's head, and he was now helping to row General Washington across the Delaware. "How can I concentrate?"

"I think it's funny," Preston said.

"Ignore him!" White said.

"Do we have names to go with the threatening emails?" Gramm asked.

"No. The names are coded. Each person is known only by a letter. After they went through the letters once, they used numbers and letters. One person is known as D3, another as P4. Our victim, Alex Sithens, also an investor, was known as *A*. Two of the assigned letters, L2 and Q were threatening. That's all we know so far," White said. "Our forensic accounting people are still looking into how much each investor stood to lose. It could be a whole different motive. It was clear that Sithens was getting antsy. He was asking Fauchard about his own personal money. He even identifies himself in his last email."

"His last email…" Preston began, glimpsed her screen, and giggled. "I never knew the Beatles were John, Paul, George, and Milo."

Milo nodded. "That's a good look for me."

Preston recovered, and repeated, "Sithens' last email said he knew everything and was threatening to blow everything up and go to the police."

"Maybe he was the target, not Cummings?" Milo suggested. "Follow the money."

"No! No! No!" Gramm argued. "Doc Smith said the woman was shot first. You don't shoot the witness first and let the target escape."

Milo was now riding Dumbo at the Magic Kingdom. "I want to read these emails. Can you send them to me?" he asked.

"Sure, but where will you be?" White asked. "Paris, Disney World, Hogwarts?"

§

Agnes stretched in her office chair. Sleeping on the couch had left her back muscles stiff. *I need another cup of coffee,* she thought. Crossing back through the gallery she was wondering where Sutherland had disappeared to when she heard him call her name. Turning around, she couldn't find him in the trees and various plants that populated the gallery. "Where are you?" she asked.

"Up in the Guiana tree with Annie," he laughed.

She doubted that but looked up anyway. Annie looked down with a stern meow as if to say, "I don't allow humans in my tree."

Sutherland raised his hand. "Over here by the windows."

Agnes saw his wave and joined him on the couch that faced the back French doors.

"I'm watching the storm. Now and then I think I see the lake through the blowing snow."

All Agnes could see outside was wind-driven white. "I fell asleep last night," she said.

"Yes, you did," he smiled.

"And you didn't wake me!"

"Confession. I fell asleep too. I just woke up earlier."

Agnes smiled. "We are too exciting."

Sutherland agreed. "Duluth Magazine has listed us as the third most exciting couple in the city."

"Third? Who are the first two?"

"People who aren't lulled to sleep on a couch during a storm."

Couple? Agnes thought. *I like that. Does he know what he said?*

15

By midmorning, the blowing snow had calmed down, and visibility had returned. The city announced the resumption of plowing which had been suspended at midnight. Milo reasoned that, if plows could be out, so could Goliath. He pushed the *cottage* button on the intercom and announced, "Goliath rides! All passengers meet me in the maintenance shed!"

Milo grabbed his newly purchased, Jamal-inspired, green, Air Force parka, descended the basement steps, and entered the tunnel system. The three tunnels were labeled: *Cottage, Maintenance Shed, Boathouse.*

"Where's Jamal?" Milo asked as he and Darian met in the shed

"Martha said I could ride without Jamal, my reward for giving up the attic room. He's not happy, but Martha promised him the next storm. Besides, he and Breanna are still moving her stuff up to the attic room, and my stuff down to Breanna's old room."

"That was big of you, giving up your room," Milo said.

Darian sighed. "It was for the best. The room wanted Breanna. All those astronomy books, she's gonna be an astrophysicist."

Milo pulled the canvas off the old halftrack. "Behold Goliath!"

Darian reached out with his mittened hand and stroked the dull-green, metal side of the halftrack. "Wow! It's huge."

Goliath wasn't built for a short nine-year-old like Darian. He couldn't reach the footrest, the metal rectangle jutting out from below the cab. Milo boosted him onto the footrest and watched as Darian maneuvered himself up to the passenger seat. Crossing to the other side of Goliath, Milo hoisted himself into place behind the wheel. "So, rooms and houses talk to you?" Milo asked.

"Sort of," Darian said. "It's hard to explain. I just get a feeling."

Milo clicked the shed door opener that was kept in the vehicle. The door creaked open revealing a massive snow drift blocking the way.

"Oh no!" Darian moaned. "We're stuck! We'll never get through that."

Milo turned the key. "This is Goliath," Milo shouted over the rumbling vibrations of the engine. "Nothing stops Goliath."

Stepping on the clutch, Milo shoved the gear shift into first. "Ready?" he asked Darian.

"We can't get through that drift; there's too much snow!" Darian shouted.

Milo lowered the plow and let out the clutch as he leaned on the gas. Goliath shuddered. "Forward!" Milo bellowed, doubled-clutching the halftrack into second before slamming into the massive pile of ice and snow in front of the door. White chunks flew into the windshield in front of Darian's face. Even more whirled past the side win-dows, making Darian lean in toward Milo. Goliath broke through the ice bank and lurched into the last gasp of the dying storm.

"Yes!" Darian shouted. "Black Panther couldn't do any better, Mr. Rathkey."

Milo had a vague idea of the Black Panther and took it as a compliment. He steered down the path, past Martha's ice-covered garden, past the tennis courts keeping Goliath in second gear. He looked over at his companion who appeared mesmerized by the power of the machine.

"Normally, she goes a little faster," Milo shouted, "but there is ice under the snow, and it takes more power to cut through it."

Darian gawked at the snow being forced to the side, and ragged slabs of ice leaping up in front of the plow. Milo asked if Goliath was happy. "I don't know about Goliath," Darian shouted, "but I am."

Martha heard the roar of a powerful engine and the bangs of the plow as it cut through the ice and snow. She looked out the cottage's attic window and saw the halftrack plowing out her parking area and access road. Jamal was Darian's age when John McKnight took him for his first ride in that monster. She was glad that Milo moved into Lakesong or else Darian would have never gotten his turn.

Jamal joined her at the window. "I wonder if he's going to let Darian drive?"

"He better not!" Martha said. "Mr. McKnight didn't let you drive at Darian's age."

Jamal smiled. "Yeah, let's go with that. But I'm taller than Darian. His feet won't reach the pedals…yet."

"You drove that thing when you were nine!" Martha looked aghast.

"I was tall for my age and quite mature," Jamal boasted.

"Let's keep that maturity thing going," Martha teased.

"Eight," Jamal whispered.

§

Jen wondered if she could ever eat eggs again. Just the suggestion made her stomach queasy. She had asked Martha for rice cereal and bananas. Now, up in her room, some of that breakfast was not sitting well.

She hadn't told anyone yet about her pregnancy, except Lars. "Lars, where are you?" she asked the room.

§

Sutherland said he was going to work out and suggested that Agnes join him. She agreed, but first needed to call Mary Alice. "I have to tell her about your tricycle riding discovery of the prohibition room before I forget."

"Okay. I'll be on my adult tricycle. It's off my living room on the right," he said.

"How will I get passed your locked door?" Agnes asked.

Sutherland was confused. "The door's not locked. It's never locked—especially to you."

As she left for her office to call Mary Alice, she was grinning.

"Are you home?" Mary Alice asked. "Do you have power?"

"I'm at Lakesong. I stayed the night. We have a generator. How about you?"

"Same here. The generator is going strong. What can I do for you?"

"Lakesong gave up another secret last night. I think you need to know about it for the party."

Mary Alice laughed. "I always thought the McKnights had skeletons in their closets."

"No skeletons, but a secret prohibition room."

"Oh my! Like a private speakeasy?"

"Exactly. It has a bar and everything."

"Where is it?"

"Under the double staircase. It wouldn't fit everyone, but people could come and go, experience a little of the 1920s."

"We could dress the bartender and servers up in 1920s costumes," Mary Alice said.

"That's what I thought," Agnes agreed. "What about the guests?"

"Getting costumes can be a pain, I think we make it optional."

§

After clearing most of Lakesong's roads, Milo stopped the halftrack to look at its handiwork. "The snow is still falling!" Darian complained. "All of Goliath's work will be covered up."

Milo shook his head. "What's coming down now is just snow. Ed Perkins, the guy who plows with his pickup truck, can handle that. He would never have been able to clear the ice. We and Goliath helped him out."

Milo drove to the shed, backed in Goliath, and turned off the engine. He went around to help Darian only to find him hanging from the door with the hopes of reaching the footrest. He was a few inches short. Milo grabbed Darian by the waist and gently placed his two feet on the concrete floor.

"Don't tell Jamal I needed help," Darian pleaded. "But Goliath was awesome!"

"Glad you liked it," Milo smiled.

Darian patted the side of Goliath's hood. "He likes it too. We are a force for good."

Milo didn't doubt that the old halftrack liked it too.

As they entered the tunnels, Darian thanked Milo and ran through the side tunnel leading to his cottage. Milo decided to leave the running to nine-year-old boys. He walked through the tunnel that led to the main house.

Milo wanted to read the Sithens emails for himself. White said that they were on the police FTP site. Milo knew what that meant but had no idea how to transfer them to his computer.

He arrived at Agnes' office just as she was finishing up a few details with Mary Alice. Poking his head in the door, he asked, "Could you come in here and finagle the FTP?"

Agnes got up, went to Milo's computer, and began to explain what she was doing. Milo held up his hand to stop her. "Don't care, just do what you do so well." Within a few minutes, Milo had the emails on his computer.

He read through some of the early ones from a year ago. Early on, people were excited to join the investment club. Apparently, the mysterious Mr. Fauchard had a great track record picking stocks. Milo moved on to the later emails, after the dividends stopped flowing. People were less excited—far less excited. He found the threatening notes from two people named L2 and Q. Milo shrugged. As threats went, these were mild.

TO: A@fauchard.com
FROM: L2@fauchard.com
SUBJECT: Where's my money?

I am getting nervous. This could not come at a worse time for my family. If we aren't getting dividends, I need my money back. I am coming to find you!

L2

TO: A@fauchard.com
FROM: Q@fauchard.com
SUBJECT: Lawsuit coming

What are you running here? A Ponzi scheme? If I don't get all my money back in two days, I'm calling the authorities. I will prosecute you to the max. See you in prison.

Q

Sithens' responses were the same. He indicated he wasn't the fund manager and that he also was on the losing end. He promised to get them more information. Milo saw that Sithens was losing patience in the last email.

TO: F@fauchard.com
FROM: A@fauchard.com
SUBJECT: I know who you are.

I need to hear from you ASAP. The investors are threatening me. One physically attacked me in a bar. Others are promising legal action. I'm the guy holding the bag here, and that's going to change. I know who you are. In fact, I know every thing! Either all of us get our money or I blow this thing up and go to the police. You have 24 hours.

Alex (The hell with this A crap)

Milo checked the date. That last email was sent the day before the murders.

§

After Agnes pedaled down a portion of the virtual Appalachian Trail, Sutherland presented her with a snowmobile suit, boots, gloves, and helmet.

"You have spare gear?" Agnes asked.

Sutherland, not wanting to say he bought it for his ex-fiancée, lied and said that Lakesong has spare everything—swimsuits, bicycle helmets, ski jackets, and snowmobile suits. "Anything you would want at the McKnight boutique," he added.

Putting on the pink snowmobile suit, Agnes noticed it was short. "Is this a petite?" she asked.

"What's a petite?" Sutherland stammered.

Agnes wondered if Miss Petite was Miss Ex-fiancée. Looking at her long legs sticking out from the bottom of the suit, she thought, *Well you're not with a Miss Petite now.*

She took off the suit, put on a double pair of Sutherland's multicolored, striped, Nordic socks, an old red Christmas sweater, and pulled the pink suit back on. She looked at her image in the mirror and laughed. The sweater sleeves and socks were sticking out of the too-small suit. "I look like a snow scarecrow."

The boots were also too small, so Sutherland found an old pair of his that were too big for Agnes. Using the trick from Martha, she stuffed the toes with a pair of Sutherland's socks. "I'm not going to be making the cover of *Snow-Go Magazine*," she laughed.

Agnes wanted to enjoy the snow on their way to the maintenance shed, but Sutherland argued that Milo and Darian could still be out there with Goliath. "We could get run over and nobody would find us until spring."

They took the tunnel. Goliath was back in the shed. Its snowy covering was melting, leaving puddles on the shed's concrete floor.

Sutherland led Agnes to the back of the building where two large automobile engines chugged away, running generators for the house.

"Isn't that dangerous, running engines in a closed shed?" Agnes asked.

"The exhaust is vented to the outside," Sutherland explained as he checked the gasoline gauges on the wall. "We're still in good shape," he proclaimed.

He pointed to a small, overlooked trailer behind Goliath covered by a blue tarp. They unfastened the tarp, whipping it back, uncovering two snowmobiles. "Chip and Dale," Sutherland said, proudly.

Sutherland drove the snowmobiles down from their sled, and offered yellow Chip to Agnes, while he rode bright blue Dale. Leaving by the shed's back door, they made their way to the side gate, which Sutherland unlocked. Once on the side road, Sutherland said, "Let's take it slow up the hill to your place. There could be plows out. We wouldn't want to run into one."

Agnes smiled. "You're so right. Slow and easy." She gunned the engine, and added, "Race you!" Her snowmobile lurched forward and sped down the sideroad.

Sutherland rolled his eyes, shook his head, and followed the yellow and pink streak. Life with Agnes was going to be challenging. By the time he reached Agnes' Lakeside bungalow, she was relaxing on her large porch, arms crossed, leaning on a post. "It seems I won!" she proclaimed.

Sutherland shut off his machine and walked through the snow to the porch. He thought of his father's words in the will accusing him of leading a structured, uneventful life. Milo was meant to shake him up a bit. Agnes, the antithesis of his former fiancée, was shaking up the other bits.

"That was fun," Agnes said, taking off her helmet. "I've never done that before."

"I thought you were Miss Sled Head," Sutherland exclaimed.

Agnes smirked. "I lied. Doesn't everybody? Mister, *what's a petite*?"

§

Milo was upset. He was having a relaxing day without his brain itching. Now, he had that feeling of unease once again. Something bothered him. Something in Alex Sithens' final email was not right. He didn't know what. He kept rereading it with no flash of insight. At some point it would become clear—it always did—but until that point, he had to walk around with the unease.

He sent a message to the group. *I am bothered by Sithens' last email.*

The fact that he threatened Mr. Fauchard? White asked. Preston asked much the same.

Gramm, who did not text, called Milo.

"Mind lint?" Gramm asked, using Sutherland's term for Milo's thought process.

"Could be. Something is stuck between my cerebral cortex and the peanut butter sandwich I had for lunch," Milo said.

"Are you still thinking money was the motive, making Sithens the main target?"

"Possible," Milo said.

"So, go investigate. We'll stay with the personal motive, Cummings. We have more than enough local suspects for her. Sithens has email suspects who might not even live in Duluth—no opportunity."

16

Weather in Duluth is often puckish—this Saturday the sun shone bright and glorious in the blue sky, a visual that screamed a pleasant winter day. The temperature, however, had taken a dive—fifteen below, wind chill of negative twenty-five.

Agnes's neighborhood still didn't have power. Yesterday's snowmobile race to her house to gather some essentials for the weekend had been a good call.

As the group was finishing breakfast, the intercom announced a visitor at the gate. Sutherland, surprised by having a visitor so early, grabbed his phone to open his Lakesong app.

"I got this," Milo said, pushing the *gate open* button on his phone.

"You're using the app?" Sutherland asked, with disbelief.

Milo shrugged. "Of course. How would I open the gate without the app?"

"But you never…"

Agnes started to laugh. "I showed him how to use it. He even practiced."

Milo held up his hand for silence. "Let's not share with the class. I need an aura of mystery. It's part of my idiom,"

"Your *idiom?*" Sutherland asked.

"I heard the word in a movie, always wanted to use it."

"Who's at the gate?" Agnes asked, watching Milo hurry to the front door.

"Mary Alice," Milo said over his shoulder.

Sutherland attempted to explain Mary Alice to Jen. "Mary Alice Bonner. She and Milo…" Remembering he was talking to Milo's ex, Sutherland modified his explanation. "She and Milo are neighborhood friends."

"We met the night I first came here and interrupted your dinner party. I would guess a lot more than friends given the speed with which Milo got up and went to the door."

Sutherland shrugged. "Close neighborhood friends?"

Jen laughed.

Milo returned with Mary Alice who had deposited her snowmobile suit and gear in the foyer. "Hello everyone," she said, entering the morning room fluffing out her blond helmet hair. "Refreshingly crisp out there."

"The wind chill is 25 below," Sutherland said.

"But the sun is shining," Mary Alice responded, glowing as brightly as her yellow turtleneck sweater. "I'm here to see this fabled prohibition room."

"Coffee first?" Milo inquired.

"Maybe after. I'm a woman on a mission. Where's this secret room?"

Following Sutherland, the troop rose from the morning room table and once again congregated between the double staircases. With dramatic showmanship, Sutherland booted the panel, causing it to swing open. Agnes clapped. Sutherland bowed.

Mary Alice stepped inside, disappearing for a bit, then reappeared and proclaimed it *perfect* for her New Year's Eve party. "Come in here. Look at this!"

"How old is this house?" Jen asked.

Sutherland was pleased to recount Lakesong's history. "My father told me it was built in the late 1800's, but records of its construction were lost in a fire in the early 1920s. We found blueprints, but they weren't dated."

"Well," Jen said, "there was no prohibition when Lakesong was built. If this room was original to the house, what was its function?"

"A closet?" Sutherland guessed.

"Why not just make a door? Why the secret Panel?" Jen asked.

"Last summer, a secret tunnel," Agnes said. "This fall, a secret staircase, and now a secret room. Who built this house? What went on here?"

"Look at this!" Mary Alice exclaimed. "This carving on the back of the bar is exquisite."

Milo and Sutherland went to inspect. The carving, a tree and a sword, was similar to the carvings that lined the walls of Lakesong's vault. "What did go on in this house?" Sutherland asked, more to himself than anyone in the group.

Mary Alice held up a dusty hand. "Not any dusting."

Agnes texted Peggy, the other party planner, to make sure that the secret room was added to the cleaner's list.

Peggy texted back, *Secret room?*

Agnes texted, *LOL. I'll call you later.*

Sutherland suggested having a second cup of coffee in the gallery, and rolled the coffee urn into the area that overlooked the glistening, frozen back lawn. A family of deer emerged from the trees to join a second group down by the lake.

Milo was making up names for the deer, trying to convince everyone that he and the deer were old friends. Mary Alice suggested that she and Jen split the remaining almond sweet roll. Jen agreed.

"My immediate need to see the secret room is all about my New Year's Eve party that will be held here at Lakesong this year. You must come."

The invitation took Jen by surprise. "I don't know," she said. "I have a situation."

"Oh, I know, but Milo's on it. It will be fine."

Agnes put Jen down as a maybe—her husband too. *Mary Alice always has an eclectic group,* she thought. *This year may top all the rest.*

§

Officer Preston sent out a second Zoom call invitation to Rathkey, White, and Gramm for eleven-thirty. Milo showed the email to Agnes who connected him. "You know, I could do this on your phone. That way you won't have to watch in your office," Agnes suggested.

"I like my office," Milo protested, swiveling in his chair.

After brief hellos, Amy Gramm leaned around Ernie so the others could see her. "Hello all. Ernie's IT person here." Looking at Milo's square, she laughed. "Milo are you enjoying the New York Subway?"

"I am, but I feel change is in the air," he said as his background morphed into the iconic photo of a snow-covered Mt. Fuji.

"Bring me back some sushi," Amy said as she disappeared from the screen.

"So, why are we zooming again today?" Gramm asked.

"Monica Sandlan's Instagram account," Preston explained.

"Refresh my memory. Who is Monica Sandlan?" Gramm asked.

"She's a nurse in Dr. Zackery's dental office who worked with our victim, Faythe Cummings," Preston said. "Cummings had thousands of followers on her Instagram page, and Sandlan hasn't wasted any time in poaching as many as she can." Preston put up a freeze frame of Sandlan dressed in a bikini and black veil, announcing the death of Faythe Cummings.

"There's more," Preston said, putting up Faythe Cummings' page. "As you can see, Sandlan posted her black-veiled-bikini-mourning photo on Cummings' page and encouraged Cummings' followers to mourn with her at *monicasandlan*."

"Nice veil," Milo said.

"Why should we care about all this?" Gramm asked.

Preston explained Instagram Influencers to Gramm, the money to be made, and how it could go to motive. "Cummings was becoming a star. She was over a hundred-thousand followers. I did the research. She could be paid as much as $200 a post plus free stuff: clothes, meals, beauty products. Also, she was paid for her personal appearances at bars and clubs."

"We have to check Cummings' financials—see how much money she was making. So, this Sandlan woman wanted in on this?" Gramm asked.

Preston nodded. "Sandlan told us Cummings was *helping* her get into the business..."

Milo interrupted. "We only have her word on it."

§

Sutherland and Agnes watched Martha's sibs in the midst of their snowball fight. Martha had relented and let them go as far as the stonewall on the back lawn, even though it was close to the unfrozen lake. Breanna claimed it first and held off two attacks from her brothers, but, in the end, the fortress was breached. Jamal bounded onto the top of the wall to claim victory and took three snowballs to the back from Darian who had decided to switch sides. Jamal relinquished his hold on the fortress to go after his younger brother, giving Breanna control of the wall once again.

"Come on," Agnes said to Sutherland. "Breanna needs help."

"Breanna?" Sutherland questioned. "I was going to help Darian."

"So be it," Agnes smiled. She raced to the hallway for her jacket, gloves, and boots. Sutherland followed, but at a much more leisurely pace.

Breanna was, once again, defending the wall by herself, Darian having switched sides yet again. Agnes made three snowballs, screamed, and ran at the boys. They were momentarily stunned as she joined Breanna at the wall.

"I thought you could use some help," Agnes said.

"Absolutely," Breanna admitted. "It's two against one."

"Sutherland is going to be on their side," Agnes pointed out, "but he can't throw straight."

Breanna laughed.

Sutherland jogged out and was immediately pelted by both sides. "Hey, guys, I'm on your side!"

"Oops! Our bad!" Jamal apologized.

Darian switched sides once again and hit Jamal in the shoulder with a snowball.

"Stop it!" Jamal yelled. "Pick a side!"

"I'm young. I get to pelt everyone!" he declared. That was followed by a barrage in his direction.

Taking advantage of the distraction, Agnes charged out from behind the wall, pelting Sutherland with snowball after snowball. To defend himself, Sutherland tackled her, and they fell into a drift laughing.

Sutherland's and Agnes's quick exit out of the house to join the post-storm snowball fight left Milo and Jen alone in the gallery watching the war on the back lawn.

"What happens with this house if those two get married?" Jen asked Milo.

"I don't know," Milo said.

§

Darian, a walking snowman who had become the target of both sides, was getting cold. Martha's hot chocolate was calling, so the sibs called a truce in the snowball war and raced back to the cottage.

Sutherland decided to show Agnes one more Lakesong secret. "I have cross-country skis in the maintenance shed. Are you game?"

"Absolutely! Let's do this."

What he didn't say was that there were ten pairs of cross-country skis, including several pairs of the waxless variety. Agnes sifted through the boots. "I hope these all aren't for petite feet," she jibed, finding a pair that worked.

Sutherland continued to look sheepish as he led the way, cutting a path toward the secret. They skied across the wide expanse of lawn to the creek that followed the south boundary of the property to the lake. Sutherland skied to the bottom of a stone bridge then stopped and began to take off his skis.

"What are you doing?" Agnes asked.

"We need to walk to the secret," he explained, "but bring your skis."

Intrigued by Sutherland's unexpected display of whimsy, she took off her skis. Sutherland squeezed between two bushes and disappeared. Agnes heard a creaking sound.

"What's happening now?" she shouted.

"Come on," he said.

She edged her way into the bushes and saw Sutherland standing by a short, open, wooden door. "Agnes, Lakesong.

Lakesong, Agnes," he said, mocking her phrase when Agnes showed him the secret staircase that she had discovered.

"Is that a tunnel? To where?" Agnes asked.

"To Patterson Park under London Road."

"You have a tunnel to a park? Who has that?"

"Mr. Patterson, Lakesong's former owner."

As Sutherland led the way, overhead lights came on, illuminating the stone walls. Agnes just shook her head. "Dad's idea," Sutherland smiled.

They emerged from the tunnel into the park. Freshly fallen snow lay undisturbed on the trails and wooden bridges that crisscrossed the frozen stream. Hoarfrost encircled the bare branches of the trees. Two deer made their way through the snow, stopping to dig for something to eat. The scene was almost too beautiful to disturb.

"Let's go," Sutherland said, throwing his skis down. "It gets even better, and you can't rush ahead this time because you don't know the destination."

"Lead on, oh mighty scout," Agnes teased.

The pair followed the stream to the center of the park where a small waterfall had frozen in mid flow. "I've never seen a frozen waterfall in person before," Agnes said, her breath visible as white puffs of frost.

"I know it's cold out." Sutherland opened his parka. "But I'm warm."

"Cross country is a fuel burner," Agnes agreed. "Let's keep moving, furnace man, or we'll freeze as solid as the waterfall."

§

By early afternoon, their private winter wonderland had become more crowded, so Sutherland and Agnes returned home to find Milo reading in the library. Annie curled by the fire, and Jet, no longer satisfied to sit on the side table, had parked on Milo's lap. He saw no advantage to this reading thing and pestered Milo to pet him.

"Where's Jen?" Sutherland asked.

Milo put his book aside. "She went up to her room to lay down."

"I am going to make Tom and Jerrys," Sutherland said, rubbing his hands together as if it was cold in the house.

"Your father's batter recipe?"

"Yes. I keep it in a safe, and the safe's in a vault, and the whole thing is under water. I have to get my scuba gear."

"It's that valuable?" Agnes laughed.

"Priceless," Sutherland said.

"John got it from a bakery in Superior," Milo disclosed. "The place was famous for its Tom and Jerry batter."

"I did not know that," Sutherland admitted. "Dad always called it his."

"I think he made modifications," Milo admitted.

Milo and Agnes left for the family room while Sutherland went into the kitchen to heat up the water. Jen, having napped, descended the stairs, and followed the voices into the family room. "A person could get lost in this house," Jen complained to Milo and Agnes.

"A number of people have," Milo said. "We hear voices and footsteps, but we've never found anybody."

Sutherland brought in the tea kettle of hot water, took the batter out of the small, family-room refrigerator, and began to mix the drinks. "I'm making Tom and Jerrys," he told Jen.

"What's in it?" Jen asked.

"The batter is eggs, salt, butter, sugar, vanilla, nutmeg, and some secret spices I cannot divulge," Sutherland said. "Hot water goes into it along with a jigger of rum and a jigger of brandy."

"Sounds delicious, but could I have one without the rum and brandy?" Jen asked. "It's a bit early for me."

Agnes smiled. Having been around her pregnant friend, Liz, this past summer, Agnes was pretty sure Jen was expecting.

17

Milo finished his Sunday morning laps in Lakesong's indoor saltwater pool. He flipped over, floated on his back, and gazed at the sunny blue sky through the glass dome. Milo was not deceived—ice was still crystalizing on parts of the dome. Another day of hibernation.

He pulled himself up and out of the pool, wandered over to the bar area, and made himself a cup of coffee. His phone erupted with the ringtone "Uptown Girl." Mary Alice invited Milo to Sunday morning brunch. Brunching with the blue-eyed beauty was worth breaking his hibernation.

Milo's day wearing blue jeans and a sweatshirt was cancelled. He upped his game to N&J black pants, a plaid shirt, and a V-neck sweater. *Going formal on a Sunday,* he thought. *Milo, what is happening to you?*

Lilly Anderson, the woman who maintained Lakesong's cars, had managed to put the heavy hardtop on the old

Mercedes, but, with all the snow, Milo opted for the estate's SUV. *Formal duds, a safe car, who am I becoming? Sutherland? Happy John?* Milo thought, thinking back to the will reading. John McKnight wanted his son Sutherland to take a few risks, and Milo his almost-adopted-son to calm the hell down. *Sunday brunch and a working car—any calmer and I'd be dead.*

The SUV's wide, four-wheel-drive tires crunched through the patches of ice and snow on lonely London Road. Mary Alice's gates were open, welcoming Milo to the Bonner estate. He drove up to the house. As he opened the car's door, Phoenix and Flash—two of Mary Alice's exuberant hounds of the manor—bounded toward him, pinning him inside the car until a confused squirrel darted past them and drew the dogs away from Milo's vehicle.

Milo used this momentary distraction to exit the car. The slamming door called the dogs back to Milo, knocking him back. "You two are liking this cold and snow, aren't you?" Milo said, petting their heads.

Phoenix kept trying to lick Milo's face. Flash, the greyhound rescue sporting a double-thick red sweater and full-length dog booties, ran to a snowbank, leaping on top and claiming it as his own before sinking down into the new soft snow.

The third dog, Luna—the female of the group—held back and was sitting by Mary Alice who was standing by the front door with her arms crossed, trying to keep warm. Flash barked. He was stuck. Milo walked over and dug out some of the snowbank with his hands. Flash broke free, covering Milo with snow. Mary Alice couldn't stop laughing.

Collecting herself, she said, "Flash thanks you. He gets cold easily."

Luna strolled up to Milo and sniffed him, returning to Mary Alice's side.

"Luna is still not impressed," Milo said.

"Neither am I if I freeze to death out here. Come inside!" The snow-encrusted dog pack bounded up the steps toward Mary Alice and Luna. Milo followed.

As they entered the foyer, Mary Alice pointed to the coat rack where Milo could hang his snowy coat. Milo mentioned that the traffic had been brutal.

"All half a mile of it?"

"There were three other cars going my direction. Three. A traffic jam of biblical proportions. I thought I'd never get here."

"You must be famished. We are brunching in the dining room," Mary Alice said, leading Milo toward the back of the house.

Milo stopped and looked around the under-construction gallery. The walls had been taken down to the bare studs, ceiling lights were hanging from wires, and the marble floors had become plywood. "Why not just tear this place down and start again?" Milo asked.

"I've thought about it. I might someday," Mary Alice said, leading Milo past the construction.

"I don't think I've been in this dining room," Milo mused. "In fact, I don't think I've been brunching as a verb."

Mary Alice looked back at him smiling, "Then it will be a morning of firsts."

Phoenix and Flash walked on each side of Milo as if the three of them were on parade. Luna stayed with Mary Alice.

As they sat down in one corner of the long, glass table, Mary Alice explained, "One of the advantages of brunch is dessert from Ilene's."

"Cream puffs?" Milo asked.

"Could be,"

The Bonner's cook, whom Mary Alice always referred to as *Cook*, arrived with mimosas.

Milo stopped her and asked, "What's your name?"

The plain, older woman with short, black hair said, "Cook, sir." She left for the kitchen.

"And you thought I was being insensitive," Mary Alice said. "Cook likes to be called *Cook*. She came that way."

"Oh, come on, she has to have a name."

"Of course, she does. Her name is Borghild—I know this because I pay her—but, if you call her Borghild, she'll hit you with her frying pan then get into a foul mood that will be reflected in her food. I respect her wishes and call her, *Cook."*

Cook returned with plates of fruit, asparagus, a tomato frittata, a cheese plate, croissants, and potatoes O'Brien. It was difficult, but Milo stifled his urge to use the cook's real name.

"Thank you for coming to my rescue with the offer of Lakesong for my New Year's Eve gala. I don't think I officially thanked you."

"I should warn you; I could lose it all. Another high-stakes poker game tonight."

Mary Alice caught her breath and went cold. Her father gambled and lost on a high stakes investment. Her son had a gambling addiction. Now Milo was betting the house. Was he kidding? "Are you serious?"

"Sure," Milo said taking a second helping of the frittata.

Trying to appear calm, Mary Alice asked, "How much could you lose?"

"A whole dollar. On bad nights, two. Ernie Gramm lost two-and-a-quarter once."

Mary Alice slugged him in the shoulder. "You are an awful person!"

"We're a wild bunch."

She started to breathe again. "Try the gruyere, *wild-man*. So, does Jen's baby make you an uncle once removed?"

"What?"

"Jen's baby. The spy I planted in your house told me."

"Jet? Jet's a spy?"

"Agnes, not Jet. So, are you happy, sad, angry, what?"

"Are you sure?"

"Haven't you noticed? No alcohol, naps, and Agnes says some foods don't agree with her. For someone who zeros in on other people, you seem pretty clueless."

Milo sighed. "Wow! Lars' disappearance must be even more frightening for Jen."

"So, does it bother you?"

"It's been ten years. Besides, I'm in a relationship."

"Relationship? Really?" Mary Alice said, flashing her blue eyes. "With whom?"

"The Widow Bonner."

"Ah, her. Are you sure you're up for the challenge?"

"I have to work on Luna first," Milo joked.

Luna hid behind Mary Alice's chair.

Milo shrugged. "It's a work in progress."

§

With Agnes sleeping late, breakfast at Lakesong was only Sutherland and Jen. Since Sunday was Martha's day off, Sutherland had a guy who delivered Ilene's pastries—a Sunday treat. He offered to make Jen an omelet. She declined. "Eggs and I don't get along these days," she explained.

Sutherland brought the goodies into the morning room. Jen had gotten herself a glass of apple juice from the refrigerator. "You can have anything in the box," Sutherland said, "but leave one cream puff because…"

"Milo goes crazy for cream puffs. I know," Jen said. "Where is Milo?"

"Oh, he's brunching with…"

"Mary Alice, right?"

"Probably."

"So how does, 'did you kill your husband' become 'sure, I'll come over for brunch?'"

"Well, as I understand it, this summer she needed a tennis partner and…"

"Oh, tennis! That makes sense. Milo is a monster on the court. Don't ever play him."

Sutherland blanched. "I already made that mistake."

"I hope he's as good at finding Lars as he is at tennis," Jen sighed.

"May I ask you a question that's really none of my business?"

Jen looked up and nodded

"Since you left Milo for Lars, why did you come back to Milo for his help? Is it just that so much time has passed?"

Jen looked stunned. "What?"

"I'm sorry," Sutherland apologized, thinking he had ventured too far. "Forget I said anything."

"No. Is that what Milo told you?"

"I guess?"

"He thinks I left him for Lars!"

"Well, he tells it with humor. It's a funny story…sort of."

"Let me set the record straight without the punchline. I didn't leave Milo for Lars! I left him because I was tired of being alone—weary of being alone. Milo, for all his laissez-faire attitude, was a workaholic. Lars and I didn't start dating for a whole year after Milo and I divorced."

"So, the dog didn't run away?" Sutherland was confused and wished he had never brought it up.

"Yes, the dog ran away. Lars found and returned him. That's how we met the first time." Jen's mood was softening. "Later, after the divorce, a friend set me up on a date with her friend, and that date turned out to be Lars. The dog already liked him."

Sutherland noticed that Jen could come up with a punchline too.

"Milo's story may be funny, but it's nowhere close to the truth." Jen sat back. "I do wish Milo well. I hope he is more available for her."

Sutherland thought for a moment. "Well, Mary Alice is a busy woman. She took over her husband's business and is making serious changes—takes a lot of time."

Jen nodded. "He found somebody just like him."

I must stop talking, Sutherland thought.

§

Retiring to Mary Alice's sitting room for dessert and coffee, Milo wondered if Mary Alice color coordinated her outfits to match the décor of her rooms—winter white, blond hair, blue eyes, and soft blue room.

"Ith tham going toth…" Milo slurred with a load of cream puff in his mouth.

Mary Alice shook her head. "Swallow. I can't decipher cream-puff speech."

Milo finished chewing his cream puff. "I'm going to restart my detective agency but take only cases that interest me."

"Really. What led to that decision?"

"Boredom," Milo said. "What keeps you from being bored?"

"My business, my son Richard, you, and remodeling this house." Mary Alice looked around the sitting room.

"Well, at least I didn't come in last," Milo joked. "Are you going to rip up this room too?"

"No! This was the one room in this monolith of a house that I designed," she said, admiring the luxurious fabrics and rounded edges of her sofa and matching chairs.

Milo realized that soon this house would lose all its James Bonner, stark white, square-cornered harshness and would be replaced by soothing blues and grays, and the softer, rounded edges of Mary Alice.

Luna got up from her place on the couch and came over to Milo. He took a bit of cream puff and held it out. The dog ate it in one gulp and sat, waiting for more.

"There you go, Milo. The lady loves cream puffs."

Milo gave her another piece with plenty of cream. "So, I have to give up some of my lovely cream puff to win Luna's heart?"

"You have to give a little bit of yourself to get a little back."

Luna jumped up and laid her head in Milo's lap.

18

By Sunday evening, the steep streets of Duluth—the city built on the side of a hill—gave up their ice and snow to salt and sand and were as clear as they could be in a Duluth winter.

At Lakesong, the weekly poker game was on with Sutherland as the host.

"Sutherland and Milo are like the Giants and Jets," Gramm said, as the players sat down around the Lakesong poker table.

"They play bad football?" Creedence guessed.

"No, they share a stadium—this great billiard room complete with Martha's tasty snacks."

"So, Martha is the concession stand?" Milo asked.

"I guess, but so much better," Gramm said, stabbing a stuffed mushroom off the top of the stacked plate.

Sutherland pointed out that he and Creedence Durant had joined the game almost a year ago as he opened a new deck and shuffled the cards. The new deck was met with hoots and hollers. "Is this the marked deck?" Pro bono lawyer and heir to the "Feinberg Pastrami Fortune," Saul Feinberg questioned.

Gramm looked around. "Are there casino cameras watching our every move?"

Milo grabbed his phone and took a picture of Gramm. "Feel better?"

"Hardly," Gramm replied.

Sutherland called the first game. "Seven card stud nothing wild." He dealt two cards down and one up.

Gramm was pleased. He professed to hate wild card games.

Milo looked at his down cards, the eight of diamonds and the eight of clubs. His up card was the eight of hearts. Creedence, with two fives down, began the bidding at a dime. Feinberg raised a dime. Milo let them lead the bidding and he matched the twenty cents as did Gramm and Sutherland.

One more card up. Milo got a King. Creedence was looking at two Queens up. He bid fifteen cents. Feinberg matched, as did Milo. Gramm folded with his usual grumble about sitting at a table of millionaires.

The third card up gave Creedence another five which led to another fifteen-cent bid. Feinberg and Sutherland folded. Milo matched. The third and fourth cards didn't help Milo or Creedence. The final down card gave Milo his fourth eight.

Creedence bid a quarter, a fortune in penny-ante poker. Gramm urged Creedence on. "Take these big-buck-guys to the cleaners!" Gramm demanded.

Milo matched Creedence's quarter and raised a quarter to the cheers of the others. Creedence, who was looking at a full house, went another quarter.

"Wow, seventy-five cents!" Feinberg laughed. "I might faint."

Milo matched his quarter, admonishing the others by saying someone had to keep Creedence honest. Creedence showed his hand: full house, fives over Queens. Milo smiled, then flipped up his three eights, placing all four in a row.

"What the?" Creedence sputtered.

Milo raked in his chips.

"How do we know it wasn't fixed?" Gramm charged. "You know, a Lakesong conspiracy. Sutherland deals, Milo wins."

Sutherland looked at Gramm. "Do you really think I would help Milo win? Really?"

"Good point," Gramm conceded.

After several more hands, none as spectacular as the first, the group took a break to devour more of Martha's poker spread. Feinberg sat back munching on a Korean barbeque skewer. "I got an invitation to Mary Alice's New Year's Eve party. The destination said Lakesong. Anyone care to explain?"

"Me too," Creedence chimed in. "Did last year's murder kinda take the shine off the Bonner place?"

"She's renovating," Sutherland said. "Getting rid of all things James Bonner. Kind of finishing what the murderer started."

"So, you offered your place?" Feinberg asked.

"Not exactly. Her first choice," Sutherland hesitated, always looking for a positive spin, "was taken off the market,"

"If she had a contract, how could they take it off the market?" Feinberg, always the lawyer, wanted to know.

"I took it off the market," Gramm admitted.

"Why do I never understand what's going on?" Creedence protested.

"Wait a minute," Feinberg said, "are we talking the Hawthorne estate—those two murders?"

"Yup. And I'm not telling you another damn thing."

"I have a question for Creedence," Milo said.

"Go ahead, ask your question," Creedence said, "because I have a long and storied history in law enforcement." Creedence stabbed a candied sweet potato piece with a fancy toothpick.

"Really?" Sutherland challenged.

"Well, I was a crossing guard for two weeks in sixth grade," Creedence boasted.

Sutherland laughed. "Why only two weeks?"

"I kept asking the other kids if they were properly investing their candy money," Creedence admitted. "It was part of a complete package. Safely cross the street, get investment advice."

"So, they fired you?" Feinberg asked.

"Yes. The principal said I wasn't paying attention to the traffic. Some of those kids are now my clients. Now, I charge for advice they could have had for free."

"I think I had a question," Milo interrupted.

"We'll get to your question," Feinberg said. "First, we have to establish Creedence's crime fighting credentials."

"I don't care about his life on the crossing guard force," Milo insisted. "I have an investment question."

"Buy low, sell high," Feinberg said. "That's all you need to know."

Creedence pushed his glasses up the bridge of his nose. "Thank you, Saul, for boiling down my entire lifetime into one neat, trite, statement."

"You still have your dinosaur toe," Sutherland said, referring to Creedence's discovery last summer of a small species of dinosaur.

"Et tu Sutherland?" Creedence complained.

"We're quoting Caesar now?" Gramm asked.

"It's not Caesar. It's Shakespeare," Feinberg corrected. "For all we know, Caesar's last words were, 'I hate wild card poker games.'"

"If that's true, then Caesar and I think alike," Gramm offered.

"I still have a question!" Milo yelled.

"So, ask it already," Feinberg said. "We don't have all night. The cards are getting cold."

"Yeah, Milo, you're holding up the game," Sutherland admonished.

Milo grabbed the last mandu dumpling, savoring it, deliberately delaying the conversation.

"Milo, ask your damn question!" Gramm sputtered.

After dabbing his mouth with his napkin, Milo asked, "What do you know about investment clubs?"

"Avoid them," Creedence said.

"How do they work?" Milo continued.

"Any way you want. The type I see the most is a group of friends who pool their money and agree on investments."

"How about one where people invest, and one shadowy guy decides where the money goes?" Milo asked.

"Shadowy?" Creedence asked. "Sounds risky. Who is the shadowy guy? What kind of investment track record does he have?"

"Don't know. He goes by the name of Mr. Fauchard."

Feinberg laughed.

Milo ignored him. "How would something like that work."

Creedence pushed his glasses up again. "Normally, a Wall Street Wizard would charge a large fee for investment services, and investors would have to trust that the wizard was worth the cost. I would not advise this for you, Milo."

"Not for me. It has to do with a case. For a while, Wizard Fauchard was returning eight to twelve percent profit. Then the money stopped flowing," Milo explained.

Creedence shook his head. "Eight to twelve percent profit in this economy? It may be a Ponzi Scheme. The main guy collects a lot of cash, pays some back to get more suckers, and then skips town with the rest of the money."

"That's illegal. Why don't you arrest this Fauchard?" Sutherland asked Gramm.

"We don't know who he is," Gramm said.

"Isn't that the bunco squad's territory?" Feinberg questioned. "Why would homicide care?"

Creedence picked up the cards and declared duces and jacks, king-with-the-axe, Gramm's least favorite game.

"Oh, give me a break!" Gramm complained.

As Creedence dealt the cards, Feinberg said, "I'd look for a dentist if I were you."

Milo looked at Gramm who asked, "Why would you say that?"

"Fauchard. Dr. Fauchard. He is the father of modern dentistry."

Gramm peeked at his two cards down. "How would you know that?"

"It came up in a trivia contest. My team has all sorts of trivial, idiotic knowledge. We win all the time," Feinberg boasted.

"Trivia. I hear that's fun. Where do you play?" Creedence asked.

"The Tip Top Tavern, every Tuesday night," Feinberg said, bidding a dime.

"Where's the Tip Top Tavern?" Sutherland asked. "I never heard of it."

"Central Entrance. In between all those car places."

Gramm added. "I've been up there a lot lately."

"Why?" Feinberg asked.

"Interviewing people of interest."

"Cop code for suspects," Feinberg challenged.

Gramm's eyebrows knitted together. "Not suspects. We were interviewing our victim's business partner and one of his customers."

The card game came to an end short of midnight with Milo the big winner, courtesy of the first hand. Gramm lingered waiting for the others to leave.

"Ernie, it's over. You lost. Go home." Milo kidded.

"That Tip Top Tavern was mentioned by Sithens' partner Van Dyke," Gramm said, ignoring Milo's urgings. "It was where Sithen's was attacked by an investor. I think it's worth checking out."

"As in it's worth *me* checking out?" Milo asked.

"Exactly. It's your theory—Sithens was the target or so you think."

19

After saying good morning to Martha, Agnes bounded into the morning room wheeling her small suitcase behind her. Sutherland looked distressed at the sight of the suitcase.

"What?" Agnes asked. "You know I'm going home today. The power's back on."

"I would prefer that you stayed here."

"That's sweet, but I'm out of clothes."

Sutherland took a deep breath and explained the threats to, and his fears for her safety. "Milo says he has a plan, but until that comes to fruition, I think it best you stay here."

Agnes sat down. "What about you? Are you going into the office?"

"I am. I'll be in an office with a lot of people. If you go home, you'll be there alone."

"I just have to change clothes, then I'm coming back here. I have to work today, remember?"

"Have Milo go with you."

"Why Milo?"

"He has a gun."

"You're serious, aren't you?"

§

Gramm sipped his coffee while watching White munching on a protein bar.

"What are we doing today?" Preston asked.

"I thought Sergeant White—with all her protein power—would confront Eddy Peterson on his lack of an alibi, while you and I struggle along and talk to Dr. Zackery," Gramm said.

"Dr. Zackery again, why?" White asked. "Milo and Kate already talked to him."

"Sunday night poker game, it was dropped that a Dr. Fauchard is the father of dentistry. That investment guy goes by the name Fauchard," Gramm explained.

"Do you really think Zackery would be dumb enough to use that name?" White asked.

"Sure. Why not? Who would know that Fauchard thing?"

"How do you know it?" White asked.

"I play poker with a trivia nerd."

"Milo?"

"Not Milo."

"Where is Milo?" Preston asked.

"He's pursuing his own theory."

"Which is?" White asked.

"With Milo, do we ever know?"

White nodded and handed Gramm her file.

"Why do I need this?" Gramm asked.

"Just in case you want to expand your interview beyond Dr. Zackery's knowledge of the father of dentistry. The file has pictures of suspects that could come in handy."

Gramm delegated, tossing the file to Preston.

§

When the Tip Top Tavern was built, land along Central Entrance was cheap, making it the favorite of car dealerships that needed large parking lots. At one time, the tavern was the main watering hole for car salesmen, mechanics, and autobody people. Over the past thirty years, Central Entrance had changed and become more suburban. The car dealerships had been joined by fast food restaurants, veterinary clinics, and one sign company—Sithens and Van Dyke Signs and Banners.

As he pulled into the Tip Top parking lot, Milo noticed the sign shop across the street. Of course, the term *across* was a bit optimistic. Anyone attempting to cross the busy four-lane highway on foot was courting a trip to the emergency room.

Two older-model cars with snow-free windows—a sign they had been driven recently—occupied the tavern parking lot, and someone was inside the bar on this Monday morning.

Milo opened the Tip Top Tavern's heavy, wooden door and stomped his feet on the floor matt placed to catch snow and ice before it was tracked into the bar. The lights of the bar were full-on bright revealing the Tip Top to be twice the size of gangster, Morrie Wolf's Rasa bar. There were numerous tables and chairs, a dance area, plus an arcade.

A female voice shouted, "We're closed. Come back at noon!"

Advancing to the bar, Milo said, "Not here to drink. I need information."

The thick, muscular woman with dark, curly hair gave Milo a side-eye and stopped wiping the bar. "Cop?"

"Sorta," Milo said. "My name is Milo..."

"Rathkey!" the woman almost shouted. "I'll be a son-of-a-bitch. Milo Rathkey! It's me, Darlene Budack."

Milo took a step back. Darlene Budack had haunted Milo's early life. She had a thing for him in high school, feelings he did not reciprocate. "Darlene? Oh, my goodness, how are you?"

Darlene smirked. "I own a bar, and I work eighteen-hour days—every day. How could I not be fine?" She turned to the man sweeping the dance area. "Hey, Deano, this is the asshole who didn't ask me to the prom."

The man shrugged and kept sweeping.

"I didn't go to the prom, Darlene."

"Neither did I, thanks to you."

Milo thought dealing with Morrie at the Rasa might be easier. Morrie never brought up the prom.

"What happened to you?" Darlene continued. "After graduation you disappeared. I kept looking for you."

Uneasy with the idea of being stalked by Darlene, Milo said, "I went into the Navy—stayed a long time. How did you become a bar owner?"

"I was between divorces and my uncle wanted to retire. I bought him out with my alimony payments. Me and the kids lived upstairs for a while. Now I got a place in Hermantown. You should visit."

"Glad it all worked out." Milo side stepped the offer. "I need some information about a fight in here a couple of weeks ago."

"Fight? I don't run that kind of bar. I got daytime suits and ties, and nighttime jeans and boots. Hell, I even have a social media following."

"Well, maybe not a bloody fight, but some pushing or shoving."

Darlene thought for a minute. "Give me a name?"

"Alex Sithens."

Darlene stopped wiping down the bar. "The recently murdered Alex Sithens?"

Milo sat down on one of the stools. "That would be him."

"He was a regular. Who killed him?"

"Don't know—trying to find out."

"And you're sort of a cop?"

"I consult with the cops. I used to be one."

"Navy and then a cop," Darlene shook her head. "Quite a straight arrow."

"I still have my wild moments," Milo joked. "Last week I did fifty-three in a forty-five zone."

Darlene resumed wiping down the bar. "Criminal."

The door to the back room slammed open and David Bonner appeared, balancing a keg of beer on his right shoulder. "We're outta Miller Lite."

"Hey, David, just in time. This dangerous guy didn't ask me to the prom back in high school."

Bonner glared at Milo. "You want me to bounce him?"

Darlene laughed. "Naw. Just want him to know I could."

Milo thought Bonner looked familiar, but he couldn't place him.

"The fight?" Milo brought Darlene back to the question.

"Yeah, I remember. Some guy came in and started yelling at Alex. I wouldn't call it a fight—some pushing and shoving—but it took my trivia guy, a bartender, and me to escort the guy out. That's why I hired Bonner here. Fights are a waste of time."

Milo didn't visibly react, but, inside his head, he called up the name David Bonner—brother of murdered James Bonner. Still focusing on Darlene, he asked, "Have you seen him since?"

"Seen who?"

"The guy you threw out."

"Nope."

"Could you describe him?"

"I can do you one better. I have cameras. Come on back," she said moving to the end of the bar, lifting the hinged top so she could walk out into the main room. Milo glanced at Bonner as he followed Darlene to the office in the back.

He looks like his brother, Milo thought. *Wonder if Mary Alice knows he's out.*

Stepping into the spacious office, Milo expected some electronics, one bad camera, and a tape machine. He got six LED monitors—all high-definition color—lining one wall of the paneled room. Milo was impressed. The Fast Mart and the Tip Top; state-of-the-art surveillance was coming into its own.

Darlene sat down at a keyboard and thought for a second. "I think the fight was two weeks ago. Let's start with Tuesday. Tuesday's trivia night," she said.

After fast forwarding through several hours of bar business, Milo identified Alex at the bar laughing with several other men. Another man walked up to him, grabbed him by the shoulder, flung him around, and appeared to be yelling in his face.

"Can I hear this?" Milo asked.

"We don't have microphones, just video," Darlene said.

Milo watched Alex retaliate. The pushing and shoving began. He wished he could get a good look at the man's face, but the camera angle was shooting down on the pair. After a few more seconds, Darlene appeared and grabbed the intruder. For one quick second Milo saw his face but wished he hadn't.

"Oh crap!" he said, slumping into a nearby chair.

"You know this guy?" Darlene asked.

"Yeah, sort of."

"Who is he?"

"The guy is married to my wife."

"Married to your wife? How does that work?"

"Ex-wife."

David Bonner came in and grabbed two cases of a trendy IPA.

Darlene smiled when Milo said *ex-wife*. "So, you're available?"

"Not really. Kind of involved." Milo had fallen down a rabbit hole.

"Who with? Anyone I know?"

Milo saw a way out of the rabbit hole—drastic, but necessary. Nodding at David Bonner, he said, "Mr. Bonner's sister-in-law, and three dogs."

David Bonner set the cases down and stared at Milo. Seconds passed like hours. If the hulking Bonner went after him, Milo didn't have a backup plan except to run. He longed for the verbal chess moves with Morrie Wolf.

Bonner picked up the same cases. "Better watch yourself."

"How so?"

"Buy me a beer."

Milo looked at Darlene who shrugged, stood up, and led the way back into the bar. She grabbed two glasses and poured the drafts. Darlene left to make a copy of the surveillance video. David Bonner sat on one stool with Milo sitting several stools away.

"Why should I watch myself?" Milo asked as Bonner downed his beer and reached over the bar to pour another.

"She shot my brother," Bonner said. "She could shoot you."

"Stan Schultz killed your brother," Milo protested.

David Bonner threw him a *don't-be-stupid* glance. "Stan Shultz was never allowed in that house. I only made it in now and then through the back door. Naw—she shot him."

"Tell the cops," Milo said.

Bonner drained his second glass of beer. "She won. She got his money and got rid of him. I got money too. I got no beef."

"I didn't kill my exes, I just divorced them," Darlene said, catching the tail end of the conversation. "That'll be ten bucks for the beers and five bucks for the thumb drive.

Make it an even twenty; I like tips." She traded the thumb drive for the twenty.

Milo walked back out into the cold sunshine and called Gramm. Lars was now a suspect. This was not good—not good at all.

§

Gramm and Preston were on their way to Dr. Zackery's office when Milo called Gramm to detail the video at the Tip Top.

"Where can we find Lars?" Gramm asked.

"He's somewhere in West Duluth. I have people looking for him. For the record, I don't think Lars is a killer."

"Milo, you're defending the guy who ran off with your wife," Gramm pointed out.

"All my life's a circle," Milo said.

"Well, circle down here to Dr. Zackery's office. Preston and I will wait for you."

"Where's White?" Milo asked.

"She's checking in on Eddy Peterson. Remember, his alibi is bogus."

"I'm on my way," Milo said.

§

Peterson's receptionist was the only one in the office when White walked in. "I need to see Mr. Peterson," White said.

"Stand in line," the receptionist snipped.

White noticed that Peterson's office was dark. "Where is he?"

"Don't know. He hasn't been in since the last time you guys were here. I'm holding down the fort, but if he doesn't come back soon, I'm going to lock up the place and look for another job."

"I'm going to check his office, see if I can find a clue to his whereabouts," White said.

"Knock yourself out."

White went through Peterson's desk. Finishing up, she still had no idea where he had run to, but she did find a framed picture shoved in the bottom desk drawer under some papers. She took a picture of the picture and texted it to everybody with the caption, *Peterson and Lerner on a hunting trip. Notice the compound bow.*

§

As Gramm, Preston, and the newly arrived Rathkey took the elevator to the fourth floor, all three received the picture from White.

"Interesting," Gramm said. "Peterson and Lerner know each other."

Preston didn't look at the text. Milo did but said nothing.

Dr. Zackery's receptionist informed them that the doctor was in surgery and it would be a while before he could see them. Milo asked if they could wait in the conference room and she obliged.

"While we're here, we should also talk with Monica Sandlan," Milo said. "She didn't mourn Faythe Cummings passing for long."

"Short mourning times are not a crime," Gramm noted, but added, "it wouldn't hurt as long as we're here."

After half an hour, Dr. Zackery walked in, adjusting a clean scrub shirt. "Sorry to keep you waiting—an impacted wisdom tooth." He grabbed two bottles of water from a small refrigerator and sat down at the end of the table. "What else do you need from me?"

Milo introduced Gramm and reintroduced Officer Preston to Dr. Zackery before asking how much money Zackery had lost in the investment club.

The bluntness of the question took Zackery by surprise, and his answer was a bad bluff, "I have many investments. I don't understand the question."

"The one run by Mr. Fauchard," Milo said. "How much did you lose?"

"Oh, that one," Zackery admitted. "It was doing pretty well then it seemed to fall off a cliff. I've got to do some follow up."

"Other investors aren't so laid back," Gramm said.

Zackery shrugged. "Like I said, I have many investments."

"Back to my question," Milo persisted. "How much did you invest?"

"A hundred grand. Why?"

"Are you the main guy?" Milo asked.

He laughed. "Me? I'm a dentist, not an investment guru."

"I'm told a Dr. Fauchard is the father of modern dentistry," Gramm said.

Zackery thought for a second. "I believe you're right, but I can assure you that I am not this *Fauchard* guy. A *fauchard* is also the name of a medieval spear. Maybe you should be looking for a knight of the round table." Zackery laughed at his own joke.

"How did you get involved in the investment club?" Gramm asked.

"I'm sorry, but none of this is any of your business. You're investigating the death of my nurse. What does that have to do with *my* investments?"

"We believe the other victim, her fiancé, was the front man for Mr. Fauchard's scheme," Milo explained.

"Front man? Scheme?" Zackery drained the rest of his water and crushed the plastic bottle. "So, I've been duped."

"How did you come to invest?" Gramm asked.

"It came up last year when we were in Montana. A couple of the guys I hunt with had already invested."

"Who suggested it?" Gramm continued.

"Hmm? I don't remember. I did get a prospectus. It looked legit."

"Faythe's latest fiancé—was he interfering with you and her?" Milo asked.

Gramm's eyebrows shot up. Preston waited for Zackery's reaction.

"You're out of line!" Zackery's nostrils pulsed. "What kind of a person do you think I am?"

Milo shrugged. "The kind of a person who has an affair with an employee."

Zackery began to drink from the second water bottle. Gramm wondered if Milo was off base. Seconds passed. Milo did not fill in the silence.

"Past tense," Zackery mumbled. "We *had* a fling. It was over."

"Faythe's other men are possessive of her. What about you?"

Zackery shrugged. "Easy come. Easy go." And finished his water.

Milo didn't believe it. "I hope this isn't out of line, but what picture went up on the wall there? One of the frames doesn't match."

"It fell. The glass broke. I'm having it fixed."

Milo picked up his phone and accessed the photo White had sent. He showed it to Zackery. "Is this the picture?"

Zackery crossed his arms. "Where did you get that?"

"From Eddy Peterson's office," Milo said.

"Why were you in Eddy's office?"

Gramm called up the picture on his phone. "I'll be damned. Peterson, Lerner, and you."

"We've been hunting together for years. So what?"

"There are five of you in the picture," Milo said. "Who are the other two?"

Zackery looked again at the picture of five smiling men standing in front of a two-engine plane. Pointing to a man on the left carrying a bow and a duffle bag, Zackery said, "That man is Bert Quince, Dr. Bert Quince. He and I went to dental school together. Maybe he's the Doctor Fauchard you're looking for. He has a practice in White Bear Lake outside the cities. The guy on the other end in camouflage, Jim Rudd, runs a TV station in Fargo. We stop and pick them up on the way to Montana."

"Why did you take down that picture?" Gramm asked.

"I didn't. It fell off the wall." Zackery stood up. "I have to get back to my surgeries. Patients are waiting."

"Who took the picture?" Milo asked, ignoring Zackery's protest.

"The extra pilot," Zackery said. "Look, I have to go."

"Could we talk to Nurse Sandlan?" Gramm asked.

Zackery narrowed his eyes. "Don't keep her long, I run a business here and patient care is primary. Next time, make an appointment."

"If there is a next time, the appointment will be in *my* conference room," Gramm threatened.

§

Joe Ripkowski, Milo's friend and fellow PI, had been looking for Lars Helvig per Milo's orders. The search had been delayed by the recent snowstorm, but now Joe was back on it. He showed Lars' picture to a number of bartenders, gas station operators, and short-stay hotels in West Duluth. Monday at noon, Joe hit the jackpot.

Walking into the Gardner Hotel, he took twenty dollars out of his wallet. Slack, the one-armed desk clerk, saw the gesture and, without looking up from his paper, rasped, "It'll cost you more than twenty."

"I haven't asked anything yet," Joe said.

"You've been showing a picture all over town. You're going to show it to me. Fifty bucks."

"Kinda steep," Joe said.

Slack looked up and smiled, "Because I know your guy."

"I haven't showed you the picture yet," Joe protested.

"So, show it. I'm busy."

Joe showed him the picture of Lars.

"Fifty bucks."

Joe added thirty dollars to his twenty.

Slack picked up the money and put it in his shirt pocket. "Upstairs, Room 308."

"You got an elevator?"

"It's broke. Stairs behind you."

Joe called Milo.

§

While Gramm, Rathkey, and Preston waited for Nurse Sandlan, Preston decided to take another scroll through Sandlan's Instagram page. "Look at this," She showed her phone to Gramm and Rathkey.

"She's advertising that she will be at the Tip Top Tavern tonight."

"Where I was this morning. It's where Lars and Alex Sithens got into it," Milo said.

"Let me check Faythe Cummings' page." Preston took her phone back from Gramm and called up Cummings' posts. "Hmm, it looks like Faythe did this sort of thing at the Tip Top at least twice a month."

"Again, Nurse Sandlan hasn't wasted any time," Gramm said.

"I haven't wasted any time doing what?" Monica Sandlan asked, walking into the conference room.

"Making personal appearances at the Tip Top," Milo stated. "It says you're replacing Faythe Cummings tonight."

"The owner needed somebody. Mondays are their slow night. Faythe brought people in. I'm not expecting to do as well, but I'll bring more than nobody."

Gramm stretched his back. "Where were you last Monday night?"

Sandlan startled. "Am I suspect?"

"Yes," Milo acknowledged. Gramm was surprised that he didn't use the usual, *we're checking with everyone* line. "Where were you, and do you know how to use a compound bow?"

Sandlan shook her head. "I was at the Tip Top doing Faythe's job. She blew that gig off to go venue-viewing with her latest fiancé. A lot of people showed up expecting Faythe, but I did pretty well."

"Cummings promised to be there and then didn't show?" Gramm asked.

"Yes. She did stuff like that all the time. I don't. That's why I'm going to go further than she did."

"I imagine people were angry," Milo said.

"Some."

"Got any names?"

Sandlan thought for a minute. "Her roommate came in early, looking for Faythe's share of the rent. She was pissed and left in a huff after I told her that Faythe was going to be a no-show. When the bar was getting busy, one of Faythe's many ex-boyfriends showed up and demanded to know why I was there, and she wasn't."

"How do you know he was a boyfriend?" Milo asked.

"He screamed it at me. He went on and on about how he and Faythe were engaged, but he wanted his ring back. Nasty guy. He was asked to leave."

"What's his name?" Gramm asked.

"I don't know. Kind of a biker dude. Good looking in a rough way," Sandlan said.

Gramm took White's file from Preston and produced a picture of Ike Granton. Sandlan looked at it. "Yeah, that's him," she said.

"Did you tell him where Faythe was?" Milo asked.

"Yes, anything to get rid of them."

"Them?" Gramm asked.

"He was with a girl, so I figured he had moved on and wanted his ring back for her or something. I didn't know he was going to kill Faythe."

"Describe the girl," Milo ordered.

"Sloppy, scowly, dirty blond hair, red smeary lipstick."

Gramm produced another picture, this one of Kayla Maki.

Sandlan laughed. "Do you have pictures of everyone in there? Yes, that's her. She seemed almost as scary as this guy." Sandlan pointed at Ike's picture. "After they left, I got on with my night. Stop by tonight. I'm fun."

20

Milo suggested that Preston and White meet him and Gramm at the Chinese Dragon for lunch. White, having failed to find a restaurant that didn't know Milo, gave in without objection.

The group was given tea at their usual back table. Hank, Milo's high school friend and restaurant owner, handed out menus to everyone except Milo. There was a pause as everyone expected Milo to object. He didn't.

"You should ask Robin why she hates your restaurant," Milo said.

"What?" White sputtered. "What are you talking about?"

"Don't fall for it, Robin," Hank advised. "I've got this."

Milo continued. "She insisted we go somewhere else the other day. You know I love this place. Your food is delicious, but for some reason Robin hates it. She made us go over the hill to some expensive sandwich place."

"I wanted to find a place that didn't know Milo," White explained, "so we wouldn't have to listen to his little dance around the specials."

"How did that work for you?" Hank asked.

"It didn't. They knew him!"

"Hello? I'm right here at the table," Milo complained. He was ignored.

"We restauranteurs meet once a month and discuss Milo. It's never good. Now, for today's special. I hired my nephew from Toronto as a sous chef. His specialty is bao buns..."

"Buns?" Milo interrupted.

"Yes, buns."

"Like hot dog buns?"

"Whatever kind of buns you want, Milo, because you're not going to order them anyway. For the rest of you, char siu bao buns, are a steamed barbeque pork bun. They are Cantonese."

White ordered the special as did Preston. Gramm ordered steamed dumplings and broccoli chicken. All eyes turned to Milo.

"I appear to be without a menu," Milo said. White looked up at the gold tin ceiling while Gramm groaned. Preston handed her menu to Milo.

"You have a beautiful ceiling, Hank," White said, still looking up.

"That's it, Milo. You have sent Robin over the edge," Hank admonished. "You're getting your usual chicken egg foo young, hold the gravy."

As Hank walked away Milo yelled, "Extra gravy!" Looking at the others, Milo explained, "I was thinking of ordering the special."

No one believed him.

"Can we get back to business?" Gramm pleaded. Pouring himself more tea, Gramm continued, "Based on this morning's interview with Sandlan, I think Granton and Maki together are on the top of my list. She guards the car while Ike paddles a canoe or raft to the estate, shoots our victims, and paddles back."

Preston shook her head.

"What?" Gramm demanded.

"She's the marksman, not him. She's won medals. We don't know if he can even shoot a bow and arrow," Preston argued.

"He shot a deer out of season."

"On his own property," White said. "He was probably up in a stand and shooting down. Not as hard as killing both of our victims from the ground, with speed and precision. That took skill."

Gramm held up his hand. "I yield to the experts. Granton watches the car while Kayla Maki does the shooting."

"Except," Milo began, "he's a hunter and we know the two victims were stalked like they were deer. Remember the talc on the trees."

"Okay, no one watches the car, they both go and shoot our victims!" Gramm grumbled.

"That would account for being able to kill both of them, especially hitting Sithens twice," Milo said.

White shook her head. "There's one flaw in all this. The arrows are thirty inches. There is no way Kayla could effectively use an arrow that long—she's too short."

"What happens if she tried?" Preston asked.

"Accuracy goes out the window, and there is no sign that any of the arrows missed. No footprints lead up to and away from the victims as if someone picked up poorly aimed arrows."

"Maybe there were three of them," Preston guessed. "Granton, Maki and Eddy Peterson. Peterson seems to have taken off."

"That was one crowded raft," White joked. "Do we know if Nurse Sandlan knows her way around a bow and arrow? We could make this canoe a yacht."

"We have no proof she does," Gramm said. "However, there is this Mr. Fauchard thing that points to her boss, Dr. Zackery."

"Why would he kill his nurse?" White asked.

Milo shook his head. "If he's running the investment scam, and Sithens threatened to expose him, he had to kill Sithens that night. It was Cummings' bad luck that she was there. Or he was obsessed with Cummings and killed her because she was leaving him."

Hank brought the food, with a small, porcelain pitcher of gravy on the side that he clinked against the plate holding Milo's egg-foo-young. "He did that on purpose," Milo complained.

"I would spill it in your lap," White said.

"What did I do?" Milo begged.

He was ignored.

As they ate, Gramm brought up another suspect. "So, Milo, tell White and Preston how your case and these murders intersect."

"You're talking about Lars?" Milo asked, cutting into his egg foo young and dragging it through the gravy. "He disappeared. His wife Jen..."

"Milo's ex," Gramm explained.

"Anyway, she asked me to find him. Remember, Sithens wrote he had a fight with an investor. I have proof the investor was Lars. My guy has found him staying at the Gardner Hotel."

"Does Lars hunt with a bow?" White asked.

"I have no idea," Milo said.

"Okay, when we finish here, Robin and I will talk with Kayla Maki and Ike Granton again," Gramm said. "And then see if we can find Lars."

Milo countered. "Let me talk to Lars."

While Gramm considered that, Preston asked, "What do you want me to do?"

"Find Eddy Peterson,"

White added, "Check hospitals and jails in other jurisdictions. Don't forget Superior."

"What about Lars?" Milo asked.

"Okay, Milo, you talk to Lars, *but,* at some point, I need to talk to him too."

"We do have Granton's phone call," White added. "It probably has no bearing on the case, but it is a loose end."

Gramm agreed. "Okay, we talk to Friendly Al first, then Granton and Maki."

As they finished their lunch, White asked Milo, "Any thoughts—something that doesn't add up?"

"Something Zackery said and Sithens' last email."

"What did Zackery say?"

"Don't have a clue. I left his office with that itchy feeling I missed something."

"Per usual, when your brain talks to you, let us know."

§

Friendly Al had three customers on the lot and didn't want to take time answering questions. Gramm insisted.

"What now?" Al complained. He smiled and waved at a young couple. "Be right with you."

"Ike Granton?" Gramm asked.

"What about him?"

"He called here last Wednesday afternoon."

"He works here."

"He was running from us when he phoned. Kind of an odd time to be calling work," White cracked.

"Can't help you. Wasn't here that day," Al said, walking up to the couple who were looking at a late model Nissan. "That's a beaut; just got that in. It's going to go fast."

Gramm and White caught up to him. "If you didn't take the call, who did?" Gramm asked.

Al shrugged, "Check with Nancy, inside." He quick stepped to another customer who seemed eager to catch his eye. "Welcome back!" Al boomed, with a strong handshake. "Ready to buy today?"

The man nodded.

"Great! Let's kick the tires and light the fires."

White and Gramm were left alone on the expansive parking lot. "I guess Nancy is the woman in the office next to Al's office," White said. "We haven't talked to her yet."

Al's business manager, Nancy Wickland, was at her computer when Gramm and White walked in. They showed her their badges as they sat down by her desk. "We need to ask you a few questions," Gramm said.

"Me? Why?"

"Alex Sithens."

Wickland took off her glasses. "Such a tragedy. We all liked Alex. He did an eye-catching job on the lot this season."

"Ike Granton, your mechanic, called here last Wednesday. Did you take the call?" Gramm asked.

"I'm the business manager, not the receptionist. If I'm busy I don't take calls."

"Who answers the phone?" White asked.

"We have an answering machine," Wickland said, pointing to a black box next to the phone. "I think Al won this thing at a chamber of commerce lunch twenty years ago." She pushed play. The machine said, *You have no new messages.*

Wickland shrugged.

Gramm felt he was being lied to. He hated that. "If you or Al didn't take Granton's phone call, and he didn't leave a message, who did he talk to last Wednesday?"

"Don't know."

"I know," Gramm said in an angry tone. "Either you or Al took that phone call."

Wickland put on her glasses, and drew her red sweaterclose around her, folding her arms. "I don't lie. Please leave."

Gramm noticed Al in the main sales area. He was closing the cabinet that held the car keys. As Al raced out the door, Gramm and White followed.

Friendly Al was handing the young couple the keys for a test drive when Gramm and White left the sales building. "One more question," Gramm said.

Al did not look friendly; neither did Gramm.

"I understand you are in a hunting party with Dr. Zackery and Eddy Peterson,"

"Is there a question in there?"

"How proficient are you with a bow and arrow?"

"I suck. I'm the only one who hasn't gotten a white tail in three years."

§

In the winter, the Gardner hotel was a warmer alternative to sleeping in the car, but only slightly more comfortable. Following Joe Ripkowski's directions, Milo passed through the lobby—and the hostile glares from Slack and two other residents—to reach the stairs, then hiked up to the third floor and knocked on Room 308.

Milo only met Lars once, ten years ago, when Lars returned Milo's lost dog, Homer. Milo and Jen were at the end of their marriage. Jen knew that. Milo was oblivious. Two months later, Milo was divorced. A year later, Jen and Homer were living with Lars.

If Lars recognized Milo, he didn't show it. "Yes?" he asked.

Milo noticed Lars still had a friendly, boyish face, but he was carrying a few extra pounds, and his hair was thinning. He looked worried, or sad; Milo wasn't sure.

"Hi Lars," Milo said.

"Do I know you?"

"Sorta. I'm Milo. Milo Rathkey. We need to talk."

"Jen's Milo?"

"Not anymore. Let me in."

Lars opened the door. For thirty-two bucks a day, $205 a week, the Gardner Hotel provided a room with a single bed, a floor lamp, a straight-back chair, and a window that hadn't been washed…ever.

Lars sighed. "Why are you here?"

"Jen hired me to find you."

Lars flopped down on the bed.

"I figured I owed you. Ten years ago, you found Homer. Now, I found you," Milo said, sitting down on the lone chair.

Lars looked at the floor. "Homer died. I'm sorry Homer died. He was a great dog…cancer." Lars looked up. Milo thought he saw tears. "He had a good life."

This guy is on the edge, Milo thought. "Lars, this is not about Homer. Why are you here in this dump?"

Lars rubbed his growing beard stubble, avoiding Milo's eyes. "We are going to have a baby. I tried to do the right thing. I failed. I lost our money. I was so dumb. I have to get it back."

"Yeah, getting the money back is only one of your problems. The guy you attacked at the Tip Top was murdered a week ago."

Lars stared at Milo in disbelief. "Alex is dead? Who killed him?"

"Right now, the police are thinking it was you. You attacked him."

Lars jumped up, crossed to the dirty window, and pushed back the faded pineapple curtain. "No! No! We had a pushing match. I came on too strong. After I got kicked out of that bar, I noticed a sign company with his name on it across the highway. I went there the next day to apologize. He was a nice guy. He said he didn't know where the money went, but he was going to find out. I believed him. That's why I'm still here."

"Okay. At some point you are going to have to tell this to the police, but for now, you need to get out of here. You can stay at my place. Jen's already there."

"Is Jen staying with you? I don't know…"

"I have a big house. In fact, if Jen is mad, you could have your own room. It's better than this one, and it's free."

21

Martha happened to look out one of the kitchen windows and saw her cottage with the telescope platform fully extended and a tall, thin man doing something with wires. She picked up her phone, thought for a minute about which Lakesong owner most likely belonged to the tall stranger, then called Milo.

"Hi Martha," Milo answered. "I'm bringing another person to stay with us for a while."

"That's nice; I'm calling about a man on the roof of the cottage."

"That would be Ed. Ed Patupick. Remember last summer Sutherland had him looking for bodies."

"Why is Ed on the roof. Please tell me he's not looking for dead bodies again."

Milo laughed. "He's fixing up the telescope for Breanna."

Martha pursed her lips; she was not pleased. "Mr. Rathkey, I thought I made it clear, I didn't want Breanna or anyone to be up on that platform. It's not safe."

"That's what Ed is fixing. The telescope will be computer controlled. If you like the idea, it was mine. If you hate it, it was Sutherland's. I don't know what's wrong with that man. He has no regard for child safety."

"If no one has to go up there, I love the idea," Martha said.

"Great. I'm glad I thought of it."

Martha's phone buzzed—it was Breanna. Martha said goodbye to Milo and took Breanna's call. "What's wrong?"

"Nothing's wrong," Breanna said. "There's a man here who is going to set up the tele…"

"I know all about it," Martha said. "How much does all this cost?"

"He said Mr. Rathkey and Mr. McKnight were paying for it. He called it upgrades to the estate."

§

Lars was puzzled as Milo stopped in front of Lakesong's wrought iron gates decorated in wreaths, bows, and silver bells. He was even more puzzled when Milo keyed in the code and the gates opened. Milo drove around the curved driveway which afforded Lars a long look at Lakesong's imposing—but cheerful—massive brick manor with its multitude of windows, each with its own candle, and chimneys, each with its own elf.

"This is your house?" Lars asked.

"I share it with a guy named Sutherland McKnight."

As Milo pulled around to the garage, one of five doors opened. "I don't know how that works," he admitted to Lars. "I think there's a chip or something they put in the car that the garage thingy reads, and the door goes up."

"Who put a chip in?" Lars asked.

"Mr. Anderson, who is really Ms. Anderson. I think her name is Lilly." Milo pulled the Honda into the garage and parked between the Bentley and Rolls.

"Whose cars are those?" Lars asked.

"They belong to the estate," Milo explained. "There is a Porsche that belongs to Sutherland, and an old Mercedes that is mine."

"Jen said you lived over a bakery."

"I moved. Long story," Milo said.

Walking into the back hallway, they were met with the pleasing aroma of cookies baking. "Martha is making her specialty," Milo said.

"Who's Martha?" Lars asked as they entered the kitchen.

"This is Martha, chef extraordinaire," Milo said, pointing to the friendly looking woman in the blue chef's coat. "Martha, this is Lars."

"Jen's Lars?" Martha asked.

Lars nodded and shook Martha's hand.

"Where's Jen?" Milo asked.

"I think in the gallery. Jet is keeping her company."

Milo led the way past the hearth room and the family room into the gallery. Lars was taking in the indoor park with its holiday-dressed trees, fake birds, and real cat when Jen stood up. "Lars!" she yelled and came running to him.

Milo slipped into the family room to mix himself a drink, thinking his job was done. He heard Jen's voice asking "Why." He didn't have to listen; he already knew the answer. Jet had followed him to the family room bar. Milo didn't know what the cat drank, so he simply said, "There's the bar, mix your own." Jet hid under the table.

After finishing his gimlet, Milo returned to the gallery to see if the reunion was a success, or if Lars would need a separate bedroom. Milo heard Jen say, "You need a shower, and we need to talk."

Milo shuddered. He had heard Jen say—many times—to him, "we need to talk." He sat down in his favorite chair by the windows overlooking the expansive back lawn running down to the lake. Jet jumped up on Milo's lap and began kneading and purring before curling up.

A meow from above told Milo that Annie, ever the calico, disapproved of young Jet's familiarity with the humans.

At that moment, Agnes entered the gallery looking for a Martha cookie. "I smell them. Do you have some?" she asked Milo.

"Some what?"

"Cookies."

"Martha is hiding them in the oven."

Agnes made a quick turn to the kitchen. Milo looked at Jet. "What are the chances she'll bring me one." Jet squeaked his answer. It wasn't hopeful.

§

Preston hung up her phone and double-timed into Gramm's office. White was already there, finishing up her much-needed afternoon coffee. "I found him!" Preston almost shouted.

"Congratulations. We knew you could do it." Gramm looked up from rereading the autopsy reports.

Preston looked pleased.

"Who'd you find?" Gramm deflated her bubble of pride.

"Eddy Peterson. You told me to find him. That was my job."

"Oh right. Where is he?"

"At the Hazline Rehabilitation Center on Mesaba. He's drying out." Preston's pride was back.

"Well done," White said. "What made you think of that place?"

"You guys said he had a drinking problem. After hospitals and jails turned up nothing, I figured that place was next."

"Can we talk to him?" White asked.

"We can."

Gramm stood up and stretched his back. "Let's go. I want to see if we can rule him out before we get to my favorites, Granton and Maki. We may solve this thing without a Milo moment."

§

Breanna was sitting cross-legged on the dormer seat studying for finals on her laptop when Ed Patupick came down from the telescope platform. "I have to test some things," he said.

Breanna watched as he booted up a large computer on the table and married it to his receiver on the platform. "Bluetooth," he said simply. Breanna put down her laptop and walked over to watch him. Ed double clicked on a telescope icon and a program came up listing Ed as the author.

"You wrote your own program?" Breanna asked.

Ed nodded. "I liked small bits of the commercial stuff, but not all of any one program. It's easier to do it myself. You push *raise* to open the roof and the telescope platform will move up into position." He pushed the button and Breanna heard the platform rising up through the cupola.

From the kitchen window, Martha watched the platform come to a halt, pleased there weren't any people on it.

Cookie seeking Agnes, came in, grabbed two cooling cookies from the rack and joined Martha at the window. "There's no one on it," Agnes observed.

"Thankfully," Martha said.

They watched as the telescope rotated from side to side and then up and down, without any visible human intervention. "Your telescope is haunted," Agnes said.

"Ed Patupick," Martha proclaimed.

Agnes bit into her first cookie. "The miracle of electronics. These cookies are yummy as usual."

Ed was pleased that Breanna knew her way around computers and telescopes. Her knowledge made explaining the software so much easier. "I have preprogrammed hundreds of stars and other targets into the software. The rest you will have to find on your own," he explained. "The icon labeled *lights* turns out all of the back-lawn lights while you are using the telescope. If you forget to turn them back on, they will do so automatically when the platform comes down."

"Does it make coffee?"

Ed, who lacked the humor gene, looked dumbfounded. "No one asked for a coffee-maker attachment."

§

The sprawling, multi-storied Hazline Rehabilitation Center towered over its Mesaba Avenue neighbors of mostly one-story commercial buildings. Even with a Christmas wreath on the door, the dark brick, and small windows gave the facility a foreboding appearance. Gramm and White parked in one of five *Special Visitor* spaces.

As they exited the car, an orderly, dressed all in white except for a black ski jacket and knit cap, came running up. "You can't park there without a pass."

Gramm showed his badge. "This pass work for you?"

The attendant nodded. He handed Gramm a cardboard pass. "Please put this in your window."

Gramm obliged. He and White entered Hazline. "I've never been in here," he said to White. Gramm showed his badge to the middle-aged receptionist and told her they were there to see Eddy Peterson.

"Patient or staff?" the woman asked briskly.

"Pardon?"

"Is Mr. Peterson a patient or a staff member?"

"Patient."

"Our patients are not allowed to have contact with the outside world while they are recovering." The receptionist seemed pleased with her rehearsed response.

White read her nametag. "Well, Ms. Hanson, call whomever you have to call because we are the outside world, and we will talk to Mr. Peterson. I'm sure you don't want a killer to remain on the loose."

The receptionist didn't have a preprogrammed response to *killer on the loose*. She nodded and called an administrator. After a short wait, a stern looking woman wearing a dark business suit arrived at the desk. She smiled and shook hands with Gramm and White. "I'm Gretchen Milne. I understand you wish to speak to one of our patients."

"We do," Gramm said. "A man named Eddy Peterson. I believe he checked in here late last week."

"Oh yes, a woman from your office called earlier. Am I to believe that Mr. Peterson is a suspect in a murder investigation?"

"He's a person of interest. We need to speak to him."

"Of course. If he agrees to see you, I must insist that I be in the room. Mr. Peterson is here for health reasons, and it's my responsibility to monitor that health."

"I have no problem with that as long as you only observe," Gramm said.

"I will stop you if Mr. Peterson shows signs of duress."

"I can get a court order, and then you can't be in the room," Gramm countered.

Ms. Milne smiled. "Let's see if we can navigate this without the court becoming involved."

"Suits me. Lead the way," Gramm said.

An elevator ride and three hallways later, Gramm and White were escorted into a conference room with comforting gray-blue walls, a small table, and five chairs. They waited for ten minutes before Eddy Peterson, dressed in jeans and a UMD sweatshirt, was escorted into the room by Ms. Milne.

"Good afternoon, Mr. Peterson," Gramm said, in as friendly a tone as he could muster. "Do you remember us?"

Peterson stared at them. "I'm sorry. I don't."

"Please sit down. I'm Lieutenant Gramm and this is Sergeant White. We visited you in your office last Wednesday."

Peterson shrugged. "I don't remember."

"We are investigating the deaths of Alex Sithens and Faythe Cummings."

Eddy startled. "Faythe's dead? Why?"

"That's what we are trying to find out. She was murdered a week ago. When we asked you on Wednesday where you were at the time of her death, you said you were with your children."

"I was?" Eddy blinked.

"No, you weren't. So, we are here again to ask you where you were last Monday night."

Peterson shrugged. "I have no idea. I don't remember last week at all."

"How did you end up in here?" White asked.

"I…I…" Peterson stopped and looked at Ms. Milne. Getting no help there, he said, "I have no idea."

Gramm indicated the interview was over and Peterson was escorted out of the room by an attendant.

Ms. Milne said, "This is not unusual, Lieutenant. Heavy drinkers often have a severe loss of memory."

"How convenient for him," White said.

"I still wonder if he's had acting lessons," Gramm added. "Who checked him in?"

"Let me check," Milne said. Making a quick phone call, she wrote down a name and hung up. "He admitted himself."

Gramm's bushy eyebrows arched up. "He's lost his memory but found this place?"

§

"Where are the pies?" Milo asked as he and Sutherland sat down to pre-dinner drinks.

"I was punched, Richard was kicked, Agnes was threatened, and all you care about are pies?"

"Pies are important."

"They're in the refrigerator."

"Cherry? Right?"

Sutherland sighed. "Yes, cherry."

"Good." Milo sat back satisfied.

"What should I do about these threats especially to Agnes?"

"Agnes had me escort her to her house this afternoon. That was a good idea. The threats will end tomorrow. Pies are powerful."

Sutherland's stomach was in a knot he couldn't untie. He wanted to know Milo's plans but didn't want to know. Instead, he changed the subject. "Tell me about finding Lars."

"Not much to tell. Joe traced him to the Gardner Hotel. I found him there and invited him to stay here."

"The Gardner? Oh no! Why there? There are much nicer places to stay in Duluth."

Milo looked at Sutherland, unsure if he was kidding. He wasn't. Milo's work on Sutherland's education was not over. "There are reasons people choose to stay at the Gardner, just as there are reasons pies are important."

Sutherland brushed past that point. "Why did he disappear?"

"He lost a substantial amount of money in a bad investment, and he was trying to get it back."

"Oh, you're saying Lars was broke, and couldn't afford anything better than the Gardner."

"Pretty much."

"How did Jen take his return?"

"A *Jen-look* and the dreaded words, 'We need to talk.'"

Sutherland smiled. "I've never been married, but I know those words aren't good. What's a *Jen-look*?"

Milo took a sip of his drink. "It's a hard set around the mouth and eyes that says she is displeased—times ten. When I no longer got that look, I knew our marriage was in trouble, but it was too late."

§

After dinner, Milo sat down to read while Jet busied himself batting a low-hanging Santa on the library tree. "Uptown Girl," the ringtone for Mary Alice, interrupted both Milo and Jet.

"Hello?"

"Has Sutherland filled you in on the threats?" Mary Alice asked.

"Tell me about this Fencig guy?"

"He worked for James—practically a James clone," Mary Alice explained. "He's big on intimidation and all-around dirty tricks. He quit when I took over and started to change things. I would have fired him anyway."

"Good to know."

"I'm worried for Richard—Sutherland too, of course—but I'm really worried for Richard. They hurt him."

"I have a plan."

"Richard mentioned cherry pies. You're going to need more than that to get Mr. Wolf involved."

Milo was once again amazed at Mary Alice. She made the connection between the pies and Morrie Wolf. "He owes Sutherland a favor."

"For what?"

"The wedding."

"Brilliant!"

22

Hearing footsteps in the hearth room, Sutherland, expecting Jen and Lars, put down his newspaper. It was only Milo and his feline entourage. "I never tire of you and your little buddies promenading to breakfast." Jet squeaked at Sutherland and stretched in a bow-like manner.

"Thank you for acknowledging my existence," Sutherland said.

"Feeling insignificant?" Milo asked as he poured a cup of coffee.

"Are you asking me or the cat?"

"I don't talk to the cats, you do."

"And it gets me nowhere," Sutherland complained.

Jet jumped in front of Milo's feet and stretched again.

"And I bow to you, young cat," Milo said, bowing.

Sutherland laughed. "Yeah, I'm the only one who talks to the cat."

"I was only being polite."

Martha brought Milo's breakfast to the morning room. "Good morning, Mr. Rathkey and feline friends."

Milo gave Annie a piece of bacon.

"Breanna was up half the night with that telescope," Martha said. "She woke me this morning excited to show me a close-up picture of a blurred something or other."

"Glad to have been of service," Sutherland said.

"Just think of all the mornings to come, and all the fuzzy pictures you'll get to see," Milo added.

Martha closed her eyes, shaking her head as she went back to the kitchen.

"Morning Sutherland," Jen said as she entered the morning room with Lars in tow.

"I'm here too," Milo said, raising his hand.

"This is my husband Lars," she said to Sutherland. "Lars, this is Sutherland McKnight, co-owner of this estate."

Sutherland stood and shook Lars' hand. "Good to finally meet you."

"Hi Lars," Milo said. "I'm sitting here at the same table as Sutherland."

Lars laughed. He had shaved and showered since Milo saw him last.

"Thank you for finding him," Jen said.

Milo looked around. "Are you talking to me?"

"No," Jen said sitting down, "I'm talking to your cat."

Jet squeaked and bowed again.

Martha brought Lars and Jen a stack of blueberry pancakes and sizzling sausages. Lars dug in. Jen mouthed a *thank you* to Martha, glad there were no eggs to avoid.

"We are heading back today," Jen announced. "Thanks, all of you, for all you've done."

Milo hesitated. "Lars needs to make a trip up to see Lieutenant Gramm before you go—to make a statement."

"A statement about what?" Jen snapped her head in Lars' direction.

"I got into a little shoving match with a guy," Lars explained.

Jen's eyes widened. "You didn't mention that. Is that guy pressing charges?"

Lars looked at Milo.

"No, he's not." Milo hoped Jen wouldn't take it any further. "Gramm just needs to get everything straight."

Jen gave Milo her *look*. After all these years it was still scary. "What's going on?"

"The guy I pushed was murdered," Lars blurted.

"Oh, good God! Are you a suspect?"

"He just has to give a statement." Milo hoped that was true.

Milo's phone rang with the *da dunk* sound that signaled an incoming call from Gramm. "We were just talking about you," Milo said.

"Who's we?" Gramm asked.

"Me, Sutherland, Jen, Lars, and the cast of *Hamilton*."

"Good, come in with Lars. Leave the others at Lakesong, although Amy would enjoy seeing *Hamilton*. We are going to interview Kayla Maki and Ike Granton this morning. I expect a confession from one or the other."

The phone went dead. Milo looked at Lars. "Gramm's excited to meet you."

"Oh, I forgot," Sutherland said, "Mr. Anderson is working on my Porsche's scratches, and she's also going to tighten the brakes on your Honda. It's a Mercedes-to-work day."

"Mr. Anderson, *she*?" Jen questioned.

"He has pronoun apoplexy. Has had it since he was a child—can't get his pronouns right," Milo said, buttering his already buttered toast.

§

Trips to the Rasa Bar in West Duluth—owned by local gangster kingpin, Morrie Wolf—were an activity to avoid, but ever since Milo moved to Lakesong, visiting the Rasa was becoming common place. Milo parked in the bar's nearly empty side parking lot, walked around to the front of the building, and pushed open the door. Mornings at the Rasa smelled of old wood, disinfectant, and stale beer—not an unpleasant odor, and one that Milo associated with his days before joining the Navy. Bennie, the bartender, was still behind the bar looking up at the TV. Morrie Wolf, in his striped sports coat and skinny tie, sat in the back booth going over yesterday's betting sheets. His bodyguard, Milosh, was sitting across from him.

Bennie turned to the sound of the front door opening. He smiled and waved, "Hey, Milo, want a beer or coffee?"

"Nothing today, Bennie, thanks," Milo said as he and his stack of three pies stepped to the back booth. Pie number four could still be found in Lakesong's refrigerator.

"Morrie, Milosh," Milo nodded in greeting. "I brought you pies from Betty's up the shore—cherry."

Morrie looked at him suspiciously. "Milo, I thought our last meeting was our last meeting."

"It was," Milo said, putting two pies by Morrie and one by Milosh. "I'm here for a friend."

"You got two minutes, but only because you brought pies," Morrie rasped.

"Remember Sutherland McKnight, the other guy who owns Lakesong?" Milo thought that at the name McKnight he almost saw Morrie smile. "He's getting threatened and got beat up by two thugs. I thought maybe you could convince them to stop."

Morrie went back to his betting sheets. "I don't get involved in other people's business."

"He did you a favor," Milo said, and then held his breath, not knowing how it would be received.

Morrie did not look up. "Milosh, refresh my memory, did McKnight do us a favor?"

"The wedding," Milosh said.

Morrie continued to check his betting sheets. "Good to see you again, Milo. Thanks for the pie."

Milo stood up. "One of the guys had a long, nasty scar on his face."

Morrie was silent. Milo, never sure a conversation with Morrie hit the mark, turned, waved goodbye to Bennie, and walked back out into the sunshine.

Morrie looked at Milosh. "You got this?"

"Scar on the face, gotta be Sid Lukovich and his brother."

Morrie nodded.

§

Gramm held court in his office, filling Preston in on the trip to Hazline. "Peterson admitted himself, but he claims that he has no memory of doing so—possible, or a well-planned defense strategy by an experienced actor."

"Where's Milo?" White asked.

"He was having breakfast with the cast of Hamilton," Gramm said. "He should be on his way in."

"I'm learning to ignore references to Milo's activities," Preston said.

"I'm just telling you what he told me." Gramm looked out into the bullpen and saw Milo heading his way with a man and woman in tow.

Milo, Lars, and Jen crowded into Gramm's office. "Lieutenant Gramm, this is Lars Helvig and his wife Jen. Lars wants to confess."

Lars went pale. Jen rolled her eyes.

Gramm nodded. "Let me ask you a question. Are you handy with a bow and arrow—do you hunt?"

"No."

"Where were you last Monday night?"

Lars stared at Gramm in panic, his brain on empty. "Monday? I think I had dinner at the Perkins near the Gardner."

"Can anyone vouch for you?"

"I remember telling the waitress the burger was good, and then I left. Oh, wait! My car wouldn't start. I called Triple-A. They jumped-started me. It took more than an hour. Is that good?"

Gramm turned to Preston. "Officer Preston would you take his statement and get an address and phone number in case we have to talk to him again."

"They're fleeing to Brainerd," Milo said.

Jen gave Milo the *look.*

White shook her head. "Don't worry, it's Milo's idea of humor."

Jen didn't stop the *look*, "Oh I am aware of Milo's *humor*."

Officer Preston stood up and directed Lars and Jen to her desk. Milo tagged along.

"So, who is Lars and why do we care?" White asked.

"He got into a shoving match with Sithens a week before the murders. I don't think he's a suspect, but we need a statement."

"Why did Milo bring him in?"

"Milo found him—his other case."

White cocked her head to the side. "Oh, the pretty woman who knows about Milo's humor is the ex-wife you mentioned."

Gramm nodded. "That she is."

White looked through the window into the bullpen. Preston was at her computer. Lars and Jen were sitting at her desk. Milo was hovering nearby. White went back to her morning coffee. "I don't want to know any more."

§

Vince Fencig looked at the dull, expressionless faces of his two henchmen—the brothers Sid and Mitch Lukovich—wondering if he had made a mistake. "Gentlemen," he began.

"I am not happy." The tall, thick, Fencig ran his hand through the side of his black, slick-backed hair. "You failed! McKnight and that Bonner bitch have not pulled their bid."

"We hit him boss. We hit them both, and Mitch even keyed his car," said Sid, defending their efforts.

Fencig's nostrils flared. "Send McKnight and Bonner's kid to the ER. This is not a school playground." Fencig smiled at the thought of putting Mary Alice Bonner's son in the hospital. *Maybe I'll send flowers.*

"Got it boss," Sid said.

§

Kayla Maki sat in the police interview room, head down, her fingers kneading the back of her shoulders. Tension was building in her body. Sergeant White had called her early this morning, ordering her to appear for more questioning.

The door opened and a handcuffed Ike Granton scuffed in. Kayla's head jerked up.

"Why are you here?" Granton demanded.

"They called me and told me to come in," Maki whispered.

Ike sat in the chair alongside Maki.

"What's our plan?" Kayla asked, searching Ike's face for reassurance.

"Our plan is to shut up," Ike hissed. "They're listening and watching."

The door opened again. Gramm and White entered and sat down opposite the two suspects. White began recording the interview, giving the date, time, and the identity of the people in the room.

Milo and Preston watched and listened from behind the one-way glass. "Why are they interviewing them together?" Preston asked.

"Gramm thinks they might turn on each other," Milo said.

White waited for the guard to release Ike from the handcuffs, warned him to behave, and then began. "Okay, let's light the fires and kick the tires."

Granton laughed. "Like everything else, you got it backwards, babe. It's kick the tires, light the fires."

"Son of a bitch!" Milo said to himself.

"It has come to our attention," Gramm began, "that you two know each other. We find that interesting."

Kayla was going to say something, but Ike shot her a *shut-up* look.

"Do you want to know why we find that interesting?" White asked.

Granton folded his arms and leaned back in the chair.

White opened her file and took out a picture of two arrows. "These are the arrows that killed Alex Sithens and Faythe Cummings—recognize them?"

Granton remained quiet. Kayla's eyes stared at the pictures.

White produced another picture. "These are the arrows we found in your barn. They are identical."

"I told you, somebody stole 'em, besides an arrow is an arrow. There's probably hundreds like that."

Kayla closed her eyes.

White smiled. "Care to fill him in, Ms. Maki?"

Kayla shook her head.

"Okay, allow me," White continued. "The length of the arrow, the type of fletching, how it's secured, and the broadhead used, combine to make this a nearly unique arrow—identical to the arrows found in your barn, Mr. Granton. That puts you in line for a murder charge."

Gramm picked up the questioning. "What we are doing today is determining if we have one murderer, Mr. Granton, or two." Gramm switched his gaze to Maki. "We know, Ms. Maki, you were searching for Faythe Cummings the night she was murdered, and, Mr. Granton, so were you."

Kayla shook her head. "I didn't kill anybody, and either did Ike. He was with me the whole night."

"Yeah, you see, one suspect giving another suspect an alibi really doesn't do much good," Gramm said. "If you confess, we can get you both a deal. You can avoid life without parole."

"We didn't do anything!" Kayla screamed.

Ike stood up. "Screw you cops!" he shouted. "I knew from the beginning you'd pin this on me!"

Kayla started banging her fists on the table and screaming, "No! No! No!"

Both Gramm and White stood up. The officer who had been standing by the door stepped toward the commotion, his hand on his Taser. "Sit down, Mr. Granton, or we will restrain you!" Gramm cautioned. "Ms. Maki, stop!"

Ike started to sit down but jumped up again. "I knew you'd accuse me of everything—every fricken thing!"

The officer placed his beefy hands on Ike's shoulder and forced him to sit down. Kayla stopped banging. Behind the one-way mirror, Milo barely took it all in, because the other nagging bit in his mind had become clear. He looked at

Preston. "I think I know who did this." He left the room. Preston scribbled out a note and interrupted the interview.

"What?" an annoyed White demanded.

Preston handed White a note. She read it and slid the note to Gramm. He told the officer to escort Ike back to his cell. "You stay here, Ms. Maki. We will have more questions."

Gramm stood up. What had Milo heard that the rest of them missed? He looked again at Preston's note. *Milo says he knows the ID of the killer. He has gone back to the bullpen.*

§

Lars and Jen sat in silence as they drove back to Brainerd. Just before Moose Lake Lars blurted, "Milo certainly does have a nice house,"

She looked at him, thinking he was comparing himself to her ex—Milo's wealth to their normal life. "I don't care about his house. I care about our home, and the home we will create for this baby."

The baby. We'll talk about the baby, Lars thought. "You're right, that was stupid of me again. Let's talk about her. Him? Her?" He smiled at Jen.

"I had to cancel my last appointment. I was in Duluth looking for you."

"We'll reschedule. We'll get everything back on track. I was an idiot, but that's in the past."

"Yes, you were, but we covered that. We're going to enjoy our little family. It's not about money or houses," Jen said.

Formula costs money. Diapers cost money. Cribs and strollers cost money. Lars thought. He knew better than to say it. "You're right. I panicked."

"Talk to me before you panic again."

"I will. Never again."

"Her," Jen whispered.

"What?" Lars asked.

"She, her," Jen smiled.

"Who?"

"The baby,"

Lars looked at Jen. "I wonder how many puppies she'll need."

23

Leaving the interview room Gramm and White found Milo in the bullpen at the computer. White stepped behind him and looked at the screen. "He's checking Sithens' emails again," she said.

"Give me a second," Milo said. "I think Sithens told us who killed him. I just didn't see it,"

White held up her handcuffs. "So, who are we arresting?"

Milo didn't answer.

Gramm sat down at a nearby desk. "We know where Maki and Granton are at present. Until Milo resurfaces from his fog, let's find out where our other two suspects are."

"I'll check Peterson," White offered. "Kate, you can check Zackery."

Gramm sat back, hands behind his head. "I love it when delegation works so well."

Milo continued at the computer, calling up one Sithens email after another.

White hung up first. "Eddy Peterson checked himself out of Hazline. He's at large."

Preston thanked Zackery's receptionist, and announced, "Zackery's gone too. His receptionist said he's headed off to the airport. He just canceled his appointments for the rest of the week, supposedly to go fishing."

"Crap!" Milo stood up, looking at the assembled group as if seeing them for the first time. "The extra pilot took the picture, so he's the main pilot. I bet he owns the damn plane."

"Who's the fixed-base operator these days?" Gramm asked, pulling on his coat. The others did the same.

"Already on it," White said, checking her computer. "It's Crème Air."

"What's a fixed-base operator?" Preston asked as they ran to the parking lot.

"It's the terminal for private planes," Gramm explained. "Let's take my car, I have lights and siren."

Milo preferred his Mercedes.

Gramm flipped on the flashing blue lights as White called Crème Air. The line was busy. Preston tried the main terminal getting through to the tower. "We are trying to stop a private plane from taking off," she said, identifying herself.

"Tail number?" the man asked.

"Don't know. Can you just stop all private traffic, maybe put plows on the runway?"

"Can't do that. You're asking that we shut down the airport. Get me a tail number and I'll stop that plane."

Milo's Mercedes tried to keep up to Gramm, but a car cut him off and he fell behind. He honked repeatedly and received a one finger salute.

White was giving directions from her phone while Preston called for backup. Gramm pulled into Crème Air and slammed to a stop inches from the green, aluminum-sided building. Preston and White dashed out and flew into the well-lighted, modern office scanning for Zackery or Peterson or both.

Preston grabbed White. "Zackery—over there."

White walked up to the man as he was buying a packet of M&M's. "Dr. Zackery!"

The dentist turned around. Recognizing Preston, he smiled. "You got me—I eat candy."

White pinned his hands behind his back, placing the cuffs on his wrists. "Dr. Andrew Zackery, I am arresting you…"

Gramm stopped by the large windows overlooking the tarmac. "Ah, guys," Gramm said, "there's a plane out there with the propellers spinning."

White and Preston turned to look.

Gramm showed his badge to the woman at the main counter. "Tell that plane to stay in place!"

"King Air N5927 hold your position. Repeat, King Air N5927 hold your position." The woman looked up. "He's not responding, sir."

The plane lurched forward, reached the runway, and was again ordered to hold, this time by the tower. The pilot ignored the order, and the plane began to roll down the runway.

Gramm walked back to Zackery. "Who's piloting that plane?"

"Ah, guys," Preston interrupted.

"What now?" Gramm yelled.

"A speeding sportscar just drove past the building onto the runway."

"Goddamn it! It's Milo!" Gramm shouted.

The plane picked up speed as it shot down the runway with Milo's Mercedes in hot pursuit. "Okay," Milo said to the car, "let's see what you can do." The car's speedometer shot up as Milo pressed the gas pedal to the floor, pushing the tachometer close to the red line.

Gramm, White, Preston, and the handcuffed Dr. Zackery watched out the window. In the background the tower could be heard yelling at the pilot to stop. Gramm looked at Zackery. "So, if you're here, who's in the plane?"

Milo passed the plane, raced as far ahead as he could, slammed on the brakes, wheeled the car to the right, and blocked the runway. Two deadly propellers, chopping through the air, were screaming toward him.

Milo dove from the car and stumbled toward the side of the runway. The pilot had three choices: slam into the Mercedes, attempt to take off without enough ground speed, or stop.

The plane lurched up, barely clearing the Mercedes, stalled, hung in the air before executing a dramatic downward turn to the right crashing into a snowy area a hundred yards down the runway.

Milo ran toward the wreckage. A ball of flame erupted from the crumpled wing of the plane, followed by an explosion. A hot force crashed into Milo's body like a wrecking ball, knocking him on his back.

"Oh no!" White yelled

The tower speaker came to life. *We have a plane down on runway 2-7. Repeat, we have a plane down on runway 2-7.*

"Let's go!" Gramm yelled, heading for the door.

"What about him?" Preston asked, looking at the cuffed dentist.

"Watch him!" Gramm ordered. He and White ran to their car.

"I didn't see Milo after the explosion," White said.

Gramm grunted.

Through the silent fog, Milo waited for pain. It came—back, legs, face. None of it sharp. The acrid smell of burning fuel was overpowering as he opened his eyes to floating balls of color. The red and blue lights of the emergency vehicles seemed wrapped in a cloud. Daylight was fading. Milo was a dark figure on a dark runway. He didn't want to survive the explosion only to be run over by a firetruck. Reaching into his pocket, he pulled out his phone and turned on his flashlight. The crumpled, glowing figure was almost a comic sight.

"I see a light on the runway. It's Milo!" White yelled.

Gramm screeched to a halt near the light. He and White bailed out of the car. White ran toward an approaching ambulance. Gramm ran to Milo. "Nice flashlight," he said.

Milo saw his lips moving but couldn't hear him. He cupped his ears and shook his head.

White, flashing her badge, waved the ambulance crew over to Milo. "There's an officer over there. He was hurt in the explosion."

The EMT hustled up the runway to the light.

"I'm fine," Milo bellowed to the approaching EMTs, barely hearing his own voice. "I just can't hear."

The EMTs checked Milo's vitals and made sure he didn't have any broken bones. One of them shined a small light in his eyes and shouted at him, asking if he had a headache.

"Yeah, and I'm sore. Do you people have an Excedrin?" This time he heard himself, but his voice was muffled.

Milo stood up over the objection of the EMTs and his colleagues. The fire had been extinguished, but Milo could not see if anyone was coming out of the crumpled cockpit.

"Please, sir, sit down. You cannot help. The pilot is deceased. I hope he wasn't a friend."

"No, no friend of mine," Milo said. "I had to stop him. If he took off, he'd be gone." Milo turned to watch the airport fire people pour foam on the wreckage.

White looked at Gramm. "Who was the pilot?"

Gramm shrugged. "We know it wasn't Granton, Maki, or Zackery, so the only one left is Eddy Peterson."

§

After Milo had been given the all clear, Gramm suggested they go back to the fixed-base operator to regroup and figure out what just happened.

White turned to Milo. "Give me your keys. You're not driving."

"Why?"

"Oh, I don't know. Maybe it's because you were knocked down by an explosion caused when the plane that almost removed your head crashed in front of you."

"So picky," Milo said.

"Keys!"

Milo handed her his keys and eased into Gramm's front seat. "We handcuffed Dr. Zackery," Gramm said. "Why was he here?"

"He was going fishing. He was the next victim. Maybe you should apologize for handcuffing him." Milo noticed White zip past in his Mercedes. "She drives too fast."

"Yeah, right," Gramm said. "How fast were you going to pass that plane?"

"Hundred, hundred and twenty…thirty…maybe forty. That part was fun."

Once inside the terminal, White undid the cuffs. Zackery's tone was subdued and distracted. "He crashed!"

"Where were you and Peterson going?" Gramm asked Zackery.

"Montana. Fishing." Zackery mumbled, rubbing his wrists and shaking his head.

Milo was puzzled. "Peterson? Where'd you get that?"

Gramm and White turned to him. "Okay, smart guy," Gramm said, "who just died in that plane?"

"Friendly Al. I thought I mentioned that."

Zackery nodded.

"*You* were going fishing," Milo said to Zackery. "I think Friendly Al was doing a bit of tidying up."

"What do you mean?" Zackery asked.

"You were going to be his next victim," Milo said. "Making it look like you were the killer."

24

Sid Lukovich was playing straight pool with his brother Mitch, at Andy's pool hall on Fourth Street. Andy's, a long, narrow room, had ten tables, only three of which were being used this Wednesday morning.

"How we gonna do this, Sid?" Mitch asked.

"We gotta lure McKnight and the Bonner kid somewhere *private*. No cameras. We can't get caught."

"It took us two weeks of tailing McKnight the last time. What we gonna lure him with?"

"Let me think about it," Sid said, sinking the two ball into the corner pocket. He lined up for his next shot.

The clicking balls and voices from the other tables disappeared. Mitch looked around. The poolhall was empty. Even the guy behind the counter had disappeared. He looked toward the door and nudged his brother. "Sid!"

"Quiet! I'm shooting here!"

"Sid! We got company."

Sid looked up to see Milosh, Benny, and two other men blocking the doorway. Milosh was big but quick. He crossed to Sid, grabbed the pool cue out of his hand, and pushed it under the frightened man's chin. Mitch tried to inch away only to bump into Benny who grabbed him by the throat and slammed him against the wall.

"Milosh, we got no beef with you," Sid gulped, the pool cue pushing against his throat.

"You been threatening a friend of ours."

Sid looked at his brother. "We wouldn't do that would we, Mitch?"

"No, we wouldn't do that, Sid," Mitch parroted.

"Aren't you going to ask me the name of my friend?"

"Sure, sure. Who's your friend?" Sid stuttered.

"Sutherland McKnight."

"Oh crap!" Mitch swore.

"We didn't know he was your friend, Milosh. We was just doing a job. We will apologize."

"You do that," Milosh said, dropping the pool cue.

"We just hit him once in the gut," Mitch blurted.

Before Sid could respond to his brother, Milosh's fist slammed into Sid's diaphragm causing the man to double over gasping for breath. "Kinda like that?" Milosh asked Mitch.

"Yeah," Mitch nodded, "Sorry Sid."

"Who are you working for?"

"Vince Fencig. We was just supposed to scare McKnight. We didn't know he was your friend."

"Now you know." Milosh and Bennie walked back to the others, "This job ends here, and you will apologize to Mr. McKnight."

Sid was still gasping.

Mitch nodded.

"Don't make me come back," Milosh threatened as he, Bennie, and the others left.

"You okay, Sid?" Mitch asked.

Sid stood up, still holding his stomach. "Call Fencig. Tell him we quit. I ain't ending up in the trunk of a car."

"How is a suit like McKnight a friend of Morrie Wolf?" Mitch wondered.

§

"My internet news feed mentioned a plane crash last night at the airport," Sutherland said, not looking up from his phone. "The report mentioned a police pursuit."

Milo limped from the coffee urn to the table, wincing as he sat down.

"It goes on to say the plane stalled, crashed, and exploded. The lone pilot died, and one police officer was slightly injured."

Milo extracted two Excedrin from the bottle he kept in the kitchen and washed them down with the coffee.

"How do you do that?" Sutherland asked.

"Do what?"

"Take medicine with hot coffee? I'd burn my mouth."

"Years of experience."

"Was the 'slightly injured officer' you?" Sutherland asked.

"I'm not an officer. I'm a consultant," Milo insisted.

Someone is at the front gate, the intercom announced. Sutherland looked at his phone. "The police have arrived to consult." He pushed the gate open button. "I'll let them in. In your delicate condition, you should stay seated."

Martha delivered Milo's breakfast, asked the identity of the new arrivals, and returned to the kitchen to make breakfast for Lt. Gramm, and plate pastries for White and Preston.

"How are you this morning?" Gramm asked as he drew a cup of coffee from the urn. White and Preston did the same.

"I died during the night," Milo said.

"For a dead man, you look remarkably well," White said.

"Better than usual," Preston added.

"I'm black and blue from my armpit to my hip. I must have bounced on my side," Milo said. "By the way, I want a blue flashing light and a siren. Some bozo cut me off on the Miller Trunk thinking the police parade had passed."

"I'll take it under advisement," Gramm offered. "Now, tell us about the current Milo mind lint."

Sutherland was pleased that his phrase for Milo's musing had caught on with Gramm.

White selected a cruller from the pastry plate while Preston took both a bear claw and cinnamon roll claiming no breakfast this morning.

"You said Sithens told us who his killer was. I read those emails. Al Lerner was never mentioned," White said.

Milo took a sip of his coffee and winced.

Sutherland placed his bottles of ginger and turmeric in front of Milo. "Once again, try these."

Milo ignored the offer. "We know Sithens was a word guy, crosswords and all that. The misspellings on the signs and banners all over the car lot had to drive him crazy."

"How does misspelling clearance fifty times solve this case?" White asked.

"There were *two* misspellings on the banners. The second one was *every thing,* spelled as two words. It's one word. In his last email, Sithens said he knew everything, but he misspelled it *every thing,* just like the banner. I checked the other emails. He never spelled that word wrong until that last email. He was telling Lerner that he knew that Lerner was Fauchard."

"Kind of remote," Preston said.

Milo shrugged. "Only one person had to get it, and he did. Unfortunately for Sithens, instead of recouping his money, it led to his death."

"So Faythe Cummings was collateral damage?" Gramm asked.

"I guess," Milo said. "He had to kill Sithens as quickly as possible. Unfortunately, she was there. I guess he didn't know if Sithens had told Cummings anything, so both had to go. Somehow, he found out where Sithens was going that night. We might never know the connection. It was a remote place, perfect for his purposes."

"Wait a minute," White almost shouted. "The arrows are Ike Granton's. How did that happen?"

Martha set Gramm's breakfast in front of him. He thanked her and dug in. Between bites, he said, "Granton whined that someone stole them. Maybe he was telling the truth."

Milo nodded. "I think Friendly Al took them when he was checking on the stolen goods."

Gramm stretched his shoulders from side to side. "So, you're saying Al was Ike's fence."

"It makes sense. My guess is Lerner's original plan was to run with the investment money and pin the scheme on Dr. Zackery. That's why he picked the name Fauchard. However, after the murders, he began to realize that Granton made the better patsy. Ike had a record plus Granton had a personal motive, Cummings dumped him. But that plan wasn't working."

"What do you mean?" Preston asked.

"We arrested Granton for receiving stolen property, but never charged him with murder. As the days went by, I suspect Lerner worried that his plan to frame Granton wasn't working, so he switched back to Dr. Zackery."

"You told Zackery he was the next victim. Explain." Gramm said, moving a fork full of hash browns through ketchup.

"Zackery's body would be found in Montana somewhere, but Lerner's would not. Lerner would then reinvent himself with the investment money safely tucked away in a numbered bank account."

"How does Eddy Peterson fit in?" Preston asked.

"He doesn't," White said. "I checked the overnight arrest log. Peterson was picked up for drunk and disorderly last night. The man has a problem."

"No acting?" Gramm asked.

"No acting," Preston echoed. "He was served with divorce papers. That set him off on his latest bender."

Returning to Milo, Gramm asked, "You said something Zackery told us triggered your mind lint. What was it?"

"He said the extra pilot took the picture of the group in front of the plane. That indicated they already had a main pilot—one of the group. It all became clear when Robin told me Lerner had been a fighter pilot."

"I did?"

Milo nodded, "Kick the tires, light the fires. You got it backward, but it's what fighter pilots sometimes said when they were ready to take off, at least they did when I was in the service."

"But how did you know I heard Lerner say it?"

"Granton corrected you during his interview. I figured he heard it from the same source—Lerner. It makes sense. Fighter pilots are adrenaline junkies. Friendly Al certainly was: fighter pilot, fence, and investment scammer. Then he upped his game to murderer."

"Can you stop calling him *Friendly* Al," Sutherland insisted. "Murderers are never friendly."

Milo looked down to see if his shoes were tied.

§

The receptionist told Milosh and Benny that Mr. Fencig was busy. Milosh walked past her and into the man's office. Fencig looked up.

"Who are you?" Fencig demanded.

"I'm your worst nightmare."

Fencig stood up, making sure Milosh saw all six-foot-five-inches of him. He walked over to Milosh, raised his middle finger, and yelled, "Screw you!"

Mr. Vince Fencig convalesced in the hospital for two weeks before going into an in-patient rehab center. Mary Alice Bonner sent flowers.

25

New Year's Eve arrived with clear skies, and balmy December temperatures hovering around ten degrees, but at least above zero. Mary Alice fretted all day about the forecasted snow. The forecast was wrong.

She kept her eye on the arrivals, greeting her guests in full hostess mode. Along with her artist and business friends, this year's party included guests suggested by Sutherland and Milo.

Teams of valets, dressed in four-pleated trousers, short, zipped jackets, and tweed hats set the 1920s tone. Each was eager to whisk the cars away to remote parts of the estate.

Continuing the twenties theme, the coat checks wore *Great Gatsby* outfits: five-button vests, double-hung watch fobs, and bow ties.

Sutherland and Agnes had also embraced the theme. Newly-bobbed Agnes sashayed about, making sure that the light caught the sequins on her emerald-green-and-black, sleeveless, flapper dress. The long fringes on the short-skirted hem swayed freely showcasing her long legs—a fun dress to wear. Sutherland strutted around in a white tie and tail *clubman* look complete with standing wing collar, pocket watch, and top hat.

Milo began the evening with a walking stick provided by Sutherland but lost it within five minutes. By coincidence, a nearby plant was seen shortly afterward supporting the same walking stick.

Mary Alice dazzled her guests in a curve hugging, black mesh, Veronique-inspired fringed dress with iridescent black sequins, and small gold beads. The subtle, art deco swirls, spirals, and shells were seen only by those who stared. Milo stared, but not at the art deco.

While mingling, Mary Alice would hint that guests should go to the wall between the double staircase and knock. "When questioned by a dubious gentleman," she advised, "say 'Milo sent me.'"

Saul Feinberg, in modern tails, with his date, lawyer Kimberly McKenna costumed in a backless, red-sequins-and-crystal gown, were the first to approach the picture of Al Capone.

McKenna knocked on the wall below the picture. Capone's picture slid back. A man snapped, "Whaddaya want?"

"Milo sent us," McKenna mimicked a gangster's voice, trying not to laugh.

A section of the wall opened; they stepped inside, and the wall slammed closed behind them. "This is…the bee's knees!" McKenna blurted, gazing at the twenties speakeasy bar and the bartenders in white shirts, bow ties, and suspenders that matched the sleeve garters.

Mary Alice's art dealer Jules joined them. "Oh my!" he exclaimed, crossing his arms over his chest, "Mary Alice has outdone herself this year. I'm in kitsch heaven."

Arial Jenkins barged into the room under the stairs with her husband Karl, in tow. "Well, no one is going to get plugged tonight," Arial proclaimed. "Murder never happens when I'm around."

"Dear, I think that's in bad taste. I understand the hostess' husband was murdered after last year's party," Karl chided.

"Of course, he was! I wasn't there! Karl, keep up!" Arial approached the other occupants of the under-the-staircase speakeasy. "Hello, I'm Arial Jenkins," she said, "I found the other venue, but it had dead bodies in it…on it…on the lawn."

Feinberg, enjoying Arial's quirkiness, held out his hand. "I'm Saul Feinberg…" He was about to introduce Kim when Arial gushed, "Feinberg? Pastrami? That fabulous house on Hawk Ridge?"

"That's me."

Arial's business card materialized out of thin air. "If you ever want to sell, I have time now. I was about to list the house of that man who killed people and blew up at the airport. Hello probate! I'll have people lined up around the block for your house, well down the hill, waiting to snap up that little jewel."

"You sell houses?" Jules stepped up. "How fabulous. I sell art. We need to talk."

"Anyone want legal services?" McKenna joked.

As the bartenders handed out drinks, they requested that the patrons return to the main party after enjoying their drinks so everyone could experience the room.

Last year, Mary Alice's long gallery easily fit the entire party. This year, the party spread throughout the many rooms of Lakesong. Along with the gallery, pockets of guests—some in twenties dress, others modern day—were mingling, chatting, and laughing in the family room, the dining room, and the billiard room.

Furniture store owner, Roger Lund and his wife Donna were the first to be approached by Jamal—clad in a white shirt and bowtie—who, along with offering hors d'oeuvres, provided advice. "If you want some action, make some Jack, I suggest the library." He disappeared into the crowd, as practiced, before a flustered Roger could ask what he meant.

Darian, dressed in a costume similar to his brother's, gripped a small hors d'oeuvres tray with both hands while complaining to his sister, Breanna, "Why do I have to be a server and you get to be a guest?"

"I'm older. Get over it; it's not going to change. Why are you standing here against the wall? You are supposed to be walking through the crowd."

"I'm short. I get stepped on."

Breanna took a stuffed mushroom from Darian's tray and disappeared into the crowd.

Donna popped a crab puff and grabbed Roger. "Let's find the library."

A man—his face obscured by his low brimmed fedora—pointed to a closed, ornately carved door. "I'd try that door if I were you. Keep your eye on your wallet."

Donna raced to the door, opened it, and dragged Roger inside. She was disappointed. It was as described, a library—just a library. They were alone, except for a fedora donned woman who was sitting at a table reading a book. She looked up and smiled, "You look like rats and mice people—craps."

"Yes!" Donna said, enthusiastically.

The woman gave a furtive glance around the room as if she were being watched. Satisfied that all was well, she rose and kicked the baseboard and the bookcase opened. The hidden stairway had been discovered by Agnes more than a month ago. The lights had been changed and the staircase was now clean, bright, and welcoming.

"What is this?" Roger asked.

Donna didn't care. She was having fun. She ran up the steps. Roger, being Roger, had no choice but to follow. The bookcase closed behind them. Once upstairs, they found themselves in another library decked out to look like a gambling hall with roulette wheels, craps tables, and vintage slot machines.

A man dressed like the bartenders, except for a green vinyl visor, welcomed them and handed them chips. "Good luck," he said, "but if you lose, you better be prepared to pay. The butter and egg man don't like people who don't pay. The *chopper squad* might pay you a visit."

"This is certainly different from last year when I was humiliated by the host," Roger laughed, referring to the late James Bonner. "Now I could be visited by a chopper squad, and I don't even know what that means."

"It's guys with machine guns, Roger." Donna accepted a handful of chips, grabbed the dice at the craps table, and put down her bet.

"How do you know that?" Roger asked. "About the chopper squad."

Donna ignored him. "Rats and mice don't fail me now." She rolled a six. The attendant picked up his dice stick and moved the dice back to her.

"A six. The lady rolled a six," the man crooned.

Donna picked up the dice, blew on them, and sent them flying. "Mama wants free babysitting."

Roger looked on in stunned silence.

After rolling another six, trying the slots and roulette wheel, Donna cashed in her chips. "You are a big winner!" the woman at the checkout kiosk said handing Donna an envelope. "Here is your prize."

"Free babysitting?" Roger asked.

"No. A free date-night, dinner for two at the Pickwick."

Donna was staring at the craps table.

Roger turned to look. "What do you see?"

"Does that huge man at the craps table know that this is just for fun?"

"I guess. Why?"

"He just palmed the house dice and replaced them with his own."

Once again, Roger wondered how his wife recognized that.

More guests arrived up the staircase, and by the time Roger and Donna rejoined the party downstairs, the gambling parlor was full. A crowd was gathering at the craps table watching the huge man having a run of rolling sevens.

One of the guests said to him, "You sure are lucky, Mr. um…"

"Call me Mike," Milosh said, palming his dice, returning the house dice to the table.

Milo's instructions as Mary Alice's escort were to mingle, observe, and check in on Mary Alice from time to time. He went into the family room where another bartender was mixing drinks. Waiting for his gimlet, Milo was joined by Martha and author Ron Bello who, like Milo, had not costumed-up. Martha, however, wore the trademark of Lady Day—Billie Holiday—a white gardenia in her hair.

"How's the book coming?" Milo asked.

"You mean my upcoming best seller on the life, death, and *redeath* of software king and lifestyle guru, Harper Gain? A case you solved. Almost done. The editor is giving it a final look. I do wish, though, that you would give it a rest."

"How so?" Milo was confused.

"My publisher wants me to write about your latest case, stopping a plane in midflight. I can't keep up with you."

"I think midflight is a bit of an exaggeration," Milo said. "I'm not mentioned in your book, am I?"

"Oh, a bit. Nothing to worry about," Bello said.

Milo received his gimlet, excused himself, and went back to the gallery.

"A bit?" Martha questioned.

"I lied," Bello smiled, really liking the Lady Day look Martha was rocking.

Milo found the golden-haired Mary Alice gliding from one group of people to another. This was the Mary Alice he first met a year ago, ever the hostess, radiating an intangible something— a something that made a man believe that he was the most important person in the room. She turned and smiled, her all-encompassing Mary Alice smile. Her sequins and gold beads sparkled in the light as she moved toward Milo. Taking his arm in hers, she said, "So, Mr. Rathkey, I understand you are new to London Road. I must learn all I can about you."

"I live in the Lakesong boat house," he joked, still getting lost in the blue eyes.

"Must be cold in the winter," she mused.

They were interrupted by Mary Alice's son, Richard. He looked much calmer than he did last year. "Mr. Rathkey," he acknowledged, shaking Milo's hand. "Are you still interrogating innocent suspects?"

Milo wondered if that was a dig or just his humor. "Lately, I've taken to shutting down airports," Milo offered. "And yourself?"

"Getting shoved and threatened—part of property development not covered in business school," Richard said.

Mary Alice smiled, "Milo took care of that small problem."

"Should I thank you?"

"Sure, why not."

Richard's attention was taken by a new arrival. "Excuse me, I see a friend."

Mary Alice watched him walk over to a pretty, young woman she had never met. "I think Richard invited a date. I wonder if she's one of the foster kitten roommates," Mary Alice said, picking an imaginary piece of lint from Milo's shoulder. "I have guards at the doors. He's not getting out of here without introducing her to me."

Milo's financial guru, and poker partner, Creedence Durant, joined them. "Mary Alice, I've seen some people disappear and I'm wondering why I'm not among them."

"I have no idea what you're talking about Creedence," Mary Alice smiled, "but I have been told by others that if you go to the picture between the staircases and knock, strange things happen. Tell them Milo sent you. After that, you may want to take a trip into the library and talk to a gentleman in a fedora."

Creedence did as he was told, laughing at the picture of Al Capone on the wall. He knocked; the picture slid back. "Whaddaya want?" the man asked.

"Milo sent me," Creedence announced, giving a thumbs up to Milo and Mary Alice. The door opened. He was greeted by Ernie Gramm and Amy waiting at the bar for their drinks.

"Lieutenant," Creedence said, "so glad you're here. I have been told there's some illegal activity going on."

Gramm smiled. "Unless you've found a body, I don't care."

Looking at Gramm's amber drink, Creedence asked if that was *the* scotch, the pre-prohibition, Macallan single malt that Milo and Sutherland found in one of Lakesong's hidden tunnels last summer.

Gramm nodded and whispered, "You have to ask for the *bad* scotch."

Ron Bello, who was standing nearby, overheard and nodded. "The really *bad* scotch."

Creedence followed their advice, watching the bartender pour the amber liquid into a glass under the bar. "Here you go, sir, the bad scotch."

Creedence took a sip and smiled. "Oh, this is terrible scotch."

"Real rotgut stuff," Bello laughed.

"As the financial adviser to this household, I must chide them for serving it so freely. It must be expensive."

Bello put his arm on Creedence's shoulder. "Do not stop the flow of the scotch. I've already been a suspect in one murder, another would be no sweat."

"Tomorrow," Creedence beamed, getting the joke. "I must chide them tomorrow."

§

Agnes' green fringes swayed, and her sequins sparkled as she checked to make sure the band was setting up in the large, empty room off the dining room. Peggy was on it. Agnes was just a guest and Sutherland's date.

She flounced over to Sutherland, giving him an affectionate hip bump. "What was that room, the empty one?"

"I have no idea. It was always empty. Milo says it was used as a kids' dining room during big parties," Sutherland said. "Not in my day."

Agnes looked around the gallery at the crowd enjoying the party. She spotted Jen and Lars talking with Feinberg and McKenna. "What is it with Milo and attractive women? Milo's ex is good looking too," she noted, "but in a different way from Mary Alice."

"Not as lovely as the beauty on my arm," Sutherland proclaimed.

The party progressed. Mary Alice circulated throughout the house, sometimes with Milo, sometimes without. She was pleased. This was a fun party. Milo found her, and they navigated through several groups, finally making their way to the ballroom.

Sutherland, in his tails, was doing the Charleston with Agnes.

The Charleston ended, and the band began a waltz. Milo thought he was leading, but soon realized that Mary Alice was in command, dancing him over to Richard and the *friend.* "Hello," Mary Alice said to the woman dancing with her son. "I'm Mary Alice, Richard's mother."

The woman stopped and looked at Richard. "Your mother is here, and you didn't introduce me?"

"Oh, it's worse than that," Mary Alice laughed. "This is my party."

The young woman gave Richard *the look* and disentangled herself from him.

Milo wondered if that look was female instinct or learned.

"I'm Sara Carsdale," the young woman said. "I am so glad to meet you. I would have introduced myself earlier if I had known."

Richard looked embarrassed.

"You throw a wonderful party," Sara Carsdale continued.

Mary Alice smiled and said, "So glad you are enjoying it. Have fun you two."

Milo watched Richard dance his partner far away.

"What's wrong with him?" Mary Alice demanded, not expecting an answer.

"I suspect he didn't introduce her because he thinks it makes her too important—too big a deal."

"What's wrong with your gender?"

"We have an imbalance."

Near midnight, the guests were ushered out onto the terrace where heaters were going full blast. The fireworks began on the stroke of midnight. Sutherland and Agnes embraced, and kissed, welcoming in the new year, as did Milo and Mary Alice.

The fireworks lasted fifteen minutes. As they ended, Jen walked up to Sutherland. "I got a check in the mail for the full amount of our losses in that investment club."

"Oh, that's great!" Sutherland said. "I wasn't aware they recovered the money already."

"The check was written from the Duranicus Recovery Fund," Jen said. "I just met Milo's financial advisor who told me all about his archaeological find, and how he got to name it after himself—Duranicus."

"Coincidence." Sutherland said.

"It's a lot of money, Mr. McKnight. Can Milo afford it?"

"I think he'll get by," Sutherland said.

"He always does."

Later, as the party was ending, Sutherland cornered Creedence. "Duranicus Recovery Fund?"

"In my defense," Creedence began, "I did not expect to meet Milo's ex-wife at this party. Who invites their ex-wife to their party?"

"Milo."

"I should have figured."

Milo was talking to Jules, Mary Alice's art buyer, when his phone buzzed. There was a message from his web page. It read:

> *Mille Greysolon here. We met at the Chester Park Festival last fall. I noticed you are in the detective business. I accidentally locked my dog, Chester, in the attic.*

Oh, good lord! Milo thought. *Is this how my New Years' begins? The page says interesting cases only.* With a sigh, he read on.

> *I found him of course, but when he came down, he had a finger in his mouth. It was just a bone, but I think it is human. I would like to know who died in my attic.*
>
> *Yours truly,*
>
> *Mille.*

Milo smiled.

MURDER AGAIN! HAPPY NEW YEAR!

If you wish to contact the authors, email us at authors@dbelrogg.com or leave a message at www.dbelrogg.com.

If you enjoyed this book, please leave a review on Amazon.

BOOKS BY D.B. ELROGG

GREAT PARTY! SORRY ABOUT THE MURDER

FUN REUNION! MEET, GREET, MURDER

MISSED THE MURDER. WENT TO YOGA

MURDER AGAIN! HAPPY NEW YEAR!

SNAP, ZAP, MURDER

CLUES, CASH, PIECES OF MURDER

OLD MURDER, NEW MURDER, WHERE ARE THE COWS.

Made in United States
Troutdale, OR
02/27/2024